The
Not-$o-Great
Depression

IN WHICH THE ECONOMY CRASHES,

MY SISTER'S PLANS ARE RUINED,

MY MOM GOES BROKE,

MY DAD GROWS VEGETABLES,

AND I DO NOT GET A HAMSTER.

By Amy Goldman Koss

ROARING BROOK PRESS
New York

Text copyright © 2010 by Amy Goldman Koss
Published by Roaring Brook Press
Roaring Brook Press is a division of Holtzbrinck Publishing Holdings
Limited Partnership
175 Fifth Avenue, New York, New York 10010
www.roaringbrookpress.com

Distributed in Canada by H. B. Fenn and Company Ltd.

Cataloging-in-Publication Data is on file at the Library of Congress
ISBN: 978-1-59643-613-8
Roaring Brook Press books are available for special promotions and premiums.
For details contact: Director of Special Markets, Holtzbrinck Publishers.

First Edition May 2010

Printed in April 2010 in the United States of America by RR Donnelley & Sons
Company, Harrisonburg, Virginia

1 3 5 7 9 8 6 4 2

To Lauren Wohl (midwife & muse)
who propped my lazy butt back up at the keys.

And with thanks to my agent, the ever delightful George Nicholson
for coaxing me off the ledge,
to my brother Barry for his belly laugh,
and to my freen Mitchell for not going irretrievably bonkers.
Aw, you guys . . .

Chapter 1
DRAGONS AND BEES

FRIDAYS AT MY SCHOOL OFTEN BEGIN WITH DISASTER. We're having this one out on the bleachers instead of in the auditorium and I'm sitting with Emily, of course. I start telling her how Creepy Carly the Creeperton almost killed me and my brother driving us to school, but Emily's barely listening.

"Hey!" I say. "I'm complaining here!"

And Emily says, "I noticed that."

"Well, where are all your sympathetic grunts and pity sounds?" I ask.

Emily shrugs.

I give her a nudge and say, "What's wrong? You sick?"

"I promised I wouldn't tell anyone," she says.

"What aren't you supposed to . . . Wait, I'm not *anyone*!" I say.

Emily bends over and puts her face in her hands.

"Who did you promise?" I ask.

"Nora," Emily says from under her hands.

"Your cousin Nora?"

Emily nods.

"She's pregnant?" That's a joke. Nora is only twelve and not the pregnant-at-twelve type.

Emily shakes her half-hidden head.

"She bludgeoned someone to death?"

Emily snorts. Nora is a teeny, tiny, bird-boned little thing.

"She's in jail? Caught the plague? Won the lottery? Got a puppy? Pierced her eyeball? Am I getting warm?"

Emily looks up. "No."

"Just tell me then. The assembly's going to start any second!"

Emily looks around as if there might be spies. We're jammed in on all sides by everyone, but I guess she decides it's safe because she whispers, "Nora and her parents are moving in with us."

"Wow! That will be fun!" I say, and I mean it. Emily doesn't have any brothers or sisters, and I think two families living together would be a blast . . . Even if Nora is a little bit whiny and the tiniest bit overly serious.

"But Jacki, they're moving in because they lost their house," Em explains, keeping her voice low.

"Why don't they just look on their old street?" I ask. "Between their neighbors? I bet it's still there."

Emily rolls her eyes.

Principal Nicholson blows into the microphone and says, "All rise for the Pledge."

We stand. "I pledge allegiance to the . . ."

I've totally heard of losing houses.

Just a few days ago, I asked my mom why there were suddenly For Sale signs all over the place. She said people couldn't afford to stay in their houses anymore.

I was so disappointed by this explanation.

"Or that's just the cover story," I said. "And the truth is there's been a horrendous mutating toxic spill that the government is hushing up so we won't all panic and go shrieking into the hills!"

"Sorry, Sweetie Pie," Mom said, "but I'm pretty sure it's just an economic thing."

". . . with liberty and justice for all." We sit.

I wonder why Nora swore Emily to silent secrecy about it, though. I can see how it would be upsetting to lose your house, but secrecy goes with something truly embarrassing or shamefully humiliating, right? I mean it's not like Nora's parents danced naked at her All School Assembly or anything.

Principal Nicholson seems to be done announcing things. She introduces today's disaster guest, a traffic safety guy. Last week we had a lockdown drill lady talking about school shooters. Before that, it was the drug police and their dope sniffing dog.

Except for the dog, who was adorable, our Friday guests are always shaking their fingers and warning us about how terrible the world is. I think we should just have all of them here on the same day and get it over with.

Yes! A Misery Marathon!

The pep squad could make signs, "Welcome Dudes of Gloom!" The kindergarten would sing a cute little song of grim despair. The elementary would put on adorable disaster skits between each lecture. First grade, catastrophic poisoning. Second grade, brush fire. How sweet they'd look in their "engulfed in flames" costumes! Stop! Drop! Roll!

Anyway, at least we're not in class, and there's a teeny bit of a breeze. Emily is drawing on my arm and the pen tickles.

We sit according to grade, so my little (fifteen months younger, but four inches taller than me) brother Mitch is below me with his class, and my sister Brooke is above. I turn around to find her, but something furry catches my eye.

Look! Cupped in Lauren's hand is a tiny brown and white hamster! He's washing his incredibly cute face with his teeny pink hands.

"Hello!"

"Shhhh!" Lauren hisses, and the hamster disappears. "Don't tell anyone!"

"No, wait!" I cry. "I won't tell a soul! Never! Not a peep! I swear!"

But Lauren doesn't bring the hamster back out. Instead she leans forward and whispers, "His name is Chubbs. He came to school in my pocket."

I start to laugh, but she shushes me again.

"Is your pocket full of hamster poop?" I ask very, very quietly.

"Worth it!" she says. Then she sits back and looks past me as if there's no tiny secret hamster stowed away in her pocket . . . as if she's suddenly interested in the safety guy who for some reason calls bike helmets "brain buckets."

I want a hamster. I *need* one. Imagine how wonderful the school day would be with a hamster curled up in my pocket!

I bet he's super soft. I'd let him run around on my desk in French. Share my lunch.

Maybe if I'm really good, and if I nag relentlessly and pass math *and* French, and am nice to Carly, and practice piano until my fingers bleed, my mom will let me get a tiny face-washing hamster of my own.

I turn around to see if maybe Chubbs is out again, but he isn't. There's Brooke, though, in the tippy top row with the other seniors. My beautiful sister. She glows.

How will I stand it next year when it'll just be me and Mitch on these bleachers? The thought makes me sad to the bone.

I look down. Oh! Emily got a little carried away. My entire left arm is a big ugly dinosaur whose toenails definitely need cutting, and whose tail is very strangely shaped and horrid looking.

"Nice," I say.

Emily smiles.

"I have a piano recital tomorrow morning, though."

Emily un-smiles.

"Think it'll wash off by then?"

Em shrugs. "Maybe. Plus you could use like, I don't know, sandpaper or something."

Ms. Kaufman turns around and points her fierce index finger at us.

"No matter," I whisper to Emily, "Mr. Rodriguez is probably going to beat me to a bloody stump when he finds out I forgot my homework again. Your dinosaur will blend with the bruises."

"It's not a dinosaur."

"Um . . . a dragon?" I ask.

"Obviously!" Emily fake pouts. "Is it or is it not breathing fire?"

"I thought it was eating a . . . well . . . maybe a blanket?"

Ms. Kaufman turns around again to hiss, "Shhhh! Girls!"

* * *

After school I've got four minutes to get to track, but first I have to find Emily because Coach Keefer said if I show up at one more practice without socks she's going to make me scrub the locker room.

There's Em!

"But Jacki," she says, "I've been sweating in these socks all day!"

"That's OK. Just hurry!"

"Eewwww!" she says, wrinkling her nose. She sits down on the floor to untie her shoes. "You know, if you'd told me at lunch, I could have taken them off then, and . . ."

"It'll be fine," I say. "You're a peach, a doll, my hero."

"I know," Emily says, peeling off her socks, and wiggling her toes. "Here ya go!" She holds them up to me by the tips of her fingers.

"Later!" I call, and take off for the locker room.

"Gator," she replies, as she has since kindergarten.

I'm holding Emily's socks under the hand dryer when I remember that permission slips are absolutely, positively due today for something. The away meets, maybe? Oops. So even with *socks*, Coach Keefer is going to kill me. Worse, she's going to make me run stairs again. That's her favorite torture.

What am I doing in track anyway? I hate everything about

6

it. Well, I like running, *zoom*, just flat out, with the wind in my face. And I love running with other people, like a herd of caribou kicking up our hooves.

But racing *against* my fellow caribou ruins everything. Then I'm a lone creature being chased by hungry lions! Running in terror instead of running to celebrate the joy of life with my pals.

I tried to explain that to Coach Keefer once and she curled her lip and sneered, "My, aren't you the little nature poet," which I guess was a deeply vile insult from her.

But while I'm running stairs at the far end of the field, panting and wheezing and feeling *this* close to puking, I wipe the sweat out of my eyes and see a mamma deer and her two babies step out from between some trees and walk right across the parking lot! Wow! One of the babies stops to look around, and I wave, "Hi, Bambi!"

A hamster on the bleachers and a family of deer in the parking lot in the middle of Los Angeles? That's *got* to be a sign, right?

* * *

You'd think I'd know by now not to tell Carly anything, but while we're waiting for my brother to get out of baseball practice, I mention that I've decided to be a veterinarian.

Carly practically sprays her diet soda all over the dashboard. "Ha!" she shrieks, all sarcastic, "I'd like to see that!"

"Well good, because you will," I huff.

"You know, there's a whole lot of math and science in being a vet," Carly says in her know-it-all tone. "I've heard that it's harder to get into vet school than med school."

"So?"

"So, you're like barely passing remedial, ninth grade, private school math, where they hold your hand and baby you through! What are you going to do when you get to college and classes are actually hard, and they expect you to work?"

I fold my arms in a knot and clamp my mouth shut so I won't blurt out what I think of her because last time I did that, Carly whipped out her phone and immediately tattled to my mom, who grounded me for a week for being rude to the *help*.

"And you know, vets have to *kill* as many animals as they *save*," Carly says. "Like, if some chick comes in and goes, *I'm allergic to my kitty, kill him*, you've got to. You can't say *no*."

Mitch drops into the backseat. "I'm starved," he announces. Mitch is always starving. A family of twelve could live for a year off what my brother eats for lunch.

But I don't say a word because I'm afraid if I crack my lips even the tiniest sliver, ghastly anti-Carly monsters and insults will squeeze out and get me in trouble.

"What's with her?" Mitch asks, jabbing his thumb at me.

"She's sulking because I don't think she could be a vet," Carly says, practically backing into the janitor's truck.

"Vet?" Mitch asks. He's getting out his iPod which means in a half second I'll basically be alone with Creep-o Carly again. But first Mitch says, "Yesterday you said you wanted to be a beekeeper. Have a honey farm."

True, the bee guy yesterday *did* have a cool job, dressed in his space suit with the mask and gloves. Even the ankles of his pants were taped closed. And the bees were amazing! Getting angrier and wilder the more he messed with the swarming, squirmy, drippy, gooey honeycombs he kept pulling out of the filter box behind our pool.

But then he stuck the buzzy slabs in the back of his Bye Bye Bees! truck, and started flirting with Crudball Carly. Gross!

He was all *Fearless, He-man, Bee-man to the rescue.* Saying how great he was for not killing the bees, but *moving* them, queen and all, to a safe place to pollinate the world's fruits and vegetables, and save the world from hunger and famine.

"All in a day's work, ma'am," he said . . . although maybe not in those exact words.

Then Carly, laying her fake French-Dutch-Texan-Brooklyn accent on thick, told him she was my "nanny." Ew. Her whole "nanny" routine is beyond lame. She's just a twerp from *the valley*, going to Santa Monica Community College in s-l-o-w motion and driving us around during the week. That is *not* a nanny.

And you'll notice the entire nanny bit totally disappears when no bee-man or grownups are watching. Then she's just, "Shut up, can't you see I'm watching *Project Runway*?"

"Your sister just thought the bee catcher guy was hot," Carly tells Mitch as she rolls through a stop sign. I guess she doesn't know he's already blasting his brains out with music. Next, she wiggles her finger toward me, going, "Buzz Buzz."

I swat her hand away from my face.

"You thought he wazzzzz cute. Right, Jacki?"

I don't say, "WRONG!" I don't say anything. But Carly is right about *one* thing: Forget being a vet. I should just become a serial killer, starting right now with her!

"Your Mom's working late again and Brooke is at ballet," Carly says, "so how about pizza at The Capri?"

I LOVE the Capri. So, OK, maybe I'll let her live till after dinner.

*   *   *

I'm in bed when Mom gets home and comes into my room. She tiptoes toward me, peering through the darkness to see if I'm awake. She can't tell that I'm looking back at her, and I'm sooo tempted to jump up and say BOO! But as hilarious as that seems, I figure that if I scare the bejeebies out of her and she has a massive heart attack and dies before she hits the ground, it won't be that funny. So I lay still and let her creep up squinting.

Then I whisper real quietly, in a tiny voice that wouldn't startle a baby mouse, "Hi, Mom."

She answers, "Hi, Sweetie Pie," and sits at the edge of my bed.

"What time is it?" I ask.

Mom straightens my blanket and says, "Late. Long, long day." She sounds beat, not her usual perky, Get-the-Job-Done self.

I skootch over and pat the bed next to me. She lays down with a sigh. It's cozy and I may have fallen back to sleep a tiny bit, when Mom says, "Feel ready for the big day?"

"Big day?" I ask.

"Your recital tomorrow," she answers.

Oh. That.

It's quiet a second, then Mom says, "I wish I could be there."

"What?" I ask sleepily.

"I know you'll do great," she answers.

"Wait. You're not coming to my recital?"

"I'd love to, Sweetie Pie, but I can't get away. There's a huge meeting tomorrow morning. I should be up preparing for it now, but I'm so tired. I just want to lie here for two more seconds . . ."

"You're not coming to my recital?" I ask again, a bit louder.

"I can't. I'm sorry."

"Well, if *you're* not going, neither am I! I hate recital-ing, I hate the piano, and the piano hates me!" I'm sitting up now. "There's no way I'm going if you're not! What's the point?"

"Please, Jacki," Mom begs. "Can we *not* have this scene right now? I'm exhausted."

I glare down at her for a while, but then my brain clicks into a happy YES! I slide back down under the blanket and snuggle in next to her.

"No scene," I say. "We just won't go."

Mom says something that sounds like "Gnorth," followed by a little snore. And that is that.

* * *

But, in the morning, I wake alone in bed. I stumble out of my room to look for my mom, and find her downstairs standing at the kitchen counter in one of her blue suits, hair and makeup done, shoes on, drinking coffee, and making notes on a big yellow pad.

"Mom?"

"Good morning!" she says. "Your father is picking you up between ten and a quarter after. If he hasn't shown up by ten ten give him a call. I hope he wears something decent. Maybe call and remind him to dress nicely."

"Huh?"

"You better hop in the shower and start getting ready," Mom says. "Wear the red skirt with the red and blue top, but have Carly give it a touch-up with the iron. She should be here shortly."

"But . . ."

Mom checks her watch. "Oh!" She takes one more gulp of coffee, puts her cup in the sink, grabs her briefcase and heaps of papers, and leans toward me for an air kiss, saying, "I'm gonna be late!"

"WHAT?" I yell. "You promised!"

"Jacki . . ." she says, with a little laugh, and tries to side-step me.

But I block the door, straddling the door jamb.

"Last night we agreed that if *you* don't have to go to my recital, then I don't either! It's both of us or neither! So don't go telling me to wear my stupid red skirt and red and blue top!" I haven't thrown a tantrum in a while, and I feel a little rusty.

"Jacki, I'm going to be late! I. Do. Not. Have. Time. For. This," she says, putting each word out on its own.

"Then. You. Should. Not. Have. Had. Kids!" I say, imitating her.

Oops. That was going too far. Mom freezes, looks at me all weird, and then I'm being hugged and squished. Mom's words are blurry but she seems to be saying that I'm right, *nothing* is more important than my recital and she wouldn't miss it for the world.

Huh?

Then she's on the phone, telling her boss that she is terribly sorry but she just can't possibly make it to the meeting, and she knows what a rough spot that leaves him in but . . . and on like that.

Wait. What just happened? How did this so totally backfire? I just wanted to get out of my recital. But instead of getting *out,* it looks like I've dragged Mom *in*! And from the sound of her groveling on the phone, I even got her in trouble at work. That's not what I meant to do!

I wave my arms and mouth the words, "No. It's OK! You can GO!" But Mom gives me a wobbly little smile and keeps apologizing to her boss.

I shake my head frantically, No! NO! NO!

Mom just blows me a kiss.

Guess I better start getting ready . . . not in the sleeveless red and blue top, because I have to cover Emily's blanket-eating dragon.

I wish I'd practiced that stupid piano piece.

Chapter 2
RECITALS AND SEEDS

I THINK DAD LOOKS KIND OF CUTE sitting next to grandma, but Mom whispers in my ear, "Hats are just a way to tell the world you're bald."

It could have been way worse. Last year Dad brought his now ex-girlfriend, Bonnie. Talk about *awkward*! And Bonnie broke up with him so soon after that recital that I've always wondered . . . well, if maybe she just couldn't like a guy whose kid was so mean to pianos.

Anyway, there's Mr. Woo, my piano teacher, at the very verge of insanity. He stresses out so badly it hurts to watch. I really don't get why he puts himself or us through this. And he'll be spraying stinky spit soon, so whatever you do, don't sit in the front row.

I find Adam B., my only semi-friend among my fellow piano sufferers. I say *semi*-friend because I only see him twice a year at our recitals and Mr. Woo's holiday concert. Adam B. is actually the only single, solitary good thing about any of this, if you ask me.

A long time ago, he told me that he's called Adam B. because there are so many Adams in his school. But he's the only one I know, so I just add the B. because it's cute.

He and I stand out of the way, so Mr. Woo won't put us to work dragging chairs or setting up teacups for after. That's why we have our backs to the room and are pretending to look out the window at the country club's empty tennis courts.

I tell Adam B. about my botched attempt at getting out of the recital.

"Ah!" he says. "The appeal to guilt."

"Lot of good it did me."

"But it *could've* worked," he says, leaning closer. "I thought about having a sore throat. But then they would've locked me in for the whole weekend. Yours was way more creative."

I accept his compliment with a smile and tell him that for my next birthday I'm going to ask to quit piano.

Adam B. strokes his invisible beard. "But they say it's good to have a musical instrument on your college applications," he says.

I cover my ears and practically yell, "I'm so entirely sick completely to death of hearing about college applications!"

"Whoa!" he says. "Easy!"

But before I can explain about my sister being a senior, Mr. Woo rings his little crystal bell.

There is the usual scramble in the audience over saved seats, but the room soon settles and the nine of us performers file in and sit in order of age. Adam B. is right next to me.

Mr. Woo gives a nervous, sweaty little speech, thanking all the "good, gentle people" for coming. See? I told you his spit flies when he's worked up. Look at it spray!

15

"Sorry about snapping at you," I whisper to Adam B.

"No problem," he answers, and gives my knee two quick pats. Pat. Pat.

Hmmmm, was that pat, pat like, *Good dog*? Or *Atta girl*? Or like *I'm madly in love with you*?

The recital starts as always, with the cute little five-year-olds who have the entire audience going "Aww" and wiping tears.

It quickly moves away from awwness though, getting more and more dreary and pathetic by the minute. Mistakes stop being cute when your feet can reach the pedals. But when a person is considering the meaning of two pats on the knee, nothing else much matters.

A whole family in the second row gets up to leave when their little darling has finished pounding on the keys. I know my mom thinks it's unbelievably rude when people do that, but who can blame them? I'd sure leave early if I could!

By the time we get to us old kids, half the folding chairs are empty. Adam B. goes right before me. He flubs about five times, and goes all the way back to the beginning to start over once, which is a heinous crime to Mr. Woo, but I think is adorable.

I'm next.

I feel Adam B. watching me, and wonder if *he* felt *me* watching him. I do a crappy job, which I'm sure surprises no one.

Afterward, Mom and Dad and Grandma surround me and I totally lose sight of Adam B. Mom says Carly (ew) is coming, and bringing my brother, and even my sister is meeting us for lunch to celebrate how lousy I am at piano. Carly is a booger with bones, and Mitch is just Mitch. But I almost never see Brooke anymore, so that'll be nice. I miss her.

Emily says it's senioritis, and that everyone acts like

Brooke their last year of high school. But shouldn't it be the exact opposite? If you know you're going to have to move to some strange, faraway place . . . well, wouldn't you want to spend every single last possible second in your own house, with your family? Especially your little sister?

But all Brooke has *ever* wanted was to go to a fancy, "back east" college, where it snows and she'll be able to bundle up in big wooly sweaters and scarves and mittens. It seems like practically everything she ever did her whole entire life was with those hats and scarves in mind.

Her friends are like that, too.

How do some people know so much about what they want to do later? Mitch wants to play major league baseball, Emily has wanted to act in musicals since we were six. Adam B. said he wants to be a marine biologist.

I understand the part of wanting to be something, but not the part about wanting to be the same thing all the time.

I know that conversation at lunch today will be entirely, one hundred percent about college. And I'm right. We sit around a table at The Clam & Crab looking like the perfect family, talking about Duke and Yale and Cornell-Princeton-Brown-Sarah Lawrence and other places that I can't keep straight or picture. At least Brooke's applications have all been sent in, so we don't have to talk about SAT scores and essays anymore.

It's usually colder at the beach, but today it's hot, way too hot to be wearing these long, dragon-covering sleeves. And I forgot to say, "No tartar sauce on my fish burger," so I have to scrape, scrape, scrape. You can never get it all off. I see Dad giving the rolls an evil eye. He is an organic baker and can spot a phony roll from a mile away.

"I'm surprised that *Getting Into a Snooty College* isn't a reality TV show yet," Dad says. "Those cable execs are missing a gold mine!"

Does Dad get that he's making fun of the most serious and important thing in Brooke's life? Everyone is dead silent, so I smile extra big.

"Remember a few years ago," he continues, "when the rumor was that the Ivy Leagues were looking for *well roundedness*? And suddenly the spawn of America's ruling class was *athletic* and *artistic* and *civic-minded*, as well as being academic hot shots with money?"

Me and Dad laugh, ho-ho-ho, but Mom and Brooke stare at their food.

"The next year the word on the street was *forget well rounded*," Dad says. "What they want is *passion*! So, that year's crop of ambitious applicants were deeply and fiercely *passionate* about human rights, or globalization or the environment . . ."

Dad pushes up his glasses and asks, "So, based on the keen wisdom of some random stranger in line at the grocery store, what magic ingredient are the Ivies looking for this year?"

Mom abruptly turns to Carly, "How's your salad?" she demands, as if she absolutely must know immediately.

"Good!" Carly answers with her mouth full. "But the croutons are a little soggy."

"Oh, I hate that!" Brooke says, and the salad conversation is up and running as if it's the most important thing on earth.

I try to think of something wonderful to pull everyone together and the first thing that comes to mind is that incredibly funny YouTube of a sneezing baby panda.

"So," I announce, "there's this video of a big fat mamma panda, leaning against the wall, just munching away on some leaves and daydreaming, when her newborn baby gives out this huge sneeze and the mom jumps!"

No one laughs.

"Well," I go on, "you can tell she totally forgot the baby was there. Maybe she forgot she even *had* a baby. It's tiny, obviously a newborn."

Nothing.

"It's hilarious," I tell everyone. "I've watched it like six thousand times."

Mitch snorts, but everyone else gives blank smiles. Even Brooke. In the old days, meaning just a few months ago, she would have made some crack about my watching too much YouTube. Or teased me about how maybe that's why I got Ds in math and French.

Mom gets *four* phone calls during lunch. She jumps up from the table and runs out on the sand to take each one.

Grandma rolls her eyes. "All work and no play . . ." she says. I'm not entirely sure what she means, but I get the feeling behind it, and it makes my lunch curl up in a ball in my gut.

I watch out the window for dolphins, but there are none today. See that gray seagull over there? The grumpy grumperton scowling because her feathers are blowing the wrong way? That's me.

* * *

The waitress hands the bill to my dad, which is stupid. We can't be the only table with a broke dad and an unbroke mom. She totally showed us her entire worldview from just where she put

19

the check: Men have money. Women don't. Doesn't that seem awfully old fashioned for a girl with enormous earplugs and a sleeve tattoo?

If I'm ever a waitress, I'm going to *ask* who gets the check. And I won't work in a snooty tourist trap like this, either. I'll work in a neighborhood diner, and I'll wear an apron, and stick my pencil in my messy, beehive hairdo, and chew gum, and call everyone *Honey*. And when my regulars say, "I'll have the usual," I'll know exactly what they mean.

* * *

The valet brings Grandma's car first, and Dad takes the keys. He has been living at Grandma's for a while and seems to have taken over the driving. As he's getting in the car, he tells me and my sister and brother to dress grubby tomorrow because we'll be gardening.

Gardening?

"Sorry, guys," Brooke says. "I can't make it tomorrow."

Grandma does the dreaded double-raised eyebrow, but Dad just nods, not surprised or mad or sad, at least on the outside. He and Grandma drive away, waving out opposite windows.

Next comes Mom's BMW, and she zooms off to work, already on the phone.

When Carly's car pulls up, Mitch calls shotgun.

I look at Brooke to see if she'll offer to take me home, but she says, "I've got a million things to do, Jacki."

I open Carly's back door and get in.

"Don't be that way," Brooke says, sounding exasperated with *me*, as if *I'd* done something wrong. "We'll do something,

20

a movie or whatever, soon. Deal? It's just that I have so many . . . And I came *today*, didn't I?"

I shut the car door.

If *I* had a little sister, I'd treat her so great you wouldn't believe it. I'd take her with me everywhere. I'd even tell my boyfriend that I want her to come with us all the time, except maybe when we're going to smooch. I'd for sure share all my clothes and jewelry and makeup and hair stuff with her. But mostly I'd share my innermost secret soul, knowing that she'd never, ever betray me, even under torture, because she'd love me more than anyone else on earth, as I would her.

Little *brothers*, like Mitch, don't count.

* * *

"Since the lawn takes so much water and gives back so little, I figure we should use the land for food," Dad says.

"If it's good enough for Michelle," Grandma says, heaping our plates with her fabulous Greek salad, "it's good enough for me."

"Michelle who?" I ask.

"Obama!" Grandma says. "Didn't you hear that she planted a vegetable garden on the White House lawn?"

My grandmother is in love with Michelle Obama. She says she's the only *real* First Lady since Jackie Kennedy Onassis. That's who Grandma pretends I got my name from, but Mom says I was named for her dead aunt Jacqueline.

"So," Dad continues, "I figure we'll tear up the back lawn."

Mitch says, "*We?*"

"Yep," Dad says. "It'll be good for you to get down in the dirt."

"Is this to build our character?" I ask.

"No, but would it be so bad if your character grew along with some zucchini and eggplant?"

"I've got plenty of character, and I hate eggplant," I mutter.

Grandma shoots me a look. "Don't disrespect your father!"

"Well, can't we at least grow something tasty?"

"Like what?" Dad asks.

"Oreos," Mitch answers.

And I say, "Strawberries?"

"Strawberries! Raspberries! Absolutely!" Dad says, jumping up. "Let's go!"

But it turns out we aren't growing anything yet. First we have to dig up Grandma's whole entire yard! Trudge, lift, grunt, sweat, worms. We're totally like the farmworkers you see when you drive up the Grapevine in the Central Valley. I can feel my character swelling up in the blisters from the wheelbarrow and shovel. Ouch!

* * *

The next day at lunch, I tell Emily about my new life as a farm-hand, and she says, "Aunt Claire was talking about growing stuff in our yard, too, so she can contribute to the groceries. But my Dad said that once you've bought the plants and the fer-tilizer, and paid for watering through the drought, it comes out to like fifty bucks a tomato."

"Ha!"

"But Nora and her mom had a garden in their old house."

"The lost one?" I ask. "They still haven't found it?"

Em shakes her head, "Nope. And my uncle Rod?"

22

"Nora's dad?" I ask.

She nods. "Well, it turns out he lost his job ages and ages ago. But didn't tell anyone."

"No one noticed that he was like . . . home?" I ask, nabbing a few of Em's fries.

She shakes her head. "No, because he got up every morning, just like normal, shaved, got dressed, left the house . . ."

"No!"

"Yes!" Em says. "Then he'd come home at night acting all normal. Complaining about regular work stuff and traffic. No one knows where he went every day, pretending he was at work." Emily chugs her milk, then says, "My Aunt Claire is sooo mad, you wouldn't believe it."

"How'd she find out?"

"I'm not sure exactly, but it turns out he wasn't paying any of their bills and he spent every penny they'd saved."

"Eewww," I say, sympathetically.

"Yep," Em agrees. "That's for sure."

*　*　*

In history, Mr. Rodriguez tells us that saying "May you live in interesting times," is a Chinese curse.

Well, if interesting times are bad, then boring times are good, which means this class is fabulous! The only things keeping me from perfect one hundred percent boredom are Olivia's hundreds of braid extensions spilling onto my desk. They snake around when she moves, or when I poke them with my light-up alligator pen.

I want to make something out of them, crochet them into

a beautiful braided I-don't-know-what. A purse maybe? No! A hat! I could sort of build it around her head into a floppy, wide-brimmed sun hat for the beach.

I don't know how to crochet, but if I did, I could bring a crochet hook, or maybe knitting needles, to class and ever so carefully and quietly . . .

Whoosh! Olivia's braids whisk away. She has turned to look at me, probably felt me scheming to crochet her. Oh, it's not just Olivia, *everyone's* looking at me. At least everyone who's awake.

"Jacki? How would you interpret that?" Mr. Rodriguez asks.

"Interpret?" I answer, attempting alert-atude.

"That curse."

"The boredom is bliss curse?" I ask.

There are scattered snickers, of course. Mr. Rodriguez crosses his arms.

Madeline stabs her hand into the air, but doesn't wait to be called on. "Actually, Jacki's right," Madeline says. "If it's a curse to live in interesting times, then . . ."

Mr. Rodriguez ignores her and says, "Ben?"

Ben's head jerks up, alarmed. He was probably reading behind his textbook. He's all Manga, all the time.

Mr. Rodriguez's eyes dart around. "Lacey?"

Lacey pockets her iPhone mid-text and tries to look like she's been paying attention.

Maybe I *don't* want to be a teacher.

I thought maybe I did. I could picture myself being beloved by a bunch of needy but adorable orphans in some primitive, dirt-floored, one-room schoolhouse somewhere. But there too, there'd probably be a Madeline with her hand raised all the time, while everyone else watched the clock, or sundial or hourglass, counting the grains of sand until I'd finally let them run off to tend their scrawny chickens.

Mr. Rodriguez just asked something else. I'd like to help the poor guy, but I have no idea what he's going on about. Zabba zabba recession, outsourcing, bank failures, national debt. He's looking for someone to call on beside Madeline, but hers is the only raised hand and she's practically dying to tell him the answer to whatever it is he asked.

He sighs in defeat and calls on her. I pity him a tiny bit.

Madeline takes a deep breath, as if this is going to need a whole lot of air. Good! If she keeps it up for six minutes Mr. Rodriguez won't get a chance to assign homework!

I don't mind Madeline. I'm sure she'll be the president of the United States and maybe the entire world one day. She's already the president of about twelve clubs that no one else wants to be president of. And she's always all frothed up about important, super serious things like global warming and endangered bugs. I'm glad that there are people like her to fix the world so I don't have to.

The bell! Yay, Madeline! But as we barrel out the door, Mr. Rodriguez yells, "Read chapters thirteen to fifteen and be prepared for a quiz."

Grrrr!

Chapter 3
A Hippo and a Slap

AFTER TRACK, tired, sweaty, and starved, I look around for Creepy Carly's creep-mobile, but it's not here. As if I'm not miserable enough after having Coach Keefer lecture me for ten hours about how *irresponsible* I am and how maybe I've been forgetting my permission slip on purpose because I really don't want to be on the team anymore, which isn't at all true, except for the part about not wanting to be on the team anymore. But that's because she's always yelling at me!

If *I* were a coach, I'd let the runners run and the jumpers jump and the throwers throw, and who cares about the exact socks and tucked-in shirts and league standings and permission slips? None of that has anything to do with anything. I heard somewhere that the original Olympic athletes competed stark raving naked, so maybe we should just . . . never mind. But the point is track should just be track, have fun, do your best, the end.

And now: no Carly.

I'm *this* far from throwing an all-out sizzling fit, when, Honk! Honk! I see Mom's silver BMW over by the tree. She's waving to me out her car window.

First my piano recital, now picking me up from school? Maybe I laid the mom-guilt on a little too thick!

I trot over to the car and get in. "What are you doing here?" I ask.

"That's a loving hello," she answers, but her voice is flat.

I correct it to, "Why are you here, loving Mother, who I love?"

But she just gives me a sickly semi-smile and says, "We have to wait for Mitch," as if I don't know the drill.

I look closer. Something is definitely wrong with her face.

"Mom?" I start to ask, but she holds up her perfectly manicured index finger and says, "Let's wait for Mitch."

This is scary. The rumbling hunger in my gut is instantly replaced by fear-juice. I say, "What's wrong?"

But she shakes her head.

My heart beats faster. "Is anyone dead?" I ask, thinking, Daddy? Grandma? Maybe Mom found out that she herself has some horrible ghastly disease and only twelve minutes to live?

Mom says, "Everyone's fine," but she doesn't smile, or scowl or act in any way even remotely normal.

Mom must've spotted Mitch in her mirror because she taps the horn and sticks her hand out the window again.

Oh, now I get it! Carly quit! Phew! The relief knocks me back against the car seat. Mom has picked us up before when sitters have quit, unless she got Dad to do it. Maybe she thinks we *like* Carly and will be upset. Ha! No worries there! I smile.

Mitch plunges into the backseat and asks, "What are you doing here? I'm starved."

Mom doesn't start the car. She just says, "I got laid off today."

I was so sure she was going to say that Carly quit, or that she caught Carly drinking and fired her, or whatever, that it takes me a second to get it.

Mitch says, "But you'll get a new job, right?"

Mom strangles the steering wheel, "Of course I will," she says. "Absolutely. But it's not a great job market right now." She gives Mitch a wobbly half smile in the mirror and I swear her nose pinks up under her makeup, like she's going to cry, which is not one tiny bit like her and practically breaks my heart.

Poor Mom, she loves her job. I don't absolutely understand what it is . . . or *was*, she did there, besides rush around with heaps of papers and her Blackberry and laptop, talking on her phone, and hurrying off to meetings, from early in the morning to late at night, but I do know she loved it.

"I'm starved," Mitch repeats. "Can we get drive-through or something?"

"Quit it, Mitch," I say. "This isn't about you!"

"It's OK," Mom says, in a flat little voice. "It's not your brother's fault." She turns the key and the car comes alive.

And in an icy whoosh, like falling into a pool, I know *whose* fault it is—entirely, one hundred percent—*mine*. If I hadn't made Mom skip her meeting and go to my stupid, stupid, piano recital, she wouldn't be here, sitting behind the wheel, looking so miserable.

Mom doesn't do drive-through, so we go to The Blue Hen, even though it's nowhere near dinnertime. I frantically text Emily, "MUST TALK NOW!!!" And when we get to the restaurant I bolt straight for the bathroom and call her. She's at play rehearsal and not allowed to talk, but this is an absolute emergency.

I wait while she finds a hiding place somewhere backstage among the props. Meanwhile, it smells of super strong stink cover-upper in here. The sneezy kind.

"It is so not your fault!" Emily says when I'm done telling her the story.

"It is too," I say, "But now what do I do?"

"Nothing! Except maybe be nice to your mom, if she's sad."

"Shouldn't I call her boss and tell him it was *my* fault she missed that meeting?" I ask.

"No!" Emily answers.

"But . . ."

"Jacki! I've got to go, but promise me you won't do anything!"

"OK, OK," I say. But I look into the smoky mirror over the sink, straight into the guilty eyes of a girl who got her own mother fired.

When I get back to our table, Mitch is telling Mom about his day, like nothing is weird. And that seems doubly weird on top of how strange it is to be sitting in The Blue Hen with Mom in the daytime.

Mom sips her limeade. Mitch scarfs down a Vietnamese chicken sandwich on bread so crunchy I can hear it from here. I can't even make myself eat a single sweet potato fry, although The Blue Hen's are the best in the world.

When I can't stand it anymore, I interrupt them to say, "But what should we *do*?"

"About what?" Mitch asks.

"Mitch!" I bark.

"You mean about my job?" Mom asks me.

I think, *well, duh*, but I don't say it. "Yes, about your job."

"Don't worry, Jacki," Mom says. "We won't starve."

"That's not what I'm worried about," I say.

"I'll put the word out there, and start job hunting as soon as I have my résumé in order," Mom explains. "Something will turn up. I'm not overly concerned, and you shouldn't be either."

I push the bottle of hot sauce around on the table wondering if we'll have to move in with Emily, too. All of us, Emily's cousin Nora, Nora's parents, Mitch, Brooke . . .

"Does Brooke know?" I ask.

Mom's brave expression caves, and her brittle half smile is back. But all she says is, "Not yet."

"Does Dad?" Mitch asks, with the sensitivity of a hammer.

Mom closes her eyes, "No."

* * *

As we roll past Carly and Brooke's cars in the driveway, Mom says, "Well, I guess Brooke knows now."

"Ew! You mean Carly knew before any of *us* did?" I ask.

"It's not a race," Mom says.

But it grosses me out anyway. I can so picture Carly oozing fake sympathy, like she always does with my mom.

The bat-cave door slides open, Mom pulls in, and the door slides closed behind us. I drop my stuff in the kitchen, kick off my shoes, and go outside to the pool, where Brooke is doing laps. I stick my hot, stinky track feet into the wonderfully cold water.

Brooke swims up, turns, and does another lap. She could've totally been on the swim team if she wasn't so obsessed with ballet. Actually she could have done anything in the world, and I'm not kidding.

When I was little, I thought I'd be like her when I got to be her age, but she keeps getting older and I keep getting older, and I'm never as cool as her for a single second. That might sound like I'm jealous, or angry, but I'm not. That would be like being jealous of the sun for being warmer than me, or of the ocean for being wetter, or jealous of a baby bunny for being cuter.

Finally, she stops at my end. She dips her head backward, to get her hair off her face and says, "You heard about Mom's job?"

"Yeah," I say. "Mom's a little shaky, but I think she's trying to be capital B Brave."

Brooke smiles. Our dad used to say people were capital H Happy if they were really, really, happy, or capital S Skinny or capital T Tall.

"Well," Brooke says, "Dad's going to be capital B Bummed if he can't squeeze spousal support or child support payments out of her while she's not working. Heavens! He might have to get a real job!"

I practically put my fingers in my ears. I hate it when my sister talks about Dad that way. It must show on my face because Brooke goes, "Oops, sorry. I forgot you're Little Miss Sweetie Pants Happy Face." And she dives back down and swims a whole entire lap away from me in one breath.

I wait till her head pops up at the bees end to yell, "I am not!"

Brooke spits an arc of pool water into the air like a whale. And then her boyfriend David arrives, shadow first, to pick her up. That means she won't be home till late.

"Hey, Jack," he says.

I don't actually like being called *Jack*, but I don't growl or bite him. I smile, smile, smile—Little Miss Sweetie Pants Happy Face.

* * *

The next night, I'm upstairs, watching a fabulous YouTube of a hippo named Jessica who opens the front door and walks right into these people's house to get snacks! Ha! Her gigantic butt barely fits through the door!

I'm about to press replay for probably the fifth time when I hear Mr. Woo's car door slam, like every Tuesday night as far back as I can remember. It must be 6:58. I check the time on my computer. Yep.

All the good Jessica-the-hippo feelings vanish. I mean, Mr. Woo is sweet, and if we could just sit around talking or playing cards for a half hour, I wouldn't mind at all. But, unfortunately, there's always the piano lesson part.

My left hand can't read music, and there's no teaching it. It is a quiet kind of hand that just wants to wear rings, and maybe help out a little with chores like buttoning buttons and putting my hair in a ponytail. Not every hand can be a musical genius. I can live with the disappointment.

And I'm sure I'm not the only one in the house who thinks it's time to give up. My brother and sister, and the neighbors on all sides, and their pets, would probably love it if we finally put an end to the torturous noise of my lessons. No one would call it *music*.

But Mom is stubborn beyond words about these things. She opens the door for Mr. Woo and calls upstairs to me, as if I didn't hear the doorbell. I trudge slowly down to the living room because the longer it takes me to get to the piano, the less time I'll have to spend sitting at it.

If I were a music teacher . . . No, even *I* can't imagine that one.

I walk in on Mom telling Mr. Woo that she thought the recital was a *perfectly lovely event*, and that she doesn't know how he manages to keep things running so smoothly with so many children.

"Actually, I have considerably fewer students than last year," he tells her. "Didn't you notice?"

Mom shakes her head, no.

I laugh, because I'm sure she's thinking it sure *seemed* like an awful lot. In fact, if one more kid had marched up to hammer out another recital piece, making the *lovely event* even three seconds longer, someone probably would have gone bonkers with a machete. And who could blame them?

But Mr. Woo looks very serious when he says, "In fact there

has been such attrition among my students, due to unfortunate and unforeseen changes in so many families' circumstances, that I'm afraid I've been forced to raise my fee to compensate."

He talks like that. Sometimes, you have to chew on his sentences a while to unwind them.

Mom nods her head, all solemn and says, "Of course."

I nearly leap off the piano bench, dying to say, *Us, too! We've had some unforeseen, unfortunate whatevers, and have to drop piano, too!* but I don't dare.

Mr. Woo goes on, "So, I'm afraid I'll be increasing my rate from thirty to thirty-five dollars a lesson. I hope that will not be burdensome to you."

It will! It will be an unbearably burdensome burden that we can't possibly bear! I want to yell. *And since it's all my fault that our circumstances have so unforeseenly and unfortunately changed, the least I can do is sacrifice the expense of my piano lessons!*

But Mom just nods and says, "Of course, that's perfectly reasonable."

* * *

I'm getting ready to get off Facebook and either do my homework or go to bed when I hear Mom yell, "Spending six hundred dollars on a dress for a seventeen-year-old is crazy, Brooke! Especially *now.*"

"It's once in a lifetime!" Brooke yells back. "My prom!"

They're having it out in the bathroom again. I don't know if they just happen to be in the bathroom when their fights break out or if they go in there on purpose because they think

Mitch and I can't hear them. Either way, this isn't their first bathroom fight this week. Or second.

I hate when they fight. They've been doing it more and more lately but as much as I hate it, I can't tear myself away.

"Plus shoes and a bag?" Mom says. "It's madness! For a single wearing?"

I creep closer.

"It's not just for one wearing! I'll wear it whenever I have someplace formal to go," Brooke insists. "And how many times is your oldest daughter going to graduate from high school? With honors!"

I've been saving money from birthdays and stuff, and I'd gladly give it to Brooke for her dress if it would make her and Mom friends again. But it's nowhere near six hundred dollars.

"The situation has changed, Brooke . . ." Mom says. "And what's wrong with the gown you wore to the winter formal?"

"You said yourself that you'd get another job right away," Brooke snarls. "You can't have it both ways, Ma. Either we're in trouble money wise, or we're not. Which is it?"

I cringe, but inch closer down the hall.

"Listen to yourself!" Mom hisses. "If I wasn't hearing this with my own ears I'd never believe any daughter of mine could speak so rudely or act so selfishly!"

"Where do you think I learned it?" Brooke says back.

Then I hear a slap!

I yank open the bathroom door and scream, "STOP IT!"

Both Mom and Brooke turn to me with their hands on their faces. For a second I'm not sure who slapped who, but then I see that Mom looks horrified and Brooke looks horrified plus red-faced on one side.

"I'M SORRY I MADE YOU LOSE YOUR JOB!" I yell. "BUT DON'T TAKE IT OUT ON EACH OTHER!"

They both stare at me.

Mitch comes up the stairs, head bobbing to his blasting iPod. He looks at the three of us at the bathroom door and says, "Are we out of Cap'n Crunch?"

Everyone looks at everyone else, eyes darting around, until Brooke starts to giggle, and Mom almost smiles.

Mitch looks confused. He pops out one of his earbuds and says, "What?"

That cracks us up completely to hysterical bits.

* * *

We end up around the kitchen table. Mitch with bowl after bowl of cereal (which had been in plain view in the pantry), me and Brooke with matching bowls of ice cream, and Mom with a zero calorie cup of herbal tea.

Mom puts her hand on mine and says, "Jacki, sweetie, three other employees, who *didn't* go to your piano recital, were also let go on Monday. It's just what's happening with the company right now."

She takes a steamy sip of tea and apologizes to all of us for overreacting to her job situation. "I'll probably get a job in no time and this whole panic will seem so silly," she says. "A minor setback."

We all nod like crazy.

"Change is good for a person," Mom continues. "I was

36

probably getting too set in my ways working there for twenty-three, no . . . twenty-*six* years."

We nod even more.

"Being set free could be the best possible thing for me!"

I'm getting whiplash from all this agreeing. But I absolutely know that even if Mom's company *had* to pick four people to fire, it must've been easier for them to pick the person who skipped the important Saturday morning meeting than someone who didn't. I don't want Mom to feel bad for me for feeling bad for her, if that makes sense, so I just keep nodding and smiling. I figure the least I can do is feel guilty *quietly*.

Meanwhile, Brooke is acting *almost* exactly like herself now, but not quite. A regular person might be fooled, but I am her sister.

I've heard of people getting abducted in their sleep by aliens who take them to their spaceship, perform bizarre experiments on them, and then return them to their beds. The people wake up suspecting that something profoundly weird has happened to them, but they're not sure what. Not that I'm saying Brooke was abducted necessarily, but still.

Brooke says that her dance teacher, Ms. Valentina, gave her a great solo in the upcoming spring concert as a goodbye gift, since it will be Brooke's last performance before college.

"You probably got that solo because you're the best dancer for it," Mom says. "Ms. Valentina's not going to do anyone sentimental favors at the expense of the dance."

I'm sure they're *both* right. I've never had a teacher who'd care one single solitary speck about me leaving anywhere, but that's Brooke. Everyone loves her, *and* she's a great dancer.

"Oh, and David got a puppy," Brooke says, as if that's not the most interesting thing he has ever done.

"A puppy? What kind?" I say.

"A black lab mix," Brooke says. "Ten weeks old."

My insides go mushy with the thought. Ten weeks is the perfect chubby, wiggly, unbearably cute age! I suddenly like David a whole lot more than I did.

"Tell him to bring it over!" I beg. "Immediately!"

"What's he going to do with it at school, though?" Mom asks. "I'm sure you can't have pets in the dorm."

"Well, she's really his parents' dog," Brooke says. "I think they got her as a way to fill the gap when David leaves for college."

We all nod, wondering who or what could fill the gap our Brooke will leave. The answer is nothing and nobody. But you've got to admit that a ten-week old puppy would sure help.

On the subject of David, though, just between you and me, I'm not exactly one hundred percent sure why my sister picked *him* out of all the possible boys in the world. I mean he's not evil or creepy, he's just . . . well, Mitch says David's a great point guard on varsity basketball, but I doubt that's what won my sister's heart.

Love is a mystery, at least that's what Emily says whenever she tries to explain why she has a crush on whoever she has a crush on. And when I once told her I didn't really see the point of David, Emily said, "Aw come on, he's totally gorgeous!"

"Humph."

"You'll never think anyone's good enough for your sister," Emily concluded. "At least not a mere mortal human being from plain old everyday Earth."

And it might be a teeny bit true that I think the right boy for Brooke should be someone extra terrific, at least a lot more extra terrific than David seems to be . . . except for the puppy, maybe.

Anyway, the subject of the prom dress doesn't come up again, and no one says anything about the slap. Brooke's cheek isn't red anymore. And we have an OK time sitting there, being us. But then Brooke's phone chirps in her pocket, and that reminds her that she has study plans, and she's gone.

* * *

I go to bed feeling guilty about Mom and wishing I had a hamster or a ten-week-old puppy, and wondering if Emily and her cousin Nora are up giggling and telling bedtime secrets, or if they're fighting over the blanket. Emily is a known blanket hog. Plus she grinds her teeth all night.

Maybe I'm the teeniest tiniest bit jealous that they get to have a sleepover on a school night, while I'm here with my crazy family, fighting and slapping, and eating bowls of Cap'n Crunch and ice cream.

Chapter 4
BEETS AND BIKES AND BOYS

"Nope," EMILY TELLS ME THE NEXT MORNING. "We were not up giggling. Nora is in major disaster mode. Her mom cries all the time, and no one knows where Uncle Rodney is, although Aunt Claire wouldn't let him in the house anyway."

"Why?"

"Well, she says he's a liar and a fake and he ruined their lives and publicly humiliated her, and it's his fault they're homeless."

"Oh."

We're sitting on the steps of the Theater Arts Building. People keep walking by, around, and over us, but we ignore them.

"Not that they're *really* homeless," Emily continues. "Both my parents keep telling Aunt Claire that she'll always have a home with us, but that doesn't seem to help."

"Poor everybody," I say.

"It's amazing how many tears the human body can cry without drying out entirely," Emily adds. "You'd think Aunt Claire would be in powder form by now."

I think about that.

Then after a while I say, "At least when my dad isn't working, he doesn't lie about it."

"Is that why he and your mom split up do you think?" Emily asks.

I shrug. "Who knows? It was so long ago. And they are so completely and entirely different in every single way that it's much easier to get why they broke up than it is to see how they ever got together in the first place."

Em rips a stick of gum in half and holds both pieces out for me to pick one. I do.

"But my dad not working was probably a big part of it," I say, unwrapping my half and popping it in my mouth. "I know my mom thinks he's lazy because whenever I'm not doing what she thinks I should be, like practicing piano, or doing homework or something, she says I'm *just like my father*. That's the worst insult she can come up with."

We chew a while. Then Emily says, "I hardly remember them being together."

"Me too," I say. "Except for weird bits and pieces."

And then out of nowhere, Emily pinches my arm!

"OW!" I yelp. "What's *that* for?"

But then I see what she's staring at. It's Brad Pitt. That's what she calls Shota, although Brad Pitt is blond and Shota has black hair. Plus Brad Pitt has an incredible body for an old guy and Shota is so skinny his pants fall off. But Emily is blinded by love.

How she can fall for boys we've known practically our whole lives and have seen every day since kindergarten, I do not know. But she does.

Shota is in the school play with her. Emily says he sings like a bird.

"You mean, tweet! tweet?" I ask.

But she just rolls her eyes.

Now he saunters over to us and says, "Hey."

Emily squirms around all wiggly. I wonder if I went wormy around Adam B.? I really, really hope not.

"Want to run lines?" Shota asks, which is drama-talk for rehearsing their play.

Emily goes, "Uh . . . er . . ." which I take as a hint.

I stand up, "Well, I gotta go . . . um," I can't think of anything to say I have to do at seven forty-five in the morning.

"OK," Emily says. "See ya."

I say, "Later."

And she automatically answers, "Gator."

Hey, I wonder if she remembers in first grade when, to be funny, Shota popped some of our class bunny's poop in his mouth, pretending it was Cocoa Puffs, then two seconds later took off screaming for the school nurse, sure he was going to die.

I can't wait to tease Emily about that at lunch!

*   *   *

As soon as I leave Emily to her crush, I run into Madeline, who's wrestling with posters that flop over before she can stick them to the wall. I catch one trying to escape. It's announcing a canned food drive for the homeless shelter up on Catalina.

That place scares me. All the people waiting on the sidewalk, their shopping carts piled high with everything they own. People wearing coats when it's too warm for coats, or going barefoot when it's too cold for bare feet. Asking if I can spare a dollar.

I never before this very second thought about how you become one of those people. Emily says Aunt Claire considers herself and Nora homeless, just because the house they're in isn't theirs. Does that count?

Madeline and I hang up four more posters. She's talking the whole time, but I can't understand half the things she says because she talks in math. Zabba number of people are homeless in the county, another zabba zabba are women and children, some zabba percent have been on the streets more than a year.

By the time the bell rings, I'm totally depressed. So in history when she asks me if I want to come with her to volunteer at the shelter some Saturday, what can I say but, "Sure."

"We mostly just watch the little kids while their moms eat," she says. "Read them stories, play games, or whatever. Babysit."

I wonder if I'd babysit the children of the people we see camped out under the freeway. Do the people sleeping in the park have kids? The family that lives in their car behind Rick's Diner does. How about that lady in Old Town Pasadena who always has a basket of kittens? How does she *do* that? Don't they ever turn into cats?

I'm about to tell Madeline that I've never actually babysat, when Mr. Rodriguez says, "Anyone not in their seat and ready to work by the count of five . . ."

And isn't it totally cosmic and psychic that he picks *this very day* to talk about foreclosures and people losing houses and stuff like that?

He says sometimes you borrow a zillion dollars from the bank to buy a house, expecting to be able to sell it later for *two* or *three* zillion, but instead, the economy goes bad and no one will offer you more than a half a zill or less. Meanwhile, you still have to pay back the bank unless you just forget it and move in with Emily.

OK. I'm *not* going to buy a house. I'll rent an apartment on the tippy top–most floor of an incredibly tall building that practically sways in the wind.

Out one window I'll have the ocean bubbling with whales and out the other, snow-frosted mountains. Between them, the city lights will twinkle their hearts out all night. Plus there will be stars and sunsets and sunrises to die for.

My hamster and I will sit on the velvet window seat, watching the world below. The buses will look like miniature caterpillars and the cruise ships like water bugs.

Oh, wait. I'm actually a tiny bit afraid of heights.

But maybe this won't count because the windows will be treated with a protective anti-fear coating.

* * *

Coach Keefer called me *the weak link*.

Maybe she's trying to get me to drop out of school or run away from home or something before my times drag our league standings too low. I mean, it's not like I'm allowed to *quit* track. The rule is that everyone at Palm Canyon Academy, from K through 12 has to be in something physical.

That's easy for people like my sister, who is a natural born dancer and my brother, who is all about baseball (except for the part of him that is about LOUD music). Even Emily is happy with fencing, in case she's ever cast in a Shakespeare play where she gets to play a boy. She says girls never, ever sword fight in Shakespeare, which is entirely unfair.

But I've been bopping around forever, from T-ball in kindergarten to soccer and basketball and swimming and tennis and back to soccer, then I don't-remember-what, and fencing just to be with Emily, then water polo, and now track. No one can say I'm not athletically well rounded, even if I do stink at everything. And my sports motto is: if at first you don't succeed, fail, fail again!

But calling me *the weak link*, is just plain *mean*.

* * *

I know, I know, it's stupid to talk to Carly, but just to kill time while we're waiting for Mitch, I tell her about my plan to go to the Catalina shelter some Saturday with Madeline.

"That'll look great on your college application," she says.

I *knew* she'd say that. Or, if not *her*, someone would. It seems like that's the only reason anyone does anything nice. If colleges suddenly stopped caring about community service I guess that would be the total end of charity.

When my sister was a sophomore, she volunteered a while at the blood bank, giving people cookies and orange juice after they donated blood. But she gained eight pounds off those cookies, so she switched to a gig as a visitor's guide at Children's Hospital, pointing people to the right elevator and delivering flowers and balloon bouquets.

Then, when she was a junior, which is the grade that the

colleges are supposed to care about most, Brooke got a volunteer job teaching ballet to underprivileged kids in the poorest parts of LA. She was nervous driving in and out of the gang neighborhoods. She said the schools had signs up reminding the kids that no firearms or knives were allowed and she had to walk through metal detectors just to get on campus even though they were elementary schools. But she really liked the actual teaching part, and loved, loved, loved the little girls. She still teaches one class a week there, and I think she wrote all her college essays about it.

Her friends do all kinds of things: read to old people in rest homes, paint out graffiti, build houses with Habitat for Humanity, clear paths and pick up litter in the state parks . . . Maybe it doesn't matter *why* people do good things. As long as the graffiti gets painted over, who cares if it is just done to impress a university, right?

"Be sure you really scrub your hands after," Carly says. "A lot of those people have bugs."

I want to tell her to shut up, but in truth I'm a little afraid of that, too. The librarian at the main library once told me that the reason they changed from comfy stuffed chairs to horrible hard ones was because of the lice and other crawlies living in the cushions!

"It's not their fault they don't have anywhere to shower," I say defensively.

"Most of them are too drunk or strung out to even care," Carly scoffs. "And if they don't care about themselves, why should we care about them?"

She is so mean! I don't know what to say back, and I'm not even sure why I'm so mad, but I am. Neither of us says anything else until Mitch flops into the backseat and announces that he's starving, for a change.

* * *

As soon as I stick one tiny nose hair into the house I know it's Hortensia Day because the house smells minty and everything gleams. Hortensia is always gone by the time I get home. Come to think of it, it's entirely possible that "Hortensia" is just a code name for Mom's secret invisible house cleaning fairies, because all I ever see of this "Hortensia" is her awesome trail of cleanliness.

I know, for instance that when I go to my room, my bed will be made so tight that it's practically shrink-wrapped. And my floor will be totally visible, from wall to wall.

* * *

Mom's reading *The New Yorker* by the pool, even though as far as I know she has never actually been *in* the pool, and she's not now, never has been, and doesn't ever plan to be a New Yorker.

She looks relaxed and tan and happy and tells us she had two really, really good job interviews back to back today and she's sure one or both will offer her a position.

"Good!" I say.

Mitch chimes in, "Cool!"

"Of course they will," Carly says. "They'd be crazy not to hire you!"

Mom smiles and suggests we go to The Coffee Table for dinner. Yumm! Mitch and I both love their tuna melt. But as she's leaving, Carly reminds us that today is Wednesday. Wednesdays we have dinner with Dad.

"Well, it's too early to celebrate anyway," Mom says with a smile. "Maybe tomorrow night."

* * *

We eat practically the second we get to Dad and Grandma's house because they are morning people. Actually Dad is such an early morning person that he's actually a middle of the night person. He gets up at three forty-five and rides his bike to the bakery in the absolute darkest dark. Then he bakes their specialty breads and rolls and bikes home before anyone else is even thinking about waking up.

Dad's olive bread is Mitch's favorite, and Brooke used to be a super fanatic fan of Dad's apricot rolls. But I have to say that the kind I love best is whichever one is in my hand, warm and smelling heavenly, on its way to my mouth.

Today it's Dad's garlic sourdough, which is unbelievably good, and I love, love, love Grandma's carne asada. Isn't eating wonderful? I'm so glad things have flavors and that we have taste buds. And I'm glad we don't just graze like cows, eating grass all day, every day. And I'm glad I'm not a worm-eating bird, or a mosquito being hated and slapped at every time I try to have a snack.

While we eat, Dad fans out little seed packets of cabbage, broccoli, beets, parsnip, and cauliflower.

"Ahem!" I say, clearing my throat. "Does anyone notice anything a little weird about these strawberries?"

"Very astute, Jack-o'-lantern!" Dad laughs, pushing his glasses up his nose for the tenth time tonight. "But the lady at the nursery said now's the time for cold-crop vegetables."

"Cold crop?" I ask. I mean look at us, the windows are

wide open, we're sitting around in tank tops and T-shirts. It's a perfect winter day.

"I think it has to do with the angle and hours of sunlight," Grandma explains, plopping more refried beans on my plate.

"She just wanted to sell you the stuff no one else in their right mind would buy," Mitch says. "Brussels sprouts for beet's sake?"

"She was very knowledgeable and helpful," Dad insists. Then with a wink, "Even kinda cute!"

"She probably didn't even work there," Mitch says. "She could've been some lunatic off the street."

"Nope," Dad smiles. "She was wearing their regulation African-safari-garden-store getup."

"Maybe she tackled and tied up the regular salesperson," I suggest. "And stole their uniform. Maybe she's from a cabbage cult planning world domination through stinky cabbage farts!"

"Jacki!" Grandma gasps.

"Well," Dad says, "you never know when free, home-grown vegetables will come in handy. In case your mother gets too broke to feed you."

"Bad joke," Mitch says.

"You're right," Dad nods. "Sorry, kiddo. I take it back."

But phew! I'm sooo glad Brooke is at ballet and she didn't hear *that!*

*　*　*

After dinner Dad brings out a graph he drew. Ta da! It's his Garden Plan. It's true, as Mom says, that Dad often gets us all fired up about his projects, but then loses interest after a while and drops them. Like his birdhouse business that I got five people to order, and then had to go back and say, *never mind, sorry, no birdhouse.*

And the summer before last, when he had us helping him weave hammocks. But his excitement is catchy and his schemes are fun while they last. Plus, the pictures on the seed packets look colorful, if not tasty.

We carefully open each little envelope, shake the seeds out onto a wet paper towel, and gently wrap them up. You wouldn't believe how teeny tiny some seeds are.

We label the "nests" in empty egg cartons. One hole is *cauliflower*. The next, *beet*. Then *cabbage*. We fill three egg cartons. Then Dad shows us how to tuck each little paper towel thingie into its nest to sprout.

"I'll keep them moist," he promises. "And we'll check on them next time."

Maybe he'll sing lullabies to them like he did to us way back before he moved out. He used to sit on the floor in the upstairs hall, equally outside our three bedrooms, and sing "Swing Low, Sweet Chariot." I have no idea what that song is about, but hearing it still makes me feel totally cozy and snug.

I love to think of Dad tending our mini nursery while we're not here, and I can tell Mitch does, too. I have a little pang wishing Brooke was part of this, but I guess I better get used to doing things without her.

* * *

We either get takeout or eat out all the time anyway, so even though there's no job offer to celebrate the next night, Mom takes Mitch and me to The Coffee Table for tuna melts. Carly is studying for a test, so Mom offers to bring her one, too. Carly has a bunch of younger brothers and sisters so she says it's lots easier for her to study at our house than at hers.

I want to say, *Haven't you ever heard of the library?* But I know Mom would totally kill me.

My sister Brooke is I-don't-know-where, getting her own dinner, I guess. We all used to share an order of onion rings when we came here. Well, not *all* of us. Mom is on a perpetual diet and spends every meal trying to get away with the least number of calories possible. Mitch tells her that if she just exercised she could eat whatever she wants, but Mom doesn't listen.

There's no job offer to celebrate the next night, either. Or the next. I tell myself to try, try, try to remember to bring a few cans to school tomorrow for Madeline's canned food drive, for good luck.

* * *

It has been so long since Emily slept over that I'm practically delirious planning it. She's coming home from school with me after my track and her fencing. I can't remember why Emily doesn't have play practice tonight, but I'm glad she doesn't.

Snarly Carly promises to take us to Trader Joe's to load up on treats, and Mitch knows that the big TV is all ours tonight.

For a minute there it looked like we were supposed to invite Cousin Nora so it wouldn't seem like Emily was sick of her. But Emily *is* so completely sick of her that the idea of inviting her practically made Emily cry. Finally, Aunt Claire said that Nora could probably use a night to herself, too. Hooray!

I guess Mitch missed Em, too, because he keeps shoving

his stinky gym clothes in her face, until I say, "Forget it, Mitch. She's in love with Shota."

Emily blushes a little and gives me a shove.

"Shota?" Mitch asks, his voice all disbelief. "But he's . . . How could you like a guy like that?"

Emily laughs. "Like what? Shota's sweet."

Mitch makes a face. "He's only the most conceited kid on the team. Ask anyone. He thinks he's so great, but like if anyone gets hits off him, oooooh boo-hoo suddenly his arm hurts."

Emily says, "Huh?"

"He gives other guys a hard time when they mess up, which is definitely not cool. And when he screws up, he's all looking for someone to blame." Mitch shakes his head. "Forget that loser," he tells Emily. "The guy's dirt."

It gets really quiet in the car. Then Carly pipes up with, "Maybe you're just jealous, Mitch, that this Shota dude is a better player than you?"

Mitch shrugs.

My brother is ridiculous in many ways, but both Emily and I know that if he says Shota is a bad sport, he probably is. That's the kind of thing Mitch knows and cares about.

It's no fun in the car the rest of the way home, but luckily it's just a few more blocks. We unload our snacks into the house then grab two bikes out of the garage. I can't actually *ask* Brooke if we can borrow hers because she's nowhere to ask, but I haven't seen her ride it in ages. Look how dusty it is!

When Emily and I were little, we used to pretend our bikes were horses and we'd zoom around the neighborhood on wild cowgirl adventures. Now we just ride for how good it feels to ride, especially downhill. Bike riding is the wonderful opposite of school. No schedule, no one to tell you what to do, or to wear the right socks or to get permission slips. It's just free and as open as the sky.

We end up at the park and sprawl under a tree. The only sounds are little kids shrieking on the swings, a basketball bouncing on the court and occasionally swishing through the chain net of the hoop, and, of course, traffic.

The grass must've just been cut because it has that extra wonderful smell. "It's weird that what smells so great to us humans is really all the little grass blades having their heads chopped off," I say.

"Think of it as a haircut," Emily says. "Not a beheading."

"You're right," I say, and take a deep breath. Mmmmm.

Emily rolls onto her belly and says, "Mitch is probably right, right?"

I know she means about Shota. "So what? I mean it's not like you're going to marry him."

"Still," Emily says, sitting up. "If the guys on his team don't like him . . ."

When I get home I'm going to kick my brother's butt for making Emily sad. "Boys like different things about each other," I say, knowing how lame that sounds. "And maybe Carly's right, that Mitch is just jealous."

Ew. Just saying the two words "Carly's right" next to each other makes me a little ill.

Then I see that Emily's not listening. "Some boys are walking this way," she whispers. And I know they must be cute by the way she tosses her hair. I shield my eyes against the sun and with a combo stomachache-thrill I see that one of them is Adam B. from piano!

Wow!

I sit up, wishing I wasn't still in my dorky school uniform. "Adam B.!" I call out.

"Jack-i!" he answers.

It's weird to see him outside, away from Mr. Woo's world of piano. His hair is soft and messy, and he's dressed like a regular boy . . . a regular *cute* boy.

"Jacki is a world famous concert pianist with the Los Angeles Philharmonic," Adam B. tells his friends as the three of them sink down on the grass with us.

I seem to have forgotten how to talk, but it doesn't matter because the boys are sort of performing for us, like clowns or court jesters, or I don't know what.

Finally Adam B. says, "So, Maestro, what are you doing here?"

I tell him I live a few blocks away.

Adam B. says, "You're kidding! How come I've never seen you around?"

"We go to Palm Canyon," I explain.

The boys look blank, so Emily says, "Palm Canyon Academy?"

Still blank. A cell phone rings. One of the boys fishes it out of his pocket and says, "Yo."

"Oh yeah," Adam B. says. "I knew you went somewhere weird. Private school, right?"

I nod.

"You live around here, too?" The dark-haired boy with long, floppy bangs asks Emily.

She shakes her head no and says, "Woodland Hills."

The kid with the phone says he's got to go. The boys stand up, but then fall over, pretending that we're pulling them back down like magnets.

"Maybe we better walk you home," says Adam B. "See if you're telling the truth about living around here, or if you fancy private school types are just slumming."

The boys don't have bikes. One has a skateboard, but the other two are on foot.

"Let's leave them in the dust!" Emily fake whispers, hopping on my sister's bike. But we don't. We half-ride, half-walk the bikes while the boys show off fancy basketball tricks, or at least *try* to. We all laugh a lot. I notice that Adam B. sticks pretty close to me, and it seems like Emily is smiling a whole lot at the one with his bangs in his eyes.

I'm glad it's a longish walk. But when we get to my house one of the boys says, "Hey, isn't this where Mitch lives?"

I say, "Mitch is my brother!"

The skateboard guy gives Adam B. a shove, "You know, man. That dude who shoots hoops with us sometimes, *Mitch*?"

The bangs guy nods. "Oh yeah, Mitch! My man!"

Then they stand around in my driveway for a while till the one who got the phone call says, "I really gotta go."

They pretend they're being pulled and torn away from us by force like by a tornado or a giant vacuum cleaner or something. They're yelling and weeping and reaching back, trying to fight it, grabbing onto trees . . . The whole neighborhood can probably hear them.

I can't believe that Adam B. lives near me and I never knew it. What a waste! But it's so amazing to see him in his natural non-piano habitat, with other members of his herd. It's like a nature show: *Boys in the Wild!*

Emily and I watch until the boys are pulled, still screaming, around a corner, then we face each other and both say, "*Mitch!*"

Chapter 5
VALENTINES AND SPROUTS

WE CRASH THROUGH THE DOOR, calling my brother's name, and thunder from room to room looking for him. We're about to run upstairs to his suspiciously quiet bedroom when Mom stops us.

"Girls, have you seen Brooke?" she asks.

"No. Have you seen Mitch?" we ask back.

"Well, when did you see her last?" Mom asks.

"Who? Brooke? I don't know," I say. "But is Mitch home?"

Mom ignores my question. "Has she called?"

OK, this is weird. "What's going on?" I ask.

Mom says, "Nothing."

Em and I exchange looks.

"Well, is Brooke like, *missing* or something?" I ask, feeling a chill of fear.

"No," Mom says. "I just want to know where she is."

"Did you call her?" I ask.

Mom nods and says, "She's not picking up."

"What about Mitch?" I ask for the tenth time. "Is he home?"

"Um, no," she says, but its like she's just guessing.

* * *

Emily and I head upstairs. "What was *that* all about?" Emily asks.

I shrug. "No idea. Brooke pretty much comes and goes whenever she wants these days. I didn't know that my mom . . . well, that she even noticed or cared, really. All they do is fight."

Emily says, "That's sad."

We peek into Mitch's empty room, then cross the hall to mine.

"I think Brooke's just nervous about the whole college thing, waiting to see what schools she'll get into. Although any school that doesn't want her is totally crazy insane!" I say. "But also, I guess that since she'll be living on her own soon, she doesn't think she should still have curfews and stuff."

Emily is the best listener in the world.

"Plus," I go on, "since my mom's been home she's been a lot nosier about everything we do. Like she wants to see my homework, and she asks us all kind of stuff, like what we had for lunch. It's weird."

"Maybe she's just bored," Emily says.

"Could be. Who knows?"

We're quiet a second and then we shake it off and start talking about Adam B. and the neighborhood boys. Emily says the guy with the long bangs is Vazken. Which, you have to admit, is a very cool name.

I tell her that Adam B. is the one I told her about from piano and she agrees that he seems really nice.

"And I could tell he likes you," Emily says.

"Well bangs-boy Vazken was sure glued to you!" I add, and we both sit on my bed smiling like two goofs.

Shota isn't mentioned again the entire night.

* * *

Many hours later, Em and I are downstairs, watching a sappy, old, black and white musical with horrendous acting, when Brooke comes tiptoeing through the room. "Mom was looking for you," I tell her.

She nods her head and keeps walking.

She doesn't ask what movie we're watching, or say hi to Emily, or even take a handful of popcorn. I remember when my sister would have joined us on the couch and cracked jokes about the actors, and maybe ordered a pizza with us or offered to French braid our hair.

Now Brooke just slinks up the stairs. Emily and I look at each other. I don't know what she's thinking, but I'm wondering if we're going to be all sneaky and moody when we're Brooke's age. I hope not. It doesn't seem one tiny bit fun.

Then the yelling begins. The clock on the TV says 1:45. I guess Mom was waiting up.

I hit pause. "Remember how we used to go hide underwater back when my parents were fighting all time?" I ask.

"Totally," Em says.

They've been divorced for over five years, so it was back when Em and I were like nine and nine and a half.

The difference is that when Mom and Brooke fight, they *both* yell. But when Mom and Dad fought, my mom would yell and my dad would get quiet. And the quieter he got, the louder she'd yell. And the louder she'd yell . . . well . . . you get it.

"So, you want to go swimming now?" I ask.

Emily says, "Sure."

I get swimsuits for us, which means going upstairs past Brooke's room where she and Mom are screaming their heads off at the same time, neither hearing a word the other one is saying. It makes my stomach hurt.

Emily and I go out into the crickety darkness.

Luckily, the water is freezing and knocks out all bad thoughts. It feels fabulously fabulous and terrible at once.

*   *   *

When we come down in the morning, Mom is hunched over her coffee. "Weekends are pointless," she says, instead of *good morning*. "The business world slams shut tight. No job interviews, no word. Just have to bear down till Monday."

Poor Mom! Imagine thinking weekends are pointless! I can tell Emily's thinking the same thing as me.

"I'm sure your luck will change Monday," Em says.

And I add, "Of course it will," although I've been saying that for weeks now.

We take two Pop-Tarts out by the pool, not to be un-friendly . . . It's just that the cloud of gloom around my mom makes it hard to eat.

A few minutes later, though, Mom comes to the back door and says, "Girls? Were you expecting company?"

My heart thumps with hope but I ask, "Why?"

"There seems to be a bicycle club going through maneuvers

in front of the house," she says. "Up and down our driveway."

Emily shrieks. We're both still in our pajamas, braless, bed-headed, morning breathed. We peek through the fence. Wow! They've multiplied. There have to be at least five boys, although maybe they're just moving too fast to count.

*　*　*

We're all on my front lawn, talking about whether we'd rather get carried off in a hurricane or a tidal wave, or be killed by molten lava from a volcano or fall into a split in the earth from an earthquake, or crushed by an avalanche or lost in a blizzard . . . I know that probably doesn't sound very cheery, but trust me, it is. In fact we're laughing so much that my face hurts when Emily's mom drives up with Nora in the car.

We wave and they both look entirely, one hundred percent shocked. Ha! I can't blame them for being surprised. I can't really believe that Em and I are out here in the center of this swarming swarm of boys, either.

Emily has to leave now though, and it won't be one bit the same without her here. The flock of boys senses it too, and buzzes away. Bye!

When we go upstairs to get Emily's overnight bag, I see Nora looking around at everything in my room. I bet she misses having her own room and her own stuff. I want to say something about it but I'm not sure if I'm supposed to know, because in the very beginning Emily said it was a secret, remember? As if it were all hush-hush and shameful.

Nora sits on the edge of my bed and kicks her feet like a little girl.

I wish I could give her something, or do something for her, but what?

Emily told me last night that Aunt Claire put their whole house full of stuff in storage, and all she and Nora have had with them all this time is one suitcase each.

Emily said her aunt Claire goes to the storage space sometimes, to figure out what she should sell, but she just ends up leaving everything there and comes home in tears.

One time Emily's dad jokingly asked Aunt Claire if she'd been visiting her furniture, but Aunt Claire took it wrong, and it hurt her feelings.

As Emily is walking out the door, she says to me, "That was a total blast!" I know she's talking about Vazken and Adam B. and all that, but I'm embarrassed to agree in front of Nora, so I just look at my feet.

* * *

Later, I'm dying to ask my brother about playing basketball with Adam B. and, well, Vazken too, but mostly Adam B., so I climb upstairs into the blast of his music. I'm a salmon swimming upstream against the current. I knock on his door and call, "Mitch?"

He doesn't hear me, of course. I bang harder, "Mitch!"

No answer.

I don't dare open his door in case he's prancing around naked or doing who-knows-what. So I get my phone out of my pocket and text him. "Knock! Knock!" and I wait.

Finally he texts back. But he says, "Who's there?" thinking it's a knock-knock joke!

"ME! At your bedroom door!" I write back, feeling pretty ridiculous.

He answers, "I don't get it."

I'm about to write that it's not a joke, but I'm suddenly so overwhelmed by the overwhelming craziness of the situation that I give up.

* * *

I'm wrapped in a towel, just out of the shower, when I pass Carly in the upstairs hall, and she says, "I hate to guess what you and your little friend are up to to get so many boys interested."

I say, "What?!"

"You heard me."

We glare at each other. I'm sputtering with things to say, but none of them turn into words. She's smiling her mean lipless smile.

Carly breaks the freeze first by turning away and saying, "I just don't even want to know."

I stomp off, hunting for my mom and I find her in the kitchen. She slams the freezer door guiltily when I walk in and holds her spoon as if she doesn't know whose it is.

"Mom," I begin, my voice shaking, "You won't believe what Carly just said to me!"

"What?"

"Well, not so much *said*, as *hinted*."

Mom rolls her eyes.

"Well, *implied*," I try to explain. Then I give up and say, "I just hate her guts!"

"That's strong language, Jacki," Mom says. "Hate should be reserved for . . ."

I cut her off. "I have incredibly strong feelings of dislike for Carly's guts. OK?"

Mom licks her spoon and tosses it into the sink. "I'm sorry to hear that," she says. "But it's important to learn to get along with all kinds of people in this world."

"Can't you just fire her?" I ask.

"Heavens, no!" Mom sounds shocked. How has she never noticed what a horrid little slimeball phony Carly is?

"Carly is an enormous help," Mom says, "and we need her."

"Why? You're not working. You could pick us up from school and shop and whatever else Carly does. I'd help."

Mom straightens up and says, "While it is painfully true that I'm not working at this exact moment, I fully expect to be employed again very soon!"

"But until then, think of all the money we'll save if we boot Carly out on her scrawny butt!"

"Jacki!" Mom gasps. "What a way to talk! And dismissing Carly would be admitting defeat."

"What?! How?"

"It would be telling the fates that I no longer believe I'm going to find another job."

"No it won't! The fates will totally get it!" I say. "The fates think Carly is a total creep, too, I swear! Let's just fire her right now, today! And the second you start a new job we could hire someone nice! OK?"

Mom shakes her head. "I know we're all under a great deal of strain right now, but lashing out and destroying an innocent woman's life, as mine has been destroyed, is definitely not the answer."

"You think your life has been *destroyed* just because you got *fired*?"

"Laid off," Mom corrects me. "And no, of course not. I was speaking dramatically. My life is simply suffering a minor setback." And she gives me a fake smile to reassure me.

I give up. But first I mutter, "Carly's NOT an innocent woman, she's a . . ."

"Jacki!" Mom barks. "Watch yourself!"

"I was going to say, *meanie*!"

* * *

On the phone, Emily says, "You didn't *destroy* your mom's life, silly! She told you herself that a bunch of other people were fired when she was."

"Not fired, laid off," I correct, although I haven't the least tiniest clue what the difference is. "And she *has* to say that, she's my *mother*."

"Well, on the subject of mothers, mine says that next time I sleep at your house we have to invite Nora. I guess she moped around all droopy while I was gone."

"Poor kid," I say.

"Which poor kid?" Em asks. "Nora or me?"

Then we sigh huge sighs at the exact same time and that cracks us up.

* * *

I'm searching for new animal videos on YouTube. So far tonight I've seen an incredibly sweet one of a momma dog nursing a litter of orphaned pink piglets, and a cute baby sloth all sleepy in a box. Now I'm glued to this web cam of a bald eagle's nest where you can watch the parents feed their fluffball chicks! I don't want to think too much about *what* they're feeding them, but still, it's amazing. Hey! That one little guy is looking right into the camera. Hello, Fuzz-face!

Mitch comes into my room, and sinks into my beanbag chair. His legs poke out a mile and he looks like a giant blue-jeaned spider. I think he's grown since breakfast.

"Mom came to my game," he announces.

I nod. Not sure what that means.

"She cheered at all the wrong places. Yelled at the ump for calling a strike. Threatened the coach." He shakes his head and adds, "We've got to get that woman back to work, like now!"

"Did she sit with Dad?" I ask, because Dad goes to all Mitch's games and my track meets and stuff.

Mitch shakes his head no and says, "At least next week's is an away game. You don't think she'd drive to Burbank, do you?"

Then I remember and yell, "MITCH! Tell me every single solitary thing you know about Adam B. and Vazken!"

"Huh?"

"The neighborhood boys you shoot hoops with sometimes at the park!"

He shrugs one shoulder.

"Come on!" I plead. "Do you like them? Do they have girlfriends? Are they nice? Funny?"

"I don't know," he says, squirming into the beans. "I guess they're OK."

"Well, are any of them any okayer than any others?" I try to stay patient and not punch him. "Adam B.? Vazken?"

Mitch shrugs uncomfortably again and he's done.

See why brothers don't count?

*   *   *

The next day Grandma says, "Well, if your mother prepared a meal at home once in a while, and didn't live like such a queen bee, perhaps this little setback wouldn't be so serious."

I hate when Grandma talks about my mom. I wonder if they *ever* liked each other.

"Learn to cook, Jacki," Grandma says, pointing her wooden spoon at me. "You'll never be sorry." I can't exactly say she's wrong, while stuffing my face with her incredibly incredible chicken piccata and Dad's warm rosemary dinner rolls.

After lunch we unwrap the tiny seed packets and inside are pale, squiggly, newly sprouted, sprout babies. Mitch tries to act like he doesn't care, but he's not fooling anyone.

The sprouts look sooo delicate. That's why I'm whispering.

We carry them outside and plant them super carefully in the dirt. It seems like it would be entirely terrifying to suddenly go from a nice warm egg carton on a sunny windowsill to the cold dirt outside full of worms and other crawlies. If I were them, I'd be scared to death.

But Dad says, "Not at all! It's their chance to grow! They're thrilled!"

I bet this is what Dad looked like when my brother and sister and I were born: all sweet and cautious, with his glasses crooked. It must really sting that his firstborn hardly even comes over anymore. I wish I could fix that.

There are more and more things I wish I could fix: Brooke's being too busy for any of us, especially Dad. Mom's work thing. And Emily says her family is falling to bits under the stress of having nonstop house guests. She says she always used to think she wanted a sister, but now that Nora's been there so long, she totally takes it all back and can't wait to be an only again.

Here's what I wish I could do: somehow get a whole huge bunch of money and hire Mom to make spreadsheets and scurry around in high heels handing them out full time. First, getting Nora and Aunt Claire's house back. Maybe tracking down Emily's Uncle Rodney and giving him a job and a second chance. And I'd have Mom give money to all the other people who are out of work and scared. And I'd give Brooke six hundred dollars for her prom dress and whatever else would cheer her up.

I never thought it would all come down to money. Fairy dust, maybe, but not *money*. It's extra sad, somehow.

* * *

When we were younger, we had to give every kid in class a card on Valentine's Day, and the only good thing about it was that my dad baked super gorgeous red velvet cupcakes for our class parties. Now the only ones who care are the kids on the decorating committee, going nuts with hearts and silhouettes of cupid all over the halls. And it's probably fun for the girls who have the kind of boyfriends who give them chocolates.

Madeline's handing out sugar-free, cruelty-free, flavor-free, politically correct candy. I ask her if she's giving them out at the Catalina homeless shelter, too, and she says, "Of course!"

I feel a guilty pang for never going with her to volunteer babysit like I said I would, but she doesn't rub it in. That's nicer of her, I think, than bringing candy.

Olivia has cut off her braids so now there is absolutely nothing to do in history besides play tic-tac-toe with myself or listen to Mr. Rodriguez. The first part of class is always current events, and today he's talking about the zabba zabba unemployment index. Unemployment? Like not being employed? Hey, my mom's in the news!

"Yeah," Emily says at lunch, "but I think a whole lot of people are in that club with your mom. Businesses are closing all over the place, like all the spooky-looking empty stores everywhere, where there used to be . . . you know . . . stuff for sale and people buying it. Like the boarded up Blockbuster and the abandoned Friday's, and that bookstore that used to be on Brand. My parents say it's entirely scary to read the paper in the morning because all the news is bad."

I say, "That's not good."

And Emily says, "Nope." Then she pulls a mangled something out of her backpack and shows it to me. It's a valentine of fluffy white kittens from Shota.

"Cute," I say, trying to be nice. I'm sure not going to be the one to mention that Emily's horribly and completely allergic to cats. In fact I'm surprised that picture isn't making her wheeze.

Emily shrugs and says, "It's a stupid holiday."

* * *

But hours later, when I get home tired, and sweaty and stinky and hungry, I find two valentines shoved in our mailbox. One has my name on it in scratchy pencil boy-printing, and the other says Emily!

I dash upstairs to call her, but she's still at rehearsal. I tear mine open, and, *yes*! It's from Adam B.! A picture of Zapp Brannigan, saying, *You get me for a valentine! I can't say I don't envy you!* which is perfect because that means Adam B. remembers that we talked about *Futurama* at the park.

I keep texting madly until Emily finally calls back all excited. "Open it! Read it to me!" she says. So I do.

"There's a picture of a rocket ship . . ." I say. I don't read the printed message though, because I'm trying to make sense of the signature. It doesn't say Vazken. "It's signed, *Ryan*." I tell her. "Who's Ryan?"

"The blond one," Emily says, sounding shocked. "The skateboard guy."

I say, "Oh."

Then I say, "That's weird."

But Emily doesn't answer. I wish I could see her face.

After a second I say, "You OK?"

And she finally answers, "I guess."

Then someone at her rehearsal calls her and she whispers, "Gotta go!" and she's gone before I can say, "Later."

* * *

All the fun is gone from getting a valentine from Adam B.

Well, not *all*, but a lot.

I trudge downstairs and find Mom in her office, paying

bills. She looks grim. "We have to have a family meeting," she says. "Tell Brooke and Mitch and Carly."

"Carly's not family," I remind her.

Mom looks up at me. "Don't start, Jacki," she warns.

"Well, I don't think Brooke's home," I say.

"Call her. Tell her to get home. Now."

Chapter 6
PANDAS AND ICE

Here's the thing: I don't understand stocks and invest-ments and bank stuff. I suppose if I squeezed my brain as hard as I could and had someone bang information about such things into my head with tiny hammers, maybe I'd get it eventually . . . if it was either that or get eaten by warthogs. But for now, when Mom says we've lost half our savings be-cause of risky investments, I'm not sure what to think, except that it can't be good.

Brooke, who got a practically perfect SAT score and has a four-point-four grade point because of her freakishly good grades in advance placement classes, says, "Huh?" Which makes me feel less stupid.

"I'm afraid we're going to have to make some drastic changes around here," Mom says. "Starting now."

"Until you get a new job, right?" Mitch asks.

"Either way," Mom says. "This morning I let Hortensia go."

I picture Mom letting go of a string, and Hortensia floating up, up, and away like a bright yellow helium balloon against the blue sky. I watch Hortensia get smaller and smaller as she heads for the clouds.

With Hortensia gone, I may never see the floor of my room ever again.

"The gardener, too," Mom says.

I say, "We had a gardener?"

Mom squints at me. "Who do you think mowed our lawn, Jacki?"

But before I answer, Brooke practically spits the words, "You mean you *fired* them? Just like *that*?"

"It wasn't *just like* anything, Brooke," Mom answers. She closes her eyes for a second. Then she says, "My stockbroker sends a statement every month. And month by month my portfolio has been sinking." She taps a stack of papers on her desk. "It's just that now, with no new income coming in . . . Well, it looks really bad."

"Wait," Brooke says, her back going stiff. "What are you saying, exactly?"

"I've been trying to remain hopeful. Thought it was just a dip in the market and we'd get past it, but I can't ignore it any longer."

"You were *ignoring* it?" Brooke asks.

"There wouldn't have been anything I could've done to stop it anyway, Brooke. If I took money out when the market was dropping, I'd have no way to earn it back if it rebounded. No one knew how to outguess this downturn. It's way bigger than me."

"Are we broke?" Mitch asks.

"No," Mom says. "But we have to be extremely careful from now on and some things have got to change."

"Like what else?" Brooke asks impatiently. "You already *fired* people!"

This seems really hard for Mom. I wish Brooke would try to act a little nicer.

"I'm fairly sure we can finish out the school year at Palm Canyon, so you can graduate with your class, Brooke. They'll probably cut us some slack on tuition in consideration of our years there. But Jacki and Mitch?" Mom turns toward me and my brother. "I'm afraid it looks like you're going to have to switch to public school in the fall."

I'm ashamed to admit that my first thought is: Wow! I'd go to school with Adam B.!

But my second thought is: *without Emily!*

And my third is pure horror.

I don't know what Mitch thinks. He's keeping his face as blank as possible. It's a boy thing.

"And . . . ?" Brooke says in a meanish way as if Mom is doing this on purpose.

"And," Mom continues bravely, "some of those colleges you applied to, Brooke, are now way out of reach for us, financially."

"Meaning?" Brooke asks, folding her arms tight.

"Meaning your college fund is not what it was, and we can no longer afford high tuition payments."

"What?" Brooke is white, and shaking.

"I'm so sorry. I thought my salary would make up for the losses . . . I know you've had your heart set on . . ."

"WHAT?!" Brooke yells louder.

"Let's hope we can still apply for financial aid to some of the less expensive schools."

My sister is on her feet, "You always said that if *I* got the grades, *you'd* take care of the rest! Now you're changing your mind? You're not keeping your end of the bargain? Is that what you're telling me?" Brooke is yelling now. "You *lost* my tuition money?"

"Brooke, it's not me," Mom tries to explain. "It's the economy . . . It's . . . We all believed . . ."

But Brooke bolts out of the room.

Mom takes off after her.

The rest of us sit barely moving or breathing. We hear the front door slam and Brooke's Prius pull away.

Mom drags back into the room looking awful. She sits at her desk, turns to Carly, and says, "I can give you two weeks' severance pay Carly, and a great letter of recommendation, but that's all I can do. I'm so terribly sorry."

Carly nods, gets up, and leaves, but with none of Brooke's fury.

It takes me a second to get what just happened. Oh! Carly got fired? It doesn't feel nearly as good as I would have thought.

There's just me, Mitch, and Mom now, looking at each other. After a while Mitch says, "Anyone for a bowl of Cap'n Crunch?" But this time no one laughs.

* * *

I'm afraid you'll get the wrong idea of Brooke. She's not really mean, or selfish, or any of the other bad things she seems to be lately. Really. It's like she's been possessed by demons. I know that my sweet, beautiful fun and funny sister is just hiding inside this new, prickly crab. I'm sure of it.

In the meantime, though, she's killing my mom.

75

"She's probably just staying at Sarah's till she calms down," I tell Mom.

Mitch agrees, yawning. It's a school night. I bet he has homework. I know I do.

Mom's jiggling her foot so hard it's shaking the couch.

I offer to call Sarah or Jennifer's house, but Mom says it's too late to wake their whole families, and we don't know their cell numbers.

It's all I can do to keep my eyes open, but I figure it's not a great night to leave Mom alone. I can tell Mitch feels the same way, but he's starting to nod off right there in the chair.

"Or she's with David," I say.

Mom gets up and pours herself a drink from the liquor bottles in the hutch then sits back next to me and resumes her nervous twitching.

I say, "Mom? Do you know what I do when I need to cheer up?"

"It's not a matter of *cheer*, Jacki, but what do you do?" Mom asks, running her fingers through my probably greasy hair. I still haven't showered since track.

I can tell Mom's just pretending to pay attention, but I say, "Can I show you?"

She checks the clock again. Then reluctantly says, "All right."

"We have to go upstairs," I explain, giving Mom's arm a tug.

She hauls herself off the couch, and lets me lead her up to my room. My brother comes, too. I sit Mom at my desk and bring YouTube up on my computer.

"Jacki, I don't know if I feel like . . ."

I tell Mom to shush and just try it. I go to my favorites and click on the sneezing panda. Mitch watches over Mom's shoulder, and I wait.

Mom doesn't fall over laughing and forget her Brooke worries completely or anything, but she does smile, and lets me play her another one. And another. The cat who flushes the toilet. The white parrot who line dances.

Mitch gives me a thumbs-up behind Mom's back.

* * *

In the middle of the night I check Brooke's room. It's empty.

I creep halfway down the stairs. Mom, still dressed, is snoring on the couch.

I go back up to my room and text Brooke. "PLEASE CALL!!"

I'm totally surprised when my phone vibrates almost immediately. The text says, "What r u doing up so late?"

And I write back, "Missing you!"

There's no answer for a while and I'm scared that was the wrong thing to say. Then the phone rings so loud I jump.

My hands go all clumsy, but I get the phone to my ear and say, "Brooke?"

She whispers, "Hi."

I go over to my window where the reception is a little better but all I can see is my own reflection against the darkness. "You OK?"

Brooke answers, "I don't know."

"Mom's worried to death," I say. There's no answer but I know she's still there because I can hear her breathing. I don't want to make her mad, but I say, "It's not her fault, you know.

Lots of people are losing their jobs and their savings. Mr. Rodriguez talks about it constantly."

"I know," Brooke whispers. "But still."

I say, "Yeah, I know. I totally know."

It's quiet a while, but not in a terrible way. Then my sister says, "Get some sleep, Wacky." She hasn't called me that in ages. I used to *hate* it, but now it sounds absolutely wonderful.

*   *   *

I zoom down the stairs and shake Mom awake. "Brooke's fine!" I say. "I talked to her!"

Mom smiles a happy, sleepy smile and folds me in next to her on the couch. We share the blue afghan, but I barely sleep.

I want to take some canned stuff out of the pantry and bring it to school tomorrow, as a thank you to the fates.

*   *   *

But the next morning I am dragging like a dead thing, and I practically fall asleep in French. I pass my brother on the green and see that he's moving pretty slowly, too. I keep looking around for Brooke but haven't spotted her yet. Palm Canyon is really spread out though, and a lot of the senior classes are way across campus. But still, I'd sure like to know that she's here.

Mom drove me and Mitch to school this morning, since there was no Carly or Brooke. We were partly late because we were groggy. I dropped my toothbrush, toothpaste side down, Mitch couldn't find his shoes . . . But we were mostly late because Mom refused to leave without first putting on her full makeup and doing her hair and dressing spiffy and all that.

Maybe she thought she'd have a car accident with some

78

successful business executive who'd say, "You know, lady, I like the way you totaled my Bentley, and I'd like to make you CEO of my company."

And she'd say, "Do I get an office with a window and tons of money and benefits and stuff?"

And he'd say, "Absolutely! And the job comes with free prom dresses, and a hamster, and full tuition to any school on earth for all your kids."

And Mom would say, "You've got yourself a deal, Bud." And they'd shake hands. The End.

* * *

"Where were you this morning?" Emily asks.

So, I tell her about last night.

Well, not *all* about last night. I leave out the part about my maybe not coming back to Palm Canyon next year. It's not like I *forget* exactly, I just don't know what to say . . . At least not yet. And Mom said she didn't *think* she could afford tuition for me and Mitch next fall. She didn't say she was absolutely, positively, one hundred percent *sure*, right?

I tell myself it's not a *lie* to wait to tell her later. It's just an I-don't-know-what. I've never kept such a big secret from Em before in my entire life, but I know it would make her so sad. And isn't just one of us being sad better than both of us?

Emily makes her little sympathetic listening noises all the way through the whole hairy story of the scene in Mom's office with Brooke storming out and Carly getting fired. At the end she says, "Eewww. That's sooo not fun."

"Way not," I agree. And we continue pushing a dusty rock back and forth in the dirt between us with our feet.

"Have you seen Brooke at school today?" I ask her.

"I don't know," she says. "I wasn't looking."

And then we get to the more serious discussion of the blond Ryan versus bangs-in-his-eyes Vazken valentine mystery. "What did Mitch say about them?" Em asks.

"My brother is useless," I warn. And when I tell her what he had to say, Emily agrees with me entirely.

* * *

Mr. Rodriguez asks something and Madeline's hand shoots up like a rocket, of course. But so does Becky's. Mr. Rodriguez is thrilled. I'm too tired to hear the actual words, but I can tell they're chewing over the same old bad news about the economy.

I don't say anything about Mom's job, of course, but I wonder how many other kids besides me have real-life, current-events stories that they're not telling.

I think about Carly leaving so quietly last night. I would've expected more drama, but I guess my sister's exit was hard to top. Carly will probably trick some other family into hiring her to *nanny* them to death in no time. But I wonder if it'll be hard for Hortensia to find another house to clean on Wednesdays. And who will we give our outgrowns and hand-me-downs to now that she's gone? Mom used to keep a *Hortensia bag* in the pantry.

Plus, without the mystery gardener (who I don't remember ever once seeing in my entire life), who's going to mow the lawn?

Maybe we'll just let the grass grow as high as an elephant's eye! That would be so cool! Wildflowers and tall wispy reeds dancing in the breeze. Sunflowers turning their giant happy faces to the sun. Among the butterfly paradise with humming-birds, an innocent-looking weed inches up the wall. At first I think it's ivy, but the stalk thickens and grows thorns. It climbs faster and quickly begins to twist and weave across the win-dows and doors! Wait! It's taking over like Sleeping Beauty's castle under the curse! The sunlight is soon blocked out com-pletely as the vine closes like a fist around our house!

Adam B. will have to draw his mighty sword and hack his way through to rescue me!

Oh. I pry my spiral notebook off my sweaty forehead and check for drool. Then I look around. Madeline's hand is still up, or up again, depending on how long I napped. Mr. Rodriguez is ignoring her, looking around for someone else to torture. Lacey is texting.

I breathe, everything is fine. This is my world . . . at least for now.

But how can I not be here next September? I try to picture this classroom without me. My desk empty. No picture of me in the yearbook for tenth grade. It gives me the same creepy stomachache that I get when I think about being dead.

Maybe I just need some real sleep. Like twelve hours. Make that fourteen.

* * *

I've gotten through most of the day without doing or saying anything particularly stupid, and am standing in the locker room, trying to stay awake while Coach Keefer yells at me about something. Zabba zabba I-don't-know-what. Is it still the permission slips? My socks? I'm too tired and punchy to care.

81

Our first track meet is this Saturday, and everybody, well not *everybody*, but some people are getting wiggy. I've seen this before, like in every single sport I've tried. The athletic kids who take sports seriously go through a monstrous transformation right before the season opens, and the coaches get even more peculiar than the kids. I try not to take it personally, although I've noticed that the sight of me makes them crazy. Have I mentioned that I'm not a particularly athletic athlete?

Now Coach Keefer seems to be done with me, and we are all trotting out to the field to begin practice. But I'm on the ground.

I'm looking at a circle of girls peering down at me, but that doesn't make sense. Coach Keefer pushes Nareh aside, and squats next to me. She grabs my ankle, OUCH!!!

I hear Coach Keefer's voice as if it's from way far away, an ant voice, looking through the wrong end of a telescope, not that I've ever looked through a telescope except a million years ago at Griffith Park Observatory when we went to see the rings around Saturn. I don't remember Saturn, but I do remember that my brother fell asleep in Dad's arms waiting in line, and was furious at us for not waking him. I bet if I mentioned Saturn to Mitch even today, he'd want to slug me.

"How the heck did you *do* this?" Keefer's asking. "We weren't even doing anything yet!"

How'd I do what? And why does she seem so little and far away?

Coach sends Nareh to call my mom and the school nurse, and then I throw up all over her leg.

"What the . . . !" Coach yells, jumping backward and half falling.

"Oh! Sorry! I'm so, so, so *sorry*!" I say. At least that's what I *try* to say.

Coach Keefer is way over there, shaking my puke off her lap, and everyone is trying not to laugh and someone tells me I'm in shock and it suddenly occurs to me that this may well be the single most wonderful moment of my life because if my ankle is broken . . . I'll be off the team!!!!

* * *

After the whole hospital ordeal it's a lot less funny, mostly because it hurts. Turns out it wasn't my ankle but a skinny bone that runs up the side of my foot. The pain, though, is everywhere. It was cool, seeing my own bones and toes in the X-ray, but now, here I am, on the living room couch because I can't walk up to my room.

The doctor, who was hugely pregnant, told me that for the first few days I shouldn't put any weight on my foot. None.

She said I should keep my foot up all the time, like on a chair. And she said to remember "ice." I for ice, C for I-can't-remember-what, and E for elevation. Oh! C for compression, which must be this clunky boot-cast-thing that Velcros on and off so I can put ice on my foot for twenty minutes every two hours. Or for two hours every . . .

But the thing about ice? It's really cold!

I called Emily a bunch of times from the hospital, "No more track!" I cheered. "I broke my foot!" And she was happy for me. But every time I talk to her I feel a twist of guilt in my belly because I still haven't told her about my maybe leaving Palm Canyon.

I've texted and called Brooke too, but I think her phone is

off. I hope she didn't drop it in the toilet again because Mom said if she drowns another one, it'll be her last.

And talk about annoying, look at my brother. I limp home, entirely clumsy and graceless on these stupid, klutzy crutches, and practically fall flat on my face, and two seconds later, Mitch is zooming around on them doing acrobatic twirls and tricks like a pro. Doesn't that just totally figure?

Mom is on the phone telling someone that it's a good thing her medical insurance hadn't stopped yet. "This would've been a pretty penny out-of-pocket," she says. "Guess I better look into getting individual coverage. That should be a wake-up call for Barry."

Barry is my dad. I wonder what Mom's medical insurance has to do with him, but maybe I don't want to know, if you know what I mean.

Poor Dad looked so scared when he came charging into the hospital, all sweaty and out of breath. It was kind of funny, but I guess not hilarious. I can picture him on his bike, pedaling like mad, bugs splattering on the lenses of his glasses. All that panic and rush and hurry, only to sit and wait, wait, wait for almost four hours before anyone looked at my stupid foot. I guess that's how *waiting rooms* got their name.

* * *

Mom finds a note in the front door, and comes in unfolding it. I'm sure it's from Adam B. and say, "Don't read that! It's private! For me!"

Mom looks at me funny and says, "It's from Mr. Woo. We missed your lesson. I'll have to call and explain about your foot."

"Oh."

Then I perk up, "Hey! Aren't we too broke for piano lessons?"

But Mom says, "The poor man depends on us, Jacki."

"So did Hortensia," I say. "And Hortensia actually *did* something useful around here. No one on earth needs me to take piano. In fact, the planet would be a happier place for just about everyone if I swore not to go near another piano for the rest of my life."

Mom gives me the single raised eyebrow, and leaves to get her phone.

Isn't there *anything* good about being poor?

"Well, at least cancel next week's lesson!" I yell after her. "I can't use the pedals!"

Mom pokes her head back in the room and squints at me.

"Pretty, pretty, pretty please?" I beg.

And she reluctantly nods.

Hooray!

Who cares about the pain and the clunky boot? This one, wonderful, tiny, broken foot bone is getting me out of *track* and *piano*! Isn't that amazing and fabulous? Now if only it could bring Brooke back home and get Mom a job, and me a hamster, life would be perfectly, entirely perfect!

Chapter 7

COUCH AND COOKIES

Remember how my life was zooming along: Mom laid off, valentine from Adam B., Brooke storming out, and Carly fired? Well now everything has slowed w-a-y down to slow motion: me, on the couch all day and all night, wishing I had a hamster. Me, on the couch every single hour of every single day, except for my big exciting trips to the bathroom.

It's day three, if you count Tuesday, which is the day I broke it. But since that was probably around three thirty, it's only really been two days I guess. Still. It feels like three. No, it feels like thirty.

The problem with Palm Canyon is that we come from all over the place. It's not like the kids you hear about who can just walk or bike over to each other's houses to hang out. I wish Emily and I could do that, but we can't. I live in Pasadena and she lives in Woodland Hills. If you don't know L.A., that won't mean anything to you, but trust me, it's really far, and no one ever wants to drive us to the other one's house.

When I have kids, I'm going to send them to the neighborhood public school so if one of them breaks their foot, their friends can come over all the time to visit.

No, actually I'll open my own school . . . in a forest! The classrooms will be treehouses and tents and caves, and everyone who goes there and teaches there will live on campus so even the broken-footed kids will still be part of everything.

The music class will play, while the art class, taught by a guy with a huge handlebar mustache waxed up crazy at the ends, makes art, and my sister's dance students pirouette through the trees. I know Brooke *says* she wants to be an entertainment lawyer, and fight for the rights of dancers and actors and stuff, but if you ever saw Brooke dance, you'd see that's *really* what she's meant to do.

Just between you and me, I think she's just scared not to be all respectable and responsible and whatever else entertainment lawyers are. Mitch says she's a mini-Mom because they're both all about super, award-winning success.

I guess I'm more like my dad.

Anyway, Emily will put on fabulous plays in our beautiful outdoor amphitheater, Mitch will run the sports department. And since my school will be on the beach, Adam B. can teach marine biology, and take us poking around in the tide pools. A tame pod of dolphins will hang out at our dock during swim lessons, we'll go kayaking with otters, and instead of crappy school food, my dad and his students will wear tall white chef hats and make us amazingly awesome meals. The air will always be full of delectable smells. And we'll all be fat and happy and sit around burping at night, with the top buttons of our pants undone so we can breathe.

* * *

Meanwhile, I watch TV, and freeze my foot, and watch Mom worry about Brooke. I totally thought when Brooke called me *Wacky,* it meant everything was fine and POOF! she'd turned back into her old self, but I guess not.

Mom called all Brooke's friends and they say she's fine, but they won't say where she is. Mom hasn't started asking their parents because she's ashamed to look like a bad mother who doesn't know where her own daughter is, although she DOESN'T know where her daughter is, so what's the point in pretending she does? Especially since not knowing is driving her absolutely bananas.

And Carly's absence is starting to show, meaning we ran completely out of toilet paper, which wasn't that funny when we had to use paper towel that we weren't allowed to flush. Mom finally went out and bought some, but it's not the normal kind and smells all gaggy in a gross perfumed way.

I don't think there would be anything wrong with Mom calling Carly to ask what kind of toilet paper we use, but Mom says she'll wait and ask when Carly comes to pick up the rest of her stuff, which will probably be soon, like maybe this weekend.

Mitch thinks Mom is embarrassed to have a masters degree and not know how to buy toilet paper, but he thinks she should be *more* embarrassed by not remembering to wash his baseball uniform.

Mom says he should learn to do it himself.

"In fact," she says, "with Carly and Hortensia gone, it's

time for everyone in this family to learn to take care of his or her own things! Laundry, bathtub rings, and no more leaving dishes in the sink for the kitchen elves! Rinse your bowls, cups, and silverware and put them in the dishwasher."

"But who's going to turn ON the dishwasher?" Mitch teases. I think it's a half serious question, though. I know the green bottle under the sink is dishwasher soap, but I have no idea where it goes in the machine.

"It's not like we have to learn to chop firewood or pluck our own chickens," Mitch says to me later. "Although I'd give anything to see Mom try!"

That cracks me up.

"Mom . . . Earth Mother," Mitch says, as if he's narrating a film. "Prairie Settler. Pioneer. Plowing her fields. Tending her goats."

I add, "Milking her cow. Spinning wool. Weaving the rough, drab cloth for her family's simple needs."

And Mitch says, "Removing her own appendix with a spoon. Buying toilet paper."

Mom pops in with my next bag of ice. We shut right up and try to look innocent. Mitch practically whistles.

* * *

Emily's working on her mom to let her sleep over tonight. And I hope, hope, hope she can because it's Friday, and I'm so bored it's almost painful. Way more painful, in fact, than my stupid foot, except when I move it or Mitch bashes into it, which he seems to do whenever he's in the room.

Emily and I haven't heard a peep from the neighborhood

boys since Monday and now neither of us is even positive we didn't imagine that whole boy story, except that I have my valentine.

Actually, I have both valentines, but I never even showed Em the one from Ryan because . . . well because what was the point? Although who knows? Maybe one day, when I'm out of this stupid boot, we'll bike back to the park and those boys will be there, and this time Emily will fall madly in love with Ryan instead of Vazken.

She'll hit herself in the head and say, "What was I thinking? Of course Ryan is way more perfectly perfect for me!" And then I'll whip out the valentine I'd been saving all along. It will be totally cosmic and romantic. And her and Ryan and me and Adam B. will live happily ever after.

Since it would totally kill my armpits and palms to crutch all the way to the park, our plan for when Emily gets here is just to plunk down on my front lawn and send powerful psychic brain waves out across the neighborhood beaming: *Boys! Come visit us!* I plan to make mine more specific: *Adam B.! Calling Adam B.!*

But Emily texts me that there's the issue of cousin Nora.

I'd be totally fine with having Nora come, too, and Mom's OK with it, and although Em is a tiny bit sick of her, she'd sure rather bring Nora than not come at all. But now that I live exclusively one hundred percent on the living room couch with my foot poking up, Emily's mom thinks it would be too much trouble to have sleepovers.

I'm not sure *who* it's too much trouble for, but there it is. Problem number one.

And problem number two is that we still haven't heard

directly from Brooke, and Mom is a basket case. Well, not a *basket case* exactly, but close. She doesn't spend every second worrying or pacing, but it's there, like a skunky smell in the air. Although at least we know Brooke is OK because Mitch asked her friend Sarah at school, and Sarah said just to give Brooke a little more time to chill.

I personally think she's been chilling long enough to get frostbite.

And talk about ice, Mom brings me my nine zillionth bag of icy-cold ice, which is really a bag of frozen organic baby peas, and says, "I'm meeting with a headhunter this afternoon."

"What?!" I say, "Gross!"

"Jacki," Mom ever-so-patiently explains, "A headhunter is someone who finds people for jobs."

"Oh. Phew! But still, don't let him near your neck."

"It's a woman," Mom says distractedly.

"Really? Do you think she shows her babies her work tools? *Here's mommy's bloody ax, her meat cleaver* . . . They go to show-and-tell with little shriveled skulls . . ."

"Jacki, *please*!" Mom barks.

Mitch is at school and Brooke is who-knows-where and Mom doesn't want to leave me alone, which seems backward since *I'm* not the one hanging around with headhunters.

"I wish Carly were here," Mom says.

"Well I sure don't!"

"But in case you need anything . . ."

"I'll be fine," I say. "It's just a couple of hours, right?"

"What if there's an emergency?"

"I'll call 911," I say holding up my phone. "And I could hop out of a fire, or an earthquake, hop, hop, hop, like a bunny. You never hear about one-legged bunnies being caught in house fires. At least I never have."

Mom squints at me.

"And if a meteor hit the house?" I continue, "It wouldn't matter how many people were here with me, right? Or if a plane crashed through the ceiling? Or the earth veered off orbit?"

"Call your father," Mom says, clearly as a last resort. "See if he can be here at one."

So I do.

He says he'd be honored to come by to keep me company today, and hints that Grandma will send over some of her super delicious, ultra-amazing peanut chocolate chip cookies.

Mom mouths, "One o'clock!" to me, so I say, "How's one o'clock?"

And he says, "Abso-root-ly!"

But it's only about nine thirty, and time, as I said, is going S-L-O-W-L-Y.

I click through the TV channels, but everything is stupid and all the laughter is fake. I wonder what disastrous disaster person is warning the students of Palm Canyon against which hideous catastrophe at the All School Assembly. I don't exactly wish I were there, but I wish I wasn't *here*, marooned on the couch with a frozen foot.

Then my phone buzzes with a text. I don't recognize the caller. My first hope is that it's Adam B., but that's just silly. How would he know my cell phone number?

"YOU BARFED ON KEEFER???? WAY TO GO! I'VE ALWAYS WANTED TO DO THAT!" it says.

I quickly answer, "Brooke?"

"AND BROKE UR LEG???" came the answer. "I TURN MY BACK FOR 1 SEC . . ."

My heart skips happily and my face practically splits in half with a grin. I write back: "Is this you?"

And my wonderful, beautiful, brilliant, talented, sister answers, "YUP."

I'm about to scream my head off telling Mom the good news when Brooke's next message comes through saying, "DON'T TELL THE MOM."

I swallow half my happiness like too big a bite of a dry PB&J. URF! You know the way it sticks there in your chest?

But I write back "OK." And add, "It's my foot not leg."

Then I write her that Dad's bringing Grandma's cookies. Maybe that will lure my sister out of hiding because Grandma puts in lots of chocolate chips and nuts, plus I think there's a secret ingredient that Grandma has written in code in a tiny, locked notebook that she keeps strapped to her body under her clothing at all times. But I'm not absolutely positive if Grandma told me that or I dreamed it.

Brooke doesn't write back, though. Maybe whoever she borrowed the phone from wanted it back. When she flew out of here Monday night I bet she didn't take her phone charger. It's not like she stopped to pack, or think. I wonder where she went? She doesn't even know Carly got fired . . .

Two seconds later my phone buzzes. Yaaay! But it's Emily not Brooke.

"Brooke's here!" Emily writes. "Staring at her right now!" I can picture Emily sneaking her phone out during All School Assembly. That's brave of her, since she has already had two phones taken away this year!

After risking her phone for me, I don't want to tell her I already know about Brooke so I just text, "HOORAY!"

*　*　*

Now Mom's dashing up and down the stairs, in and out of the room half dressed, half shoed, half painted. "Is this instead of going to the gym?" I ask her.

"I can't *find* anything!" she says. "Help me look for my gray shoes. The ones that go with the gray silk."

I turn my head this way and that.

"Any luck?" she calls from back upstairs and I giggle. How long will it take her to remember that I'm permanently rooted to the couch?

"Found them!" she calls.

I know Mom misses Carly way more than I do. Which isn't saying much, of course, because except for the toilet paper, I don't miss Carly the least tiniest speck. But she kept Mom's world of dry cleaning and gray shoes running.

"How do I look?" Mom asks, standing straight and pretty and executive- businessy-woman in front of me.

"Beautiful!" I say. "They'll hire you for sure!"

"This is the headhunter," she reminds me.

I shiver.

Mom checks her watch. "You're sure you told your father to be here at one?"

"Yes. Don't worry. He'll be here any second."

Mom pauses.

"And I'll be totally, totally, one hundred percent fine!" I say.

Mom checks her watch again.

"Go!" I command.

So she does.

* * *

And then it's sooo quiet that I start to fall asleep, when someone knocks on the front door!

Uh oh! Did Mom lock Dad out? I'm not supposed to get up!

The doorbell!

No, it can't be Dad. He'd know to come around the side. We *always* use the side door, even though sitter number three, Gladys, told us it was bad feng shui to come and go through the same door we use for the garbage.

No one uses the front door but company. Does Dad think of himself as *company* now? That would be so sad.

More knocking and ringing!

I yell, "Go round to the side!" but I doubt my voice reaches all the way outside. I try again, "DAD! TRY THE SIDE DOOR!"

I feel so stupid, sitting here like a lump. I start to haul myself up to hop to the door, but it's impossible not to put my bad foot down just a little and OW! The pain plops me right back down on the couch.

Hey. The ringing and knocking have stopped and no one came in. Dad wouldn't just go away, would he?

No.

So it must have been someone else. Adam B.! No, it's the middle of a school day. How would he know I'm gimped out at home?

It's more likely robbers who've been staking out the house

and saw Mom leave and were just knocking to make sure no one else is home and the coast is clear. And since no one answered the door, they're sharpening their nefarious, cruel and unusual, life-of-crime burglar supplies, including ropes to tie up and gag any stragglers they may find still inside.

I pull the blue afghan over my head and hope I look like a harmless lumpy old couch when I hear the side door click open. Eeek! I hold my breath. It's absolutely quiet for a long, long, second, then Dad calls out, "Jack-o'-lantern?"

* * *

"Grass is getting a little long out there," Dad says. "Gardener on vacation?"

I'm not sure if it's a secret that we're going broke, so I just shrug.

Dad is pacing. It must feel weird to be back in the house he once lived in, but he doesn't say so. It's at least ten cookies since he got here, and he has tromped the big circle from living room to dining room, past the hall bathroom and Mom's office, through the den, past the kitchen, and back to the living room at least twelve times, when someone knocks on the door.

Adam B.?

No. It's a delivery guy telling Dad that he was here earlier but no one was home. I guess that explains the knocking.

"You don't look thrilled," Dad says, putting Palm Canyon's Get Well Flower Arrangement on the coffee table next to my broken foot.

"Well, it's the same one school sends when you get your tonsils out, or your grandfather dies, or your mom has triplets, or your entire family is wiped out by the bubonic plague," I explain, eating another cookie. It's going to be hard at this rate to even save crumbs for anyone else.

"Dad, pleeeeease sit down!" I beg, as he passes by *again*.

He reluctantly perches on the edge of the chair and asks me what time Mitch and Brooke get home.

"Mitch gets out of baseball at four fourteen," I tell him, "and Brooke, hasn't been here since Valentine's Day."

Dad says, "Huh?"

Oops. Maybe I wasn't supposed to say that. "She and Mom are fighting," I say, feeling like the world's lowliest tattle-telling worm.

"About what?" Dad asks.

"Money."

He nods. "Yeah, that's a big one for your mother. So where has Brooke been staying?"

Now would be an excellent time for that meteor to crash into the house, but it doesn't. And Dad is peering at me through his thick glasses, waiting for an answer. I shrug.

"You don't know?" He's shocked. "Brooke's just out there somewhere in the world? Since Monday? And this is Friday? And no one called the police?"

"She's at school today," I say trying to fix it.

"*Today*?"

Dad demands the whole story.

Now he's back up on his feet. As he retromps his circle, he repeats, 1. As her father, I'm entitled to know these things. And 2. Anytime you need a break from your mother you can stay with me and Grandma.

* * *

Mom calls to makes sure I'm OK, and to tell me she's on her way home. That's code for me to tell Dad so he'll leave and they won't have to see each other. I tell Dad but he doesn't take the hint.

Uh oh. There's going to be a scene, and I can't even get off this couch to hide! It's like watching huge, dark, storm clouds gather from horizon to horizon, and not be able to run for cover.

I wish I hadn't said anything! I wish I didn't break my foot! I wish I didn't make Mom go to my stupid recital and get fired! I wish I'd told Emily about my maybe leaving Palm Canyon so I wouldn't have to feel guilty all the time. I wish I could go back to the boring old days. That's too many wishes for a regular Three-Wish Genie. I need a Super-Genie.

"These must be the *interesting times*," I tell Dad. But I don't think he knows what I mean.

Chapter 8
WINKS AND SEA LION PUPS

MY PARENTS HOLD THEIR SEETHING, snarling, blamefest in the kitchen, way, way, too close to my couch, if you ask me. Each of them accusing the other of being a terrible, zabba zabba, selfish, parent.

Remind me never to do that, and for sure not in front of my kid.

Actually, they started out remembering that I was trapped right here in the living room, and they kept their voices and accusations to a low hiss for a while. But then they threw themselves into battle with greater gusto and just let it rip.

I want to hear and eavesdrop on everything, but at the same time, I totally don't. Do you know what I mean? So, when it gets too intensely intense, I grab my crutches and lurch outside.

It takes a while, but eventually I get out by the pool and land, panting and sore, in a lounge chair. I can still hear my parents, though, so I start singing as loud as I can: camp songs from Brownies, all the patriotic "America the Beautiful"-type songs that I can remember, "Rudolph the Red Nosed Reindeer," and a few rock classics.

I'm sure the neighbors enjoy it.

Then it gets quiet.

I haul myself up and stump over to peer in the window. Dad is on our land line, and Mom on her iPhone, tracking down Brooke. And then without a peep to me, they zoom off in Mom's car. Where? Why? To see Brooke? To get her? What about Brooke's car? And who's going to get Mitch from school?

I go back inside to my couch, wondering what's going on.

Mom calls a while later to tell me that they'd gone.

I don't say, *No kidding?* I just say, "OK."

Dad doesn't own a cell phone, or I'm positively sure he would have called too. Twice, probably, since they're in score-keeping mode.

I call Emily a few hundred times, while flipping through the channels. I land on a nature show about sea lions, and it's fine until a mamma sea lion starts ignoring her fuzzy newborn pup.

I keep watching, thinking that everything will work out. They wouldn't show a tragic animal story to animal lovers, right? And who else watches animal shows? So I don't turn it off even when the baby sea lion looks around for help, and the other moms growl and snap at him with mean angry faces!

"Hey! Cut that out!" I yell at the TV. My voice sounds weird in the empty house.

But none of the sea lions has the least speck of pity for the poor little guy! He just floops away alone, and sad until . . . No! The tide comes in and washes him out to sea!

WHAT?!

I turn it off and try to catch my breath.

What a horrible, horrible program! I can't believe they let something like that be on TV! Shouldn't there be a warning at least, flashing: *BEWARE! Most upsetting show on earth!*

If I had a TV network, i'd just show happy, healthy animals playing and being cute and having fun. At one o'clock: frisky puppies. One thirty: wooly lambs.

Hard day at school? Watch tiger cubs pounce and tumble. Lose your job? Tune in for waddling ducks. Can't sleep? Watch furry forest animals cuddle up in their cozy nests. Everyone would watch, right? I totally would!

Finally Mom, Dad, Brooke, and Mitch all tromp in. The whole happy animal family. But a very, very, quiet version of it.

* * *

I never did get the full story of exactly where Brooke was the days and nights she was gone, but now we're on week three of The New Rules: in exchange for Mom making Brooke's car payments, and paying her car insurance and gas, (which Mom has been doing all along anyway), Brooke has to drive me and Mitch to and from school. And that's *three* trips because now that I'm track-free, I can leave an hour and a half before Mitch gets out of baseball.

When Brooke has club meetings or something after school, I sneak in and watch Emily rehearse for the play, although sneaking on crutches isn't exactly like tiptoeing. Sometimes Emily can sit with me between scenes.

And now I've seen so many rehearsals I practically know the whole entire play by heart. In a pinch I bet I could play any one of the Guys or the Dolls, sing all their songs, do their dances . . . except that I can't sing or dance.

Anyway, besides driving Mitch and me, Brooke has to be home by eleven o'clock on the dot every night, unless she has special permission to stay out late. Plus she's in charge of changing everyone's sheets on Sunday and washing towels. She says David calls her Cinderella.

And who does that make me? One of her ugly, evil, step-sisters? But I don't mention that. We all have to be very, very careful about every little thing we mention to my sister because she could go off like a bomb at any second. Like today, on the way home from school. All I said was, "Maybe we should put on Halloween masks and rob a bank." When BLAM! Brooke totally exploded!

"Where have you been, Jacki!" she yells, as if I'd suggested we kill Mom. "The whole point of this mess is that the banks don't have money anymore! As you'd know if you paid any attention at all to anything and weren't all *Tra-la-la. Drive me here. Take me there. I'm going to be a fireman. Can Emily come over?*"

I scrunch down in my seat. *That's* what I sound like to her?

"The banks don't *have* money, Jacki," Brooke overly explains. "Because they loaned it all out to people who can't pay it back. They threw it away. It's gone."

"I just thought I could wear my Sponge Bob mask from second grade . . ."

"No, you didn't *think*!" Brooke snaps. "You never do. If banks had money wouldn't I be getting student loans to get out of here and go to school? Huh? Wouldn't I?"

See what I mean?

* * *

Brooke's not the only one with New Rules. Mitch has to unload the dishwasher and take out the garbage, and he's in charge of his own stinky laundry and skimming the leaves and dead bugs out of the pool.

Mom is in charge of shopping and general cleaning.

Once a week someone has to mow the lawn with our brand new lawnmower. My brother did it the first week.

"It's not entirely terrible," he said. "You put on some tunes, build up your pecs."

The next week was Mom's turn and she said it made her shoulders ache and gave her itchy sneezes.

Mitch flexed his skinny arms and called Mom a wuss, so she showed us her polka-dot, flea-bit ankles. That shut him up.

It'll be Brooke's turn this weekend. I wonder what she'll think. Maybe she'll do it *en pointe*! The Lawn Mowers Ballet! Can't you picture that?

Oh, and everyone has to do at least one major chore each week when asked, such as wash the kitchen floor or vacuum the living room and den. That is, everyone but *me*. I don't have to mow or do anything else until I get off these stupid crutches. Well, except sort and fold laundry. That may not sound like much, but you should see how high it heaps up around me on the couch and coffee table and chair! I've become a brilliant folder-of-towels and matcher-upper of socks, though, if I do say so myself.

* * *

Mom drags in just a few minutes after Brooke and I get home.

"Good!" Brooke tells her. "You can get Mitch this time."

But Mom shakes her head and says, "I've got to put my feet up. I'm exhausted." She kicks off her shoes and wiggles out of her pantyhose right there at the door.

I brace myself. Maybe Brooke got all her meanies out at me over the Sponge Bob bank robbery, but she could still have more for Mom. You just never know.

And right on cue Brooke starts to whine about having homework and stuff before ballet, but then she changes it to, "Were you on a job interview?" See what I mean about never knowing? She can switch from mean to nice in a microsecond.

Mom collapses in the chair. "More like a cattle call. There are so many applicants for every job . . ." Mom's voice trails off.

"Hazel, you know Hazel, right?" Brooke asks.

Mom and I nod.

"She's been volunteering at the humane society as a cat socializer."

Mom raises her eyebrows.

I ask, "A what?"

Brooke dismisses it with a flick of her wrist, saying, "She plays with kittens so they'll be tame when people adopt them."

Wow! That sounds like the most amazingly wonderful job on the planet! I've totally found my calling!

"That's her community service?" Mom scoffs, as if it's not utterly perfect.

"The point is," Brooke says, "that they advertised for a new associate director and got stacks of applications from all kinds of people. Pink-slipped teachers, advertising account executives, a CPA from some fancy company, journalists . . .

According to Hazel, the director was interviewing people who were way more glamorous than herself, and they were begging her for this puny job."

Mom nods. And she and Brooke look sweet together for the first time in a while. Sweet and sad.

But a *cat socializer*! How fabulous!

I try to honor this serious moment of sorrow and bonding between my mom and sister, but when I can't take it anymore I blurt out, "Tell Hazel I would seriously, totally, and completely *love* her kitty job when she leaves for college!"

My mom and sister both look at me like I'm something stinky stuck to their shoe. I know they think I should be more depressed every second of every day, but all this unending sad stuff is getting ridiculous.

I glance out the front window and there, on the street, are boys! *My* boys! Some are walking, some on skateboards, others on bikes. There's Adam B.!

I scream, "WAIT!" and both Mom and Brooke jump. I grab my crutches and struggle off the couch. "Don't let them get away!"

The boys are moving slowly, the ones on bikes circle back so the walkers can catch up.

I finally get to the front door. Stumble through unlocking all the locks, Hurry! Hurry! I throw open the door and yell, "HI, GUYS!" as loud as I can. This is *not* the time to play hard to get. "Yoo hoo!" I shriek like some crazy loon. And it works! They're coming back!

I teeter down the three steps and totter on the front walk. Up comes Adam B. and . . . well . . . who cares who else?

"Whoa!" he says, straddling his bike. "What happened to you?"

I wish I'd thought up a good story, but too late now. "Well, after playing my Beethoven solo at The Bowl," I explain, "my fans threw so many roses on the stage that when I came out for my encore, I tripped." Not great, but not bad for spur of the moment. Better than: I fell over my own feet and threw up on my coach.

"Oh yeah!" Adam B. says with a soft smile. "I heard about that concert."

His friends hover. One does board tricks. One asks if Emily is here but I'm not sure which one because I'm busy grinning my head off at Adam B.

"Thanks for the valentine," I say.

Adam B. nods, "No problem." Then he tells me they're on their way up to the high school to watch a friend of theirs play. "Want to come along?" he asks.

I think yes! Yes! YES! But how? I look down at my stupid boot, and he says, "Oh. Right."

The other boys are anxious to get going. One of them says, "B, you coming or what?"

So he gives me a helpless kind of smile and goes with them, although I can absolutely positively tell he wants to stay.

"See ya later," he says.

And I say, "K!"

He rides down my drive and pops a mini-wheelie. One of the other boys reaches over and bonks him in the head, teasing him about *me* I bet.

Adam B. turns around to see if I'm still watching, and waves an adorable little wave.

* * *

"Which one asked if I was there?" Emily asks as I absolutely knew she would. We're on the phone so she can't see me cross my fingers before I say, "Ryan."

Emily moans, "I wish I was there!" She doesn't sound too disappointed about it not being Vazken, although for all I know, it actually *was* Vazken.

"What kind of game?" Emily asks.

"I dunno. Baseball I guess. Football?"

"Well, I gotta get back to rehearsal anyway," she says.

"Later."

"Gator."

* * *

Brooke is crazed, hurrying me to her car after school.

"I can't go any faster," I whine, stopping to show her how red and sore the palms of my hands are from my crutches. "And my armpits are like . . ."

"Move it, girl!" she yells. "You can show me your wounds later! Just hurry!"

She peels out of her parking space before I even have my seatbelt on and drives like Carly.

"Hey!" I cry, grabbing the door handle as I'm thrown sideways. "What's this about?"

"Jerry doesn't get to us until almost five because we're at the end of his route," she says, "unless he has a sub. Subs make up their own delivery schedule and you never know when Jerry's going on vacation or is sick or whatever."

Huh? I watch cars blur as we swoop through traffic.

"Subs can get there anytime," Brooke adds.

Oh, *Jerry* our mailman. This is about college acceptance letters!

Now Brooke jiggles in her seat and drums on the wheel, trying to make the red light turn green faster.

"But wait. I thought you said the letters come at the end of March."

"This is *wink letters*, Jacki," she says, as if I'm supposed to know that. "Sarah got one today from Middlebury!"

The light changes and we're off! We just miss a parked car, but NASCAR Brooke doesn't even tap the brake.

I can barely croak out the words, "Wink letter?"

"Some schools send them if they really, really want you, and want you to know that before the official acceptance letters go out."

"Why?"

"In case *everyone* wants you, and you have to decide which school to go to," Brooke answers, squealing onto our street, and up our driveway in record time. I wonder how many poor innocent cats and squirrels and pedestrians are mowed down on wink letter days. My sister is inside the house before I've taken off my seatbelt.

I climb out of the car, balance my backpack and hobble my way inside. Brooke didn't even leave the door open for me, but I don't blame her, today. There is mail flung around in the foyer, but no other sign of my sister. I lurch from room to room, then listen at the bottom of the stairs and hear the heartbreaking sound of my poor sister crying, all alone, like Rapunzel, way, way up in her tower.

I haven't actually tried stairs yet. Well, I've done the few (exactly three) out the front door to catch Adam B., and the two into the building where my French class is, but there must be fifty of them here.

If I bump up backward on my butt it shouldn't be so, so, impossibly hard, right? I just have to hold my foot in its fifty-pound boot up in the air in front of me. Of course Brooke's room is the last one at the far end of the hall.

* * *

OK. This isn't so bad. I'm more than halfway up in just a few little minutes.

Then Brooke appears at the top, and says, "Oh!" at the sight of me. Her eyes and nose are entirely red and she's still sniffing. Then she's on her way down *toward*, then *past* me on the stairs.

Hey! She's across the living room and practically out the side door before I get it. "Brooke!" I call out. "Wait!"

She stops and turns.

"Did you . . . um . . ." I suddenly don't know how to ask exactly, and end up saying. "Did the mail come?"

She turns and continues out the door saying, "Yes." And then she's gone.

So, here I am. Stranded halfway up the stairs without a paddle. I can't figure out if those were tears of sorrow because she *didn't* get winked at, or tears of sorrow that they *did* wink at her but she doesn't have the money to go? Or were they tears of joy? No, forget that last. Those definitely did not look like happy tears.

Ah! I'm finally back in my nest, surrounded by the snacks I lugged, snack by snack, from the kitchen to my couch.

My computer is humming away on YouTube, although it's ready, at a moment's notice, to switch to homework. And my textbooks and folders are spread around in a scholarly A+-looking way that would impress the daylights out of anyone who noticed.

When Mom comes home, I watch her from my couch as she, too, attacks the mail. She doesn't cry, but she sure looks grim. I guess we're still losing money every month and there's nothing Mom, in spite of her MBA, can do about it. I can tell she's on the phone with her broker, because her voice has to force itself out past her clamped teeth. If she were a dog, this would be that really low, quiet but scary growl they make.

I hear her say, "It's like bleeding to death from a thousand tiny paper cuts." That's *not* something I want to picture.

Mom ends her call, turns around, and notices me. "Is your brother home?" she asks.

"No."

"Did Brooke go to get him?"

"I don't know."

"Well, where is she?"

"I don't know," I say. "She left crying."

"What? Why?"

"I'm not sure. She either *got* or *didn't get* a wink letter."

Mom squints at me. Is it my imagination or is she squinting at me more and more lately?

* * *

Brooke comes home not all *that* late, but Mom is steamed because she had to get Mitch herself in spite of The New Rules. And because I'm on crutches, and what if I'd needed help, which I absolutely didn't.

"Zabba zabba, shirking responsibility . . ." Mom rants. "Wink letters no excuse . . . Zabba helpless little sister . . ."

Me?

It's not pretty. And I hate being put on the anti-Brooke side. Mom lines us all up like a firing squad pointing our rifles at my poor, blindfolded sister. Not in real life, of course, but you know what I mean. Mitch probably feels bad about *his* part in getting Brooke in trouble, too, but he's drowning his sorrows with music up in his room, so who knows for sure?

* * *

It turns out Brooke *didn't* get any wink letters, but she says that only a couple of schools sent them today. The others could come at any time over the next couple of weeks, and not all schools send them at all!

Oh great. We get to go through this every day for weeks? How will any of us stand it? Especially Brooke.

"When it's me applying to colleges," I say. "I'm just going to . . . well, I don't know what I'm going to do. But I'm going to try not to get too upset."

"It'll be different for *you*," Brooke says.

I know she means it as an insult because I'm not as smart

as her or as good a student, and I'm not the type for colleges to go winking at left and right.

"That's OK," I say. "I *want* it to be different!"

Brooke makes a mean little sniff, and huffs out of the room. Hey, why's she so mad at *me*? Does she think I tattled on purpose? Does she think I *liked* getting her in trouble for not babysitting me like a big baby?

Chapter 9

FRITOS AND BALLET

EMILY AND I ARE LYING BESIDE THE POOL. I can tell Nora wants Emily to come back in the water with her, but since I'm permanently beached by my boot, Emily has to go back and forth between us.

Having Nora around is a teeny tiny bit like having a little sister, so I try to be the sister I always thought I'd be: patient, generous, and not at all resentful when she cuts into my time with my best friend, or gets whiny and sulks if we talk about people she doesn't know.

Strictly speaking, no one is allowed to swim when there's no grownup at home, but I figure Emily is almost fifteen, Nora is twelve, Mitch (up in his room) is thirteen, and I'm fourteen and a half, so if you add us all together . . . well . . . that would be math. But I bet we'd come out older than my mom!

Brooke's ballet recital is tonight and Mom got tickets for Emily and Nora, which was nice considering she says she's trying to spend less money.

She's at another interview right now. Won't it be nice if she comes home all happy? Bam! She'll throw open the door from the garage and yell, "Kids! Great news!"

Mitch will hear her because it will be the quiet second between songs. He'll come barreling down the stairs, Emily will run, I'll hop in, and Nora will splash over leaving wet footprints on the wood floors but Mom won't mind. She'll throw her arms around all of us in a giant hug. Nora will be getting Mom's blue silk suit all wet, but who cares? Mom's got a great new job and we're all so happy, happy, happy!

We'll tell Brooke right before she goes onstage and it will make her leaps higher and her pirouettes even more perfectly twirly. The entire audience will be utterly astounded!

* * *

Emily checks to make sure Nora's not listening, then leans closer to me. "I have something amazing to tell you about my uncle Rodney," Emily whispers.

"Amazingly good or amazingly bad?" I ask.

"Amazingly amazing," Emily answers. "Later."

I answer, "Gator," even though no one is going anywhere.

I hear the garage door open and my mom's car purr in, so I yell, "Nora! Quick! Get out!"

We'd planned this drill. Emily's already holding up a towel for Nora to cocoon herself in, and fall onto her lounge chair to pretend she has been there all day, dry and toasty.

Success!

Mom calls out her hello, but she can't hear my answer over Mitch's sound system. After a few minutes she tracks us down and stands next to the pool looking way too dressed. Suit jacket and skirt, blouse, stockings, pumps, jewelry. She says, "Hello girls," and I instantly know something's wrong. I'm not sure how. Her voice? Her face? The way she stands?

"Brooke home?" she asks.

I shrug, although I know she's not. I'm not sure if Brooke was allowed to go out today before her performance but I'm not touching that with a ten-foot pole.

Mom doesn't have to ask if Mitch is home. He's very, very, easy to track. That's not always true, though. When he's wearing headphones you can never find him no matter how loud you yell, unless you happen to trip over his body.

I say, "What's wrong?" But Mom says, "Nothing," which I'll bet is a total, complete, one hundred percent . . . well . . . I don't want to call my mom a *liar*, but I really don't believe she's telling the absolute, capital T Truth.

Mom goes back into the house, her high heels clicking on the flagstones. I wonder what creepy creepiness is in store for me and Mitch and Brooke after Em and Nora leave. Whatever is worse than losing her job and half her investments I DO NOT WANT TO KNOW!

Meanwhile, Emily and Nora are giving each other high fives and giggling over tricking my mother. But I don't think it counts if Mom's got some huge, gigantic monster worry filling her brain. That's practically cheating. There's a trail of puddles across the deck, and Nora has completely soaked through her towel, so if Mom didn't notice it's because she's just totally distracted.

Nora and Emily's giggles are getting on my nerves. I almost tell them to cut it out. My lips are one teeny sliver of an inch from saying "It's not *that* funny," but I shove a handful of Fritos into my mouth instead, and chase it with a huge gulp of lemonade.

Now Nora and Emily are talking about fooling their mothers or something yesterday; about how they weren't supposed to eat some food they ate, so they faked it all fluffy to make it look untouched. And it worked, no one knew they'd eaten some.

It's not a particularly interesting story. Or maybe I'm not listening hard enough. Emily and Nora seem to have a lot of stories like that, now. I'd say they were like sisters, but look at me and *my* sister, we don't have even a trace of *just us, her & me* stories. If I sound a teeny microscopic bit jealous of Nora and Emily becoming such pals, it's because I totally am.

But when Nora goes inside to change into dry clothes, Emily scoots her chair close to me and says, "So . . ."

"So what?"

"So the amazingly amazing story," she says.

I lean closer.

"Well, it turns out that not only did Uncle Rodney spend every cent he and Aunt Claire had in savings and stuff, but he also borrowed money from everyone they knew."

I wait for her to go on.

"Not *my* parents, natch, but practically all their friends. And my aunt never had a clue! So, like they'd be out to dinner with friends and Aunt Claire would order a big old expensive steak or something, not knowing that she was sitting across the table from people she owed money to!"

"Well, *she* didn't owe it," I whisper back. "Uncle Rodney did."

"But they're married! Their money is shared. And the point is," Emily looks around to make sure Nora isn't coming back. "That Aunt Claire had no idea that he was borrowing like that. But their friends didn't know that she didn't know. They thought she was wasting their money on steak, and lobster and clothes, and trips, instead of paying them back! Can you imagine? My aunt is so embarrassed she just wants to crawl in a hole and die!"

"But it's not her fault! And now she can explain it to them, right?"

"She doesn't even know how much Uncle Rodney borrowed or from which friends! It's so awful. She only found out because her best friend Nancy wants to be paid back. Not in a mean way, or anything, it's just that Nancy and her husband work in construction, but since no one is hardly building houses anymore, they need the money they loaned to Uncle Rodney."

"Ew!" I say.

Emily nods, "Nancy thought Aunt Claire knew all about it!"

Emily and I stare at each other wow-eyed. Then she says, "Now my poor aunt is calling everyone she can think of and asking them, *Did my no-good husband borrow money from you?* And so far practically everyone is saying *yes!* Even the parents of some of Nora's friends from her school! But since they all know that Claire and Nora are homeless and broke, no one wants to tell her how much he borrowed! Isn't that unbelievable?"

"Isn't what unbelievable?" Nora asks.

Emily's eyes go absolutely gigantic but I say, "How many calories there are in Fritos! Look!" and I show her the side of the bag.

Remember how I said I was jealous that Emily and Nora were such chums? Well, I take it back.

*   *   *

We all get dressed up for Brooke's dance recital, except Mitch, of course, who always wears jeans and band T-shirts every single day and won't change for anyone no matter what, except to put on his baseball uniform. We look, if I do say so myself, fabulous. We take a few hundred pictures of ourselves with our phones. I make sure they only shoot me from the knees up, because my stupid clunky boot definitely wrecks the look. Nora says she's going to post the glam shots on her MySpace page because she's the kind of girl who knows how to do that.

We're waiting for Mom, who takes longer to get ready than anyone else on earth. I check the time on my phone and say something about what a slowpoke she is.

Nora says, "My mother is like that, too. So when we got evicted we hardly got anything out of the house."

I say, "Huh?"

"The police said we'd have as long as it took them to change all our locks to gather up whatever we could."

I'm totally not getting this.

"So," Nora continues, "first you have to subtract the time my mother and I just stood there with our mouths hanging open, going *HUH?* and *This must be a mistake*! And while we were doing that, one of the cops had already unpacked his tools and started to drill out the lock on our front door."

What? Drill out locks? Cops? I shake my head a little to clear it.

Nora says, "Finally, my mother stopped arguing with the guy, and we started packing. But we *so* didn't get it still, that we were folding stuff into suitcases and making trips outside to put them in the car. By then the lock-changer-cop had finished the front door and was getting ready to start on the back. I'll never, ever forget the sound of that power drill."

Emily must already know this story because she isn't gasping and her eyeballs aren't boinging out of their sockets.

Nora smiles at me. "Finally we started running from room to room, grabbing anything we could, and hurling it out on the front lawn to worry about later. I never saw my mom move so fast, swearing her head off the whole time. Words I didn't think she even knew!"

Nora laughs as if there is anything even one teeny tiny bit funny about this horrible story. I have to tell myself to blink.

"Like a cable reality show," Emily says. "How Much Can You Get Out Before You're Locked Out!" Emily and Nora chuckle and I get that creepy nightmare feeling, like when nothing around you makes sense.

Then Nora says, "One of the cops said *he'd* give us more time if it was up to him but he had thirteen evictions to secure that day and his shift ended at seven. That's what he does all day, every day, lock people out of their houses. Not a job I'd want."

Em says, "Me neither."

"Why didn't they give you any warning?" I ask.

Nora's voice gets quieter. "Maybe my dad got some warning but didn't believe them, or tell us," she says. "It's just lucky we were there when they came or we could've come home and found ourselves locked out with *nothing*."

Lucky? She thinks they were *lucky?*

Emily pipes up, "I saw a news show on the same kind of thing. This family had, like, fifteen minutes to get out, with a bunch of babies and strollers and highchairs and no car to load up and nowhere to go."

I can't picture Emily watching such a depressing and horribly NPR-ish show. I know I'd turn it off at the speed of light.

"And," Em continues, "the landlord complained that when he gives his renters any warning they trash the place, steal the lightbulbs, or whatever."

Both Emily and Nora are talking about this so *normally*, while here I am with the hairs standing up on my arms like a porcupine.

"They let us in a week later," Nora says with a shrug. "To move everything out in a more civilized way. You know, like with a moving van and all."

Emily says, "My parents say that if there's an earthquake I'm supposed to grab photo albums. They think everything else is replaceable."

I look around. What would I grab if I only had a few minutes? Actually, once I'd grabbed my crutches, my hands would be full. Hmmm, if I didn't take my backpack would I still be expected to turn in my homework?

Mom comes in and yells, "Let's go, girls!" as if it's *us*, not *her* who's making us late.

Mitch has been in the car all this time.

* * *

I know Mom wants us to sit with her as a buffer against Dad and Grandma, but she has to settle for just my brother because Emily and Nora and I go sit in the front. Normally, I'd sneak backstage before the performance to say hi, and watch the dancers scurry around in their leotards and makeup, but my boot and crutches, plus Nora and Emily, make that too hard.

I turn around and watch the dance studio fill up. David comes in and looks for a seat. Brooke's best friend Sarah waves him over.

I recognize the families of other dancers who have been coming here to drop off and pick up and watch recitals forever like us. I won't *miss* them exactly, but it feels saddish anyway.

In the old days, before Brooke and her friends could drive, Mom used to bring Sarah and whoever else Brooke wanted to bring, to these recitals, and we'd all go out for ice cream afterward. Brooke would keep her stage makeup on. And I'd like it that total strangers knew I was with a star!

I wonder if we'll all go out after tonight's performance or if Brooke will just go with her friends. Actually, that would be fine, especially if she doesn't come home till after I'm asleep because I know Mom wants to talk to us about something, and I'm pretty sure I do *not* want to hear what she has to say.

I know that will just put it off till tomorrow, but every extra little second of happiness counts, right? And tomorrow is Sunday so we'll go to Dad's house, which means maybe we can stall Mom's bad news till tomorrow night. And then . . .

Yes, I know I can't avoid it forever. I remember Grandma saying that if you don't let bad news in the door, it'll just come in a window. At least I *think* that's what she said. But I feel like after Nora's horribly horrible eviction story, one more tiny speck of sad terribleness and my head will explode.

In any case, if I'm wrong, and Mom turns out *not* to have

some kind of nasty, bad thing to tell us, then Monday I'm absolutely taking six cans of food to Madeline's canned food drive, in thanks. Make that seven. Ten!

"Yoo hoo!" Emily says, waving her hand in front of my face. "Anyone home?"

"Oops, sorry," I say, shaking my head. "This might be the last time I see my sister dance for a while."

Emily smiles a sad sympathetic Emily smile at me because she understands.

The lights go dim, then dark. The music starts and we hear the dancers run onstage, their toe shoes making that funny *thunk thunk* sound as they take their places. The curtain ripples open, the lights come up, and there's my amazing sister, second from the left. Her hair tight in a perfect bun. Her legs perfectly straight, her neck long and lovely, her arms floating up as if they weigh nothing at all. She is the most beautiful girl in the world.

At intermission I can't believe anyone can talk about anything besides how gorgeous Brooke is.

After her solo, I'm the last one to stop clapping. And when the whole program is over I'm the first to stand up, stumpy boot and all, for a standing ovation.

But when Brooke comes out into the lobby afterward, still in her white tutu and tights, before anyone has a chance to say anything about how amazing she is, she grabs David's arm and says, "Great news! David got winked at by Dartmouth!"

Everyone, meaning the adults and Sarah, congratulate David and make a big gigantic fuss over him. Grrrr! What about how fabulously Brooke danced?

"Both my parents went there," he tells us, meaning Dart-mouth, like anyone cares.

I pull Emily and Nora away from the David scene.

"Ooooh," Em says. "Do I smell anger? Jealousy? A little hatred?"

"Well, why should we give two figs where his stupid parents went to college? And doesn't that just show that he's a total copycat with no mind of his own if he can't even pick his own school?"

"Parents totally love that sort of thing," Emily explains. "My mom is dying for me to go to University of Michigan to relive every second of her college life. And I'm positive that my dad wants me to be his clone at Columbia."

Nora nods like none of this is news to her, either.

"They call it Legacy, like when you've got a big old family alumni tradition, eating turkey on Thanksgiving and going to Harvard." In a male voice, Emily says, "I'm a Harvard man. My father and his father were Harvard men. We proudly kill any children in our family who are not Harvard material . . ."

"Hmmm," I say. "I don't even know where my parents went to college. How mysterious that they never told me!"

"Maybe you just didn't listen," Emily suggests, and it is one hundred percent possible that she might be right.

"My parents are either going to have to cut me in half," she adds, "or I'm going to have to drop out of high school and skip the whole college thing to make everyone happy."

Nora giggles.

But wait. It never, ever occurred to me for a single second that Emily and I might not go to the same college and be roommates in the dorm. Anything else would be totally and completely unacceptable. Does that mean I have to go to Michigan or wherever Columbia is? Emily is a much better student than I am. But she's got three years to get some Ds so we get accepted to the same schools.

Emily's still ranting about the other thing. "No one gets it that they only get *one* life to live," she says. "Parents think they've got *their lives*, and then as a bonus for being so terrific, they get *ours*, too!"

Nora and I laugh, making Mom squint over at us. See what I mean about the squinting?

* * *

Brooke gets special permission to stay out late tonight, not to celebrate her amazing dancing, but to celebrate David's stupid legacy wink.

In the car Mom says, "I happen to know, having just helped Brooke with her applications, that tuition at Dartmouth University is thirty eight thousand, six hundred and seventy nine dollars a year. Room and board, an additional eleven to twelve thousand. Textbooks, an average of twenty one hundred, plus miscellaneous expenses."

I say, "Wow! You could buy a whole lot of very cool, fun stuff for that kind of money. A pet snow leopard. A camel. A houseboat to travel the world . . ."

"I bet you could have a gigantic statue made of yourself," Nora says.

"Out of tuna salad!" Emily adds.

My brother says, "Gross," although I could have sworn he wasn't paying attention.

"Times four," Mom says, still thinking about the money. "Since undergrad is four years. Fifty-three thousand dollars a year, times four, is well over two hundred thousand big ones. And, if you go on to graduate school . . ."

I hate when people talk math. How am I supposed to know what two hundred thousand dollars means besides *a lot*. Might as well say ninety squillion, ga-prillion. Or just say: more than we've got, or have any chance of digging up or stumbling over before classes start in August.

I'd much rather think about the houseboat I once saw in *National Geographic* magazine at the dentist. It was a floating mini-barge with an adorable little house on it with window boxes of pink flowers. It had a tiny front lawn and a white picnic table, and a little black goat all drifting down a swampy-looking river with spooky Spanish moss hanging off the trees all Halloweenish.

I bet that houseboat cost way less than Dartmouth.

And which sounds more fun? To study and stress and take hard tests, or to float with our toes trailing in the water and pet the goat and feed it whatever goats eat?

"I totally want a houseboat," I tell Emily. "With a goat."

And she says, "Fine. We'll get a houseboat with a goat."

"Me, too?" Nora asks.

"Of course!" Em and I chime at the same exact time.

* * *

Maybe I was wrong about Mom having new bad news. Maybe she's just in a cruddy mood. Or maybe she only seems worse because the old bad stuff isn't going away. I guess fresh, new, bad news is better than old, stale bad news that's beginning to rot and smell nasty with spots of fuzzy green mold on it. Or is *old* bad news better than *new* bad news because you get used to it?

We drop Emily and Nora at their house, and then drive home, listening to the NPR people talk about how whole cities are going broke and firing teachers and police officers and closing libraries and clinics and zabba zillions of people don't have the money to get the medicine or operations they need. I absolutely do *not* see why that's fun for her, but Mom barks at me if I try to change the station.

When we get home, I'm hobbling into the house when Mom stops Mitch from bolting upstairs and says, "Time for a family meeting, guys."

See? I told you! But getting to say that *I told you so* doesn't much help.

Mitch moans. Maybe I do too. I know I *feel* like moaning.

I'm about to whine about Brooke not being here, but I give up and follow Mom into the kitchen. Mitch's legs take up most of the space under the table, and my crutches take up the rest.

Mom is at the stove, making tea and saying, "It's only a distant possibility, but I feel I have to try, in good faith, for whatever comes up. And going for the interview doesn't mean I'd necessarily accept the position if it is offered. You have to remember that a job interview is for both the prospective employ*ee* and the prospective employ*er*, to see if it looks like a good match all around."

Mitch says, "Mom? Are you talking to us? Because you're not making a whole lot of sense here."

I giggle a little tiny bit. Nervously.

Mom blinks.

Mitch continues, "I'm just saying that maybe you left off the topic sentence. Or a noun or two?"

I can't help giggling a teeny bit more, because he's right. I have no clue what she's talking about either.

Mom opens and shuts her mouth. Then she abandons her teacup on the counter, takes the Ben and Jerry's Cherry Garcia out of the freezer, and plunks it on the table between me and Mitch.

She jerks open the silverware drawer with a clatter, grabs three spoons, hands one to Mitch, one to me, and keeping the third, she sits down in Brooke's usual chair, and digs out a huge spoonful. After she has her first taste, Mom says, "There's a position in Casper, Wyoming, that fits my skill set and experience to a T. They are flying me out for an interview Monday. Well, I'm going to go Sunday night, so I'm fresh for the interview Monday morning. Then, if it goes well, there will be further talks on Tuesday, before I return home."

Mitch says, "Casper?"

And I say, "Wyoming?"

Mom nods. "Casper, Wyoming."

But to tell the truth I'm more shocked by Mom not using a bowl and eating ice cream right out of the carton than I am about her having an interview in Casper, Wyoming, wherever that is. At least until Mitch says, "And if you got this job you'd what? Like . . . move there?"

Mom nods, already on her next giant spoonful. One drip drips on her pretty aqua blouse.

"And you'd expect . . . ?" Mitch points to me, then himself, then back at me again.

127

"Of course!" Mom says. "You're my children! We'd all go."

Mitch drops his spoon and pushes back from the table.

I freeze, inside and out. My voice sounds all weird. "You mean move away completely? To whatever, Wyoming?"

"Casper," Mom says.

Mitch is up out of his chair. "No way," he says. "It's not happening. I'll live with Dad."

"It's just an interview," Mom says. "There may be dozens of applicants. Probably nothing will come of it."

Mitch shakes his head and reels out of the kitchen as if he's pretending to be drunk. It's quiet after he's gone.

Just to break the silence I say, "He's more of a Rocky Road than a Cherry Garcia kinda guy."

Mom smiles as if I'm her favorite kid of all, so this probably wouldn't be a good time to tell her that I think she'd be crazy to move so far away just for a stupid job, and if she does, I'd want to stay here with Daddy, too.

Chapter 10
BRINE SHRIMP
AND BOUGAINVILLEA

GRANDMA COMES RUSHING OUT to help me get my stuff out of Brooke's car, which is nice, but I'm so used to my crutches that I don't really need it.

"It smells like heaven in here!" I tell her, when we get inside.

Grandma smiles, "Your father and I are making homemade pasta, with a garlic basil sauce. Hungry?"

"I am now!" I laugh.

Grandma's house is flat with no stairs, so I'll get to sleep in a real bed in a real room instead of on the living room couch. Mitch will share Dad's room, and Brooke and I will share the guest room, which I'm totally excited about, but I also keep telling myself not to get my hopes up too incredibly high in case she's not in a sisterly mood, although she's been totally sweet all morning and last night, too! Don't tell her I said this, but I'm glad she's semi-grounded and can't go stay at Sarah's or anyone's house while Mom's gone.

Grandma and I lug my stuff to the guest room, where

Brooke is already sprawled on one of the beds. Then Grandma goes back to the kitchen to help Dad weep over the onions.

"Italy's still here," Brooke says pointing.

I look at the ceiling, "Yep!" I remember when she told me the crack on the ceiling looked like Italy. I'd thought it was so worldly and sophisticated of her to know what Italy was shaped like. I bragged to Emily about it at school the next day and Emily said, "Like a boot?"

"Huh?"

"Italy. It's shaped like a boot, Jacki. Even *I* know that."

I told myself to check next time I either looked at a map or Grandma's ceiling to see if that was true, and it was.

* * *

This whole room is full of memories, even though it's not full of much else. Two twin beds with a dresser between just about fill it up. The far wall is mostly window with a view of the street. The yellow curtains are wide open.

I sit on the edge of my bed and watch two squirrels chase each other around and around the trunk of the grapefruit tree, making a chitt-chitt sound. Is it a tongue click? Teeth chattering? I try it a few ways and Brooke laughs at me, but in a wonderfully Brooke-ish way.

The only tiniest not-so-great-part is that I couldn't make myself wish Mom luck on her Casper, Wyoming, interview, and now that she's gone, I feel bad about that. Not that I want her to have good luck if it means the people in Wyoming love her and hire her to move there immediately.

But I could have wished her luck to maybe meet some great guy on the plane who'd offer her a fabulous job here in Los

Angeles, or who is so sweet and fun that they'd fall instantly and completely in love and he'd propose and Mom would happily accept and be all hearts and flowers and white doves tying satiny ribbons and going *cooo*.

And he'd turn out to be a zillionaire and set Mom up in a terrific business of her own that she'd love, here in L.A., of course. And she could hire all the other out-of-work people and give everyone great jobs with enormous salaries, and no one would have to move, and NPR would have to talk about something else for a change.

Plus, he'd think Mitch and Brooke and I are the world's greatest kids and we'd absolutely adore him, too, but in a totally different way than we love Dad, so no one's feelings would get the least bit hurt and no one will be even the teeniest bit jealous. Is that too much to ask?

But there's no point in thinking about that right now. It's a beautiful, sparkly day.

"Hey, look! There's a dog!" Oh! It darts across the lawn, and disappears up a neighbor's driveway. But ten seconds later it's back sniffing, running, wagging its tail like crazy.

Brooke raises on one elbow and looks out. "Like Lady, from *Lady and the Tramp*," she says, and flops back down.

She's right! I watch Lady run one way, then circle back and run across the street again without stopping to watch for cars. I get up and go to the window to check the block as far as I can see in either direction. No person.

"I think she's lost!" I say, hoping that she'll have no owner and no collar and will be mine forever! Her curly ears flop up and down when she runs. Her tongue hangs out the side, and she looks incredibly soft.

I crutch at top speed down the narrow, dark hall, across the tiny living room and out the front door. There she is!

"Come here, Lady," I call. "Come on!" And as if she has known me all her life, she comes trotting right up to me.

I say, "Hello there!"

And she says "Hi!" back with a jump that practically knocks me off my crutches, but in the most wonderful way.

I sit down on the lawn and Lady is all over me, licking, jumping, wiggling. Her tail whamming around like a whip, but a nice one.

Oh darn, she's wearing a collar. That means she has a home. She's too bouncy and wiggly for me to read it, but then I do, and it has a phone number, and says her name is Daisy.

"Hello, Daisy."

"Forget it," Brooke says from the front step. "Grandma will never let it in the door."

"Well, she has tags. We have to call her owner!" I hear the whine in my own voice.

"Maybe she wanted to get away," Brooke says. "And she's not ready to go back yet."

I stop myself from saying, "Like you?"

Brooke sits next to me and Daisy is instantly all over her. Wag! Lick! Jump! There's no way Daisy ran away from home all furious and angry like Brooke did. Daisy is pure happiness with fur. I bet she's never been mad for one tiny second of her whole wagging, wiggling, panting life.

Mitch comes to call us for lunch, but sees Daisy and joins us on the lawn. Daisy knocks him flat and stands on his chest to lick his face. I think Mitch is going to pee from laughing so hard.

Then Grandma is clapping her hands loud and yelling, "Shoo! Shoo!" She comes bearing down on Daisy in a scary way. Daisy stops mid-wag, mid-lick, and cowers low like she thinks Grandma is going to hit her!

"Shoo!" Grandma yells again, and Daisy slinks away to the edge of the yard.

"But Grandma!" we all protest at once.

"Come eat, and we'll discuss it afterward, if the dog is still here," Grandma says.

"But she'll run in the street!" I cry. "She doesn't know anything about cars!"

Grandma turns and heads back inside. My sister and brother get up and follow.

Daisy, meanwhile, has run next door, her tail back in full wag. A big dog behind a fence barks at her, and Daisy runs over to sniff noses.

My sister looks to see if I'm coming and says, "Oh, let her have her adventure, Jacki. Not everything needs to be mother henned."

Mother henned?

Daisy is now three houses down. Maybe she knows where she lives and is headed home. But maybe she's just getting more lost. I watch her trot happily, stupidly, into the street and cross at an angle. A car comes barreling up and I shriek. But no need, the car slows to let Daisy casually trot up a driveway and onto another lawn before it zooms past.

A girl could have a heart attack watching this dog! But Daisy just smiles and holds her tail high. I shake my head at how clueless and cheerful she is. Miss Sweetie Pants Happy Face. Hey, wait. Isn't that what Brooke called *me*?

I start after her, calling, "Daisy!"

She looks at me, but doesn't come.

And then my dad is at my side. "That dog runs loose all the time," he says. "I see him out here two, three times a week."

"Her," I correct. "Daisy."

"She'll be fine," Dad says. "Just let her be."

"But she's so dumb about cars!" I insist.

"Come on, Jack-o'-lantern," Dad says, putting his arm around my shoulders. "It's time for lunch."

Daisy is way up the street now.

"Dad?" I ask.

"Hmmm?" he answers.

"What will happen to *you* if we move to Wyoming?"

"We'll worry about that if and when the time comes," he says, giving my shoulders a Dad-squeeze.

"But would you visit there or what?"

"Of course I would! And you'd come back for vacations and holidays, at least until you made so many friends and had such a wonderful and jampacked fun-filled life there that you didn't want to anymore."

"Would you bring Emily?" I ask.

Dad smiles. "The pasta is getting cold," he says.

* * *

Lunch takes forever and I can barely even look at Grandma. The second she gets up to clear the dishes, I crutch out the front door, calling Daisy's name as loud as I can. She doesn't answer and I don't see her anywhere.

At least there's no run-over Daisy in the street. And maybe she just went home to someone just like me who loves her to bits and is beyond thrilled and relieved that she's back, safe and happy. And Daisy is super happy, too.

I call her name a couple more times, just in case, but there's no answer so I go back inside.

Grandma doesn't ask me to help with the dishes, so I don't.

"Where's Dad?" I ask her.

"In the garden."

"Where are Brooke and Mitch?" I ask next.

She answers, "Their rooms, I guess."

Neither of us mentions Daisy.

I go out the back door. Wow! Look how much our garden has grown! There are such cute rows of baby green plants looking so perky and optimistic. They all wave in the tiny breeze. Hi, guys!

Dad is weeding. I sit next to him on the ground, shoving my crutches behind me and sticking my boot foot straight out.

"The dog went home, eh?" Dad asks.

"I guess so. I hope so."

"I'm sure he did," Dad says.

"She."

Dad smiles. Then he points to a weed. "Want to pull that?"

So I do. And we pull weeds together.

I'm not sure what my dad's thinking about but we don't say that much at first. It's nice, though, being quiet together, sitting on the ground, playing in the dirt.

My brother and sister and I haven't stayed here all together for a long time and for sure not on school nights. I guess it will be like a mini-rehearsal for what life might be like for real if Mom moves to Casper, Wyoming, which I hope, hope, hope she won't do.

"Did you ever have a dog?" I ask Dad.

"No."

"Did you want one?"

Dad's quiet a second. Then he says, "I remember desperately wanting the miniature sea monkeys they advertised on the backs of comic books."

"Wow! Miniature monkeys!" I say. "Cool!"

"*Sea* monkeys," Dad says. "It showed them waving and smiling. Next to the ads for X-ray glasses that could see through women's clothing, and trick gum that turns your friends' teeth black."

"Did you get them?" I ask.

"Grandpa kept telling me it was a lie. That there were no monkeys that lived in the sea. He even dragged down our encyclopedia and we looked up primates."

"This isn't going to end happily, is it?" I ask him.

"You remember Grandpa, right? A no-nonsense man."

I nod.

"But, despite all evidence to the contrary, I *believed* in sea monkeys. And finally used my own birthday money to send away for them."

"Uh oh," I say. "Here comes the tragic part, right?"

"You guessed it. There are no sea monkeys. They sent me dried brine shrimp that came to life for a little while in a jar of water, then died in a putrid clump."

"So when you asked for a dog, did Grandpa say there's no such thing as dogs?" I ask.

Daddy laughs, "No. But that's something like what's happened to our economy."

"Huh? Where did *that* come from?"

"Everyone believed in sea monkeys because they wanted to. Buying things they couldn't afford because the banks said they could. We were lied to, told we could just keep owning and buying and taking and having and borrowing and polluting and harvesting and mining forever and ever. And now look."

I look at him.

"I just want you to understand that it's not your mother's fault. She didn't do anything wrong."

I absolutely do *not* see the connection between brine shrimp (whatever they are), and Mom losing her job and our college funds. But I guess Dad doesn't want to talk about dogs. At least I'm glad he doesn't think the global economic crisis (as Mr. Rodriguez calls it) is totally Mom's fault.

I say, "I bet the pictures of sea monkeys were cute, though. I totally would have wanted them too."

* * *

Dad and Mitch left for Mitch's game. Grandma is taking a nap.

I'm in the shower, amazed how the dirt went everywhere! I even blew some out of my nose, although all I did was sit there and pull a few weeds. It's not like I rolled around in it or blasted it all over myself with my trunk like an elephant.

Maybe ants and zillipedes crawled in my sleeves, dribbling dirt as they went. Eewww! But how else did dirt get all the way into my bra?

It's a tricky business, showering one footedly, but since

they don't have a bench like ours in their shower, Grandma gave me a white plastic lawn chair to sit on.

Grandma and Daddy's shower-bathtub thing is nothing like any of ours. They have one bar of regular old white soap, one bottle of shampoo, period. The end. Like pilgrims or cavemen!

And this is their *only* shower, which isn't very many for five people, especially when one of them is my sister. There *is* another bathroom, but it's only a sink and toilet and that's not enough for Brooke. She could completely fill both these bathrooms wall to wall with Brooke-ness in no time.

When I get back to our room she's on the phone so I eavesdrop. Whoever she's talking to must be upset because Brooke is making a lot of sympathetic little sounds like Emily does. I wonder if I do that.

I look out the window but Daisy's still gone. That's good, right?

Brooke hangs up and says, "The company Sarah's dad works for just went bankrupt."

I know that's one of those bad, bad words for going super broke, but I'm not exactly, one hundred percent sure I know what it means.

"And," Brooke says, "he totally didn't see it coming. Sarah says he heard about it on the car radio, while he was driving in to work. She's amazed he didn't get in a wreck learning about it that way."

I try to picture someone hearing about themselves on the radio.

"At least *Sarah's* dad had a job to lose," Brooke says.

I wince, and shoot a look at the bedroom door. It's open!

"Dad has a job," I whisper.

Brooke rolls her eyes, "Part time," she sneers. "*Baking*."

I hope Grandma didn't hear that.

While my eyes and ears are scrunched closed, Brooke hops off her bed. I guess she's going to Sarah's. I know it's mean and selfish of me to want her to stay here, when her best friend needs her, but . . .

Brooke says, "Want to go for a walk?"

"*Me?*"

Brooke laughs. "We'll see if we can find where Miss Daisy lives."

I grab my crutches and off we go.

* * *

My sister notices so much more than I do. Walking with her is like wearing magic Brooke glasses. She points out a woodpecker hammering holes in the side of a palm tree. How can he stand sideways like that? Does he hook his little bird toes in somehow? And look, you can see a whole bunch of his old holes, perfectly round, drilled all the way up.

It reminds me of Nora's story about policemen drilling out locks but I don't want to think about that.

Brooke points out a waterfall of bougainvillea that is such a bright, capital M Magenta that my whole head is instantly magenta-filled, ear to absolute ear, leaving no room for creepy thoughts. Good!

The next house has silly, sculpted shrubs like poodle pom-poms. I guess I usually just watch my feet when I walk. But never again!

All kinds of dogs bark at us as we pass, but none of them are Daisy.

HONK! I jump.

It's a car full of boys hollering and whistling at my sister. She doesn't react.

"You get that all the time, right?" I giggle.

"It doesn't mean anything," she says, flicking it away with her wrist. "It's just noise."

I can't wait to tell Emily that. "Well, not everyone gets that kind of *noise*," I tell her. "They don't honk and drool and all that when you're with David, though, do they?" I ask.

"We broke up," Brooke says matter-of-factly.

I almost pitch forward off my crutches. "You *what*?"

Brooke nods.

"When?" Brooke hasn't been crying or anything. When did I see David last? At the ballet! His Dartmouth wink letter. They went out to celebrate . . .

"Look!" Brooke says, and there, mangling the curtains, and barking her head off out the front window of a pink house, is Daisy!

"Hi, Daisy!"

"You never liked him," Brooke says. "I could tell."

"Who, David?" I stall.

"It's OK," Brooke says. "Really."

"I . . . um . . . *tried* to like him," I stutter. "And . . . I didn't *hate* him at all."

Brooke smiles.

"And Mitch said he was a good something-or-other in basketball," I add, trying to be nice. Then I say, "But if he hurt you . . . Are you OK? Because if he made you sad, I'll totally kill him."

Brooke laughs.

"No really," I insist. "I will hunt him down and show no mercy. Emily will help for sure. We'll . . ."

"I'm fine," Brooke says. "You can let him live. And anyway, he's not worth you and Emily going to prison."

"But . . ."

Brooke shrugs, "Our lives are going in such different directions. Dartmouth for him . . ."

"Where *is* that?" I ask.

"Dartmouth? It's in New Hampshire. And Los Angeles for me."

"Los Angeles? You're going to stay *here*?" Boom! That's my heart leaping!

Brooke stops walking. "Jacki, what did you think this was all about?"

I'm stammering again, afraid she's going to get mad. Afraid to ruin the good feelings and seem totally stupid. "Well, I know we can't afford the super-duper, fancy-shmanski expensive schools back east, but, I figured . . ."

"What did you figure?" she asks.

"That you'd go to a cheaper school out there."

"No such thing," Brooke said. "There'd be room and board wherever I'd go. It's too late to apply for financial aid or scholarships for this year, and no one's giving out student loans. Mom's broke and Dad never got it together to save a dime for me . . ."

Wow! It never occurred to me that Brooke might stay *here*! I know, I know, I know I shouldn't be happy if she's not, but I practically want to cheer. I'd feel terrible about how selfishly mean and rotten I am, but I'm too happy!

I clamp my mouth shut. The safest thing is not to say

anything. But then I remember where this all started and I ask, "But why did you break up *now*? There's still March, April, May . . ." I count the months off on my fingers. "Five months till college starts, right?"

Brooke shrugs. "Why wait?"

I know absolutely for sure that there's a whole lot more to this story, but even *I* can tell Brooke doesn't want to talk about it. Dad doesn't want to talk about dogs, Brooke doesn't want to talk about David. I don't get it. I want to talk about everything, all the time! Well . . . except that I still haven't told Emily about you-know-what. But if Mom gets this job and we move to Wyoming, there's no reason for Em to know that we wouldn't have gone to school together anymore anyway, even if I stayed, right?

Brooke points to a cactus garden and I pretend to be interested although just between you and me, I think cacti are mean, with their spikes out all the time like everyone and everything is their sworn enemy.

Chapter 11
PENS AND MUSHROOMS

I DON'T USUALLY EAT A BIG BREAKFAST, but Dad got home from the bakery with fresh cinnamon raisin bread before we left for school. I'm bringing a slice to Emily but even though I'm stuffed to the rafters, it's making Brooke's car smell so yummy that I might have to eat it myself. Emily will understand. Especially if I don't tell her.

To take my mind off raisin bread, I ask Brooke if it's icky to see David at school and she says, "I guess." Which means she *still* doesn't want to talk about it. We had fun sharing a room last night though, at least I did. We didn't talk about anything massively important, just little things, like what it feels like to spin on one foot, on one *toe*.

"It cleans every single thought completely out of your head," Brooke said. "You just become pure movement. You're totally about that turn, and there's nothing like it." Brooke was quiet a second then said, "But you know a pair of Russian pointes, my toe shoes?"

"Yeah."

"They're seventy-five bucks a pair and I can dance them soft in two or three weeks, easy."

"Death by raisin bread," Mitch groans from the backseat, and I can totally imagine. I ate an awful lot, but he had even more.

* * *

Emily devours every crumb. "If you can't burn it to a cinder on the grill, my father has nothing to do with cooking it," she says, hunting through the folds of the crunched napkin for hidden raisins.

I tell her about Daisy the dog and how Grandma hated her, and about Brooke and David splitting up, and Brooke staying here next year. And Emily tells me that Nora has the flu and was up coughing and hacking and moaning all night in the same room.

"Her gooey snot-wad tissues are *everywhere*," Emily says with a shudder. "I stepped on like ten of them with my bare feet!"

"Ew!"

"So incredibly eewww!" Emily agrees. "And my play is this weekend! If I catch it . . . I totally swear . . ."

"You won't," I assure her. "Just eat like seventy or eighty oranges every day till then."

Emily nods, "Good plan."

* * *

Oops, I forgot to do my French homework.

And now Mr. Rodriguez says he told us to be ready for a history quiz.

"You didn't say anything about a quiz," Ben says, and Lacey agrees.

I brace myself for Madeline to raise her hand and say some horrible thing like that he *did* warn us yesterday at ten twenty-seven exactly, and she has the word-for-word notes on her laptop to prove it.

But she doesn't! Yaaay, Madeline!

Oh, wait. Her hand isn't up *at all*. That's not right. I poke Olivia in the back and she turns around. "What's the matter with Madeline?" I ask her.

Olivia shrugs, "Beats me," she says.

Now Mr. Rodriguez is droning on about bailouts of major industries and banks. Zabba zabba, NPR-type stuff. Then he gets strangely quiet and everyone looks up to see why.

"Palm Canyon Academy relies heavily on endowments," he says. "Does anyone know what that means?"

Madeline does not raise her hand! This is seriously, seriously weird.

Becky calls out, "Fund-raising? Like our car wash and bake sale and stuff?"

Mr. Rodriguez shoves his hands in his pockets. "Alumni give money to the school, as a way of saying thanks," he says, "after they make it big. And as a tax write-off. What do you suppose happens to this, or any institution that relies on charitable giving, in a recession?"

Still no peep from Madeline. Oh, God. She must be sick or dying or worse!

"Anyone?" Mr. Rodriguez asks.

No one says anything.

"Well," he begins. "If you're worried about paying your

own bills, and feeding your own family, and keeping a roof over your head, aren't you going to be less likely to give money to charity?"

It occurs to me I still haven't brought anything in for Madeline's canned food drive. I don't even know if it's still going on! Now *that's* embarrassing. I super quietly tear off a corner of my notebook page and write, "You OK?" on it. I fold it six hundred times, then I nudge Avi awake next to me and give him my note. "Pass it to Madeline," I whisper quiet as a bug.

But Mr. Rodriguez spots it halfway and makes Riley hand it over.

"Who sent this?" he asks, all stern and angry and full of wrath and thunderbolts.

I squeak, "Me."

"What was so important that it couldn't wait till after class?" he asks.

"I was asking Madeline if she was OK because she hasn't raised her hand once this whole class," I say.

Some kids snicker, of course, but Madeline's head whips around to look at me, and she seems so startled. Oh, I embarrassed her. Sometimes I just make me sick.

Mr. Rodriguez tosses my note in the trash and goes back to talking about how horrible everything is in the whole entire world and how probably even here at Palm Canyon there will be layoffs and some programs will be cut.

I look closer at him. Is he talking about *himself*? Is he saying he's going to be fired, too?

Enough! I want to jump up on my desk – whip an impossibly gigantic Bugs Bunny STOP sign out of my pocket, and give my shiny cartoon whistle an ear piercing blast!

But I raise my plain pinkish-beige-yellow-brown hand instead, and say, "There's something I don't get. If the banks and the government suddenly don't have any money, and neither do the regular people . . . well . . . This might sound stupid, but . . . Where *is* it all?"

I picture a huge, beaming, mountainous mountain of sparkly coins and million dollar bills, forgotten somewhere. And if we could just *find* that . . .

"Excellent question!" Mr. Rodriguez says, which has *got* to be a first, at least for someone talking to *me*.

He comes over to my desk and picks up my light-up alligator pen. "Let's say you bought this for a dollar," he says.

I didn't buy it. It was a gift from my gator pal, but I don't say that.

"That dollar is what it cost to make it: the raw materials and supplies, labor, overhead to run the pen factory like electricity and running water and rent. Then packaging and shipping. Plus some profit for the pen company and for the store who sold it to you. All that adds up to a unit price of one dollar per pen."

I don't say so, but I bet it cost more than that. I mean, it *lights up*!

"But *suddenly* everyone in this room wants your pen and they're willing to pay more than your original dollar. The pen hasn't changed in real value, correct?"

I nod. A few other heads nod around me, so maybe I'm not the only one who doesn't totally understand this whole disappearing money thing.

"Now, with so many people interested in your pen, people who are willing to pay more for it, it's suddenly worth maybe five dollars. Wow! You've got a five-dollar pen! Its value has increased by four dollars! Quadrupled!"

He holds it up higher for everyone to admire it. "But let's say you come to class tomorrow, thinking you have a five-dollar pen, but no one wants it anymore. You can't sell it. You think, *Hey! What happened to my four dollars?* But really, that money never existed. They were fantasy dollars. Never actual cash."

He gives me back my pen, and I don't tell him that actually, it's priceless because I'd never sell it for any money in the world. Well, maybe enough to get Mom to relax, and to buy a prom dress and a bunch of toe shoes for Brooke, and buy a hamster and maybe a houseboat with a goat and a dog like Daisy . . .

"Does that help?" Mr. Rodriguez asks me.

I nod.

"Now let's complicate things," he says. "Say you borrowed money against the value of your pen. Maybe yesterday, when everyone in class was clamoring for it, you told Ben here that if he sold you his lunch *today*, you'd pay him three dollars for it *tomorrow*, as soon as you sold your pen.

"Ben agreed and handed over his lunch, which you gobbled up, on credit. But when you can't sell your pen the next day, how are you going to pay him back? And where does that leave Ben?"

Mr. Rodriguez is looking at me, waiting for some kind of answer. Was that a *question* question? Or just a question? I don't know what he expects me to say, so I look at Ben and say, "Sorrrrrry!"

Why this cracks up the whole class, I have no idea.

Someone taps my arm and I spin around. Spinning on crutches is a very bad idea if you're me. Especially wearing a backpack. There's a stumbling sort of clamor, books and papers fly, one crutch skids across the floor heading straight for Coach Keefer. Uh oh!

Madeline catches me and props me up. Kids chase my scattering books and pencils. Coach Keefer does a weird little dance step over my crutch and just keeps walking.

"Sorry, sorry, sorry!" Madeline gushes. "I just wanted to tell you that I'm fine, and thank you for caring."

"No problem," I say, trying to balance myself and all my junk. "But how come you didn't raise your hand today?"

"I don't *always* raise my hand," Madeline answers.

"Yes, you do."

"No, I don't."

"You do, too!"

"Don't."

If I didn't know better I'd think we were about to throw punches, so I giggle.

Madeline jams my pencil case back into my backpack making me wobble again. "And it's not funny!" she says, stomping off in a huff.

Now *that's* what I call weird.

* * *

Brooke suggests we go out for ice cream after school, to kill time until Mitch gets out of baseball. I know she just doesn't want to drive back and forth endlessly to Grandma's but still,

I squeal, "Just you and me?" as excited as Daisy, jumping up, practically wagging my tail. I am so deeply and profoundly and completely uncool.

Walking to Brooke's car, I say, "You know that super A+ goody-goody kid Madeline in my grade?"

Brooke nods. "Sarah's little sister?"

"Oh yeah, I totally knew that!"

Remember Brooke's friend Sarah whose dad heard on the radio that he lost his job? Well, Sarah and Madeline are *sisters*. It's just that they're such totally and completely different kinds of girls that . . . Well . . . people are probably equally shocked by me and Brooke, right?

"That totally explains it," I say.

"Explains what?"

"Well, they have the same dad!" I explain.

"That's often what it means to be sisters."

I ignore the sarcasm and ask, "Is Sarah still real upset about her . . . *their* dad's company's bankruptcy thing?"

"Yeah," Brooke says, "But I told her we'd go to community college together and make it fun."

I laugh tee-hee, because even *I* know girls like Sarah and Brooke don't go to community college. Community college is for people with crappy grades . . . like, um . . . Well like *me*.

Brooke glances at me. "I missed the joke," she says.

I quit laughing. "There're a whole bunch of other colleges in California," I say. "Tons! The UCs, the Cal States . . ."

"Yeah, but I didn't apply to any of them," Brooke says. "And now it's too late. At least for next year."

"Ick."

"Ick is right," Brooke says. We're stopped at a light and

her phone chirps. I watch her check to see who's calling, but she doesn't pick up.

And then, without absolutely *meaning* to, I tell her about Adam B. And guess what? She doesn't tease me or say anything mean or sarcastic! She just asks me if I've called him.

"No. I don't know his number," I explain. "Or even what his *B* stands for."

My sister smiles her beautiful Brooke smile and says, "Capital B Boyfriend!"

* * *

At Swork I get a pineapple gelato, of course. And Brooke gets an iced cappuccino.

"Wow, it's really expensive," I say, surprised that I'm so surprised.

"It's all right," Brooke says. "I've switched to drugstore makeup. No more Kiehl's or Sephora or department store. Could you tell?"

She turns her face to me and bats her eyelashes. The guy behind the counter hands Brooke her drink and says, "Looks pretty darn good to me!"

She says, "Thanks," as if everyone gets compliments like that and it's just how people talk to each other. The coffee guy watches her walk to a table. Other heads turn to watch her too. She has no idea.

Her phone rings again. She checks it and ignores it.

"I guess I never noticed how expensive this stuff was," I continue, "because Mom's usually here to whip out her credit card."

Mom.

I ask Brooke if she thinks Mom will get the Casper, Wyoming, job.

"I used to know everything," she answers. "I knew exactly how my life would go; I'd graduate at the top of my class, with honors, and go to a fabulous school on the East Coast in pre-law with other smart kids from all over the world, who *also* graduated with distinction.

"I'd probably meet a terrific guy there, someone a lot like me. Hardworking, ambitious, nice . . ."

"Cute," I add.

Brooke smiles, "I'd go to a great law school and study entertainment law, be editor of the law review, get the perfect internship over summer. Then I'd graduate magna cum laude, land an amazing job with a prestigious firm doing important work for artists' rights. I'd travel a lot, make great money, and eventually marry and have two kids, a boy and a girl. And they'd grow up and graduate at the top of *their* class, with honors . . ." Brooke plays with her straw.

"So, does that mean you think Mom *will* or *won't* get the job?" I ask again.

"It means I don't even *guess* about the future anymore," Brooke says, slurping the last of her frozen cappuccino.

After a while I say, "That doesn't mean it has to be bad, though, does it? Just because you can't predict it? I mean you can still have a fabulous life with a happy ending, right?"

"Hope so," Brooke answers, reaching her spoon over for a taste of my gelato.

* * *

Mom calls after we get Mitch.

"Mom! How was the interview?" I yell into the staticky phone.

"Everyone was very nice," she says. "It's static-static beautiful here," she says. "Static everyone there?"

"Good! We're good! Did you get the job?"

"What?"

"Did you get the job?"

Mom laughs, "There's a breakfast static tomorrow. And I static with static-static committee tomorrow afternoon."

"Well, good luck!" I'm sooo glad to finally get to say that!

I want to add that Brooke and David broke up, but I don't. I just say, "Brooke's driving but do you want to talk to Mitch?"

"Static please," Mom says. "Love you!"

I echo, "Love you, too!" and hand my phone to Mitch.

"She doesn't know yet," I tell Brooke. "More interviews tomorrow."

Mitch is telling Mom something about baseball, "RBI zabba zabba grounder zabba." I bet Mom doesn't know what he's talking about, either. I think she just likes the sound of his voice.

Meanwhile, Brooke has ignored her phone about eight times. Finally I ask, "That's David calling all the time, right?"

And Brooke nods the teeniest nod.

Of course he wants her back! Who wouldn't?

* * *

Grandma's making dinner at home again tonight. When the three of us tromp in she asks if we want to help her. Mitch

and Brooke quickly explain that they have tons of homework, projects due, papers to write, pyramids to build stone
by stone with their bare hands, they need to discover the
wheel and devise a method for turning toenails into gold by
morning.

I probably have homework, too, but I wouldn't do it right
now anyway, so I say, "OK."

We're taking last night's meatloaf and yesterday's pasta
leftovers and making a whole new dish out of them. Grandma
has me washing lots of mushrooms, all different kinds.

"I've joined a mushroom hunter's club," Grandma says,
"And I'm learning to recognize edible mushrooms that grow
wild around here."

"In the wilds of *Los Angeles*?" I ask, pulling my hands out of
the water. I look suspiciously at the mushrooms bobbing in the
sink. "But . . . um . . . if you guess wrong we all die, right?" I
ask. "I mean, aren't some mushrooms totally poisonous and
deadly?"

"Yes, but I fancy myself a natural mycologist." Grandma
peers at me and says, "Mycology is the study of mushrooms."

"Well where did you find *these*?" I ask, eyeing the weird-
looking mushrooms in the sink.

"Trader Joe's," she answers, and it takes me a second to
realize she's teasing me.

"Grandma!" I bark, splashing her with mushroom-sink
water.

So even if she doesn't like *dogs*, Grandma's still Grandma.
That doesn't mean I want to *live* here every day full time, but
still, it's good to know. And our mushroom, meatloaf, pasta

invention is fabulously delicious. I sneak back and eat more of it before bed.

*   *   *

I'm minding my own business in history the next day when a note plunks onto my desk. I glance around, but no one's claiming it that I can see. Mr. Rodriguez is busy zabbaing at the board. I turn it over and see my name printed very, very neatly on it. There's only one kid whose writing is that perfectly tidy: Madeline. But *Madeline*? Passing notes in class?

I unfold it. Inside, it extra neatly says, "Sorry, Jacki."

When she turns around I give her a thumbs-up and she smiles back.

*   *   *

Emily is totally stunned when I tell her. "No way!" she says, all disbelief and amazement. It's so satisfying to tell Emily stuff.

"Next thing you know," Em says, "Madeline will be ditching class to sneak smokes in the bathroom!" We both crack up at that.

"But," Em giggles, "I guess people *do* change."

"Well, don't *you* go changing anything," I say.

"Not even my underwear?" Emily asks. "Or my ring tone?" Then she looks down and says, "And anyway, *you're* the one who's changing everything."

"Am not!" I say. "Like what?"

"Like your address . . . if you move to Nebraska."

"Ew, don't remind me!" I say giving her a shove. But too late.

Now I'm totally reminded practically to tears. "It's Wyoming," I mumble, "not Nebraska."

* * *

Mom caught an early flight and she's standing in the kitchen when we get home from school. She doesn't know if she got the job yet, and is afraid she'll jinx it if she talks about it.

"Jinx?" I say on the phone to Emily. "Is she going to start crossing her fingers and wishing on stars and wishbones?"

"Wearing Lucky brand jeans," Em adds. "Eating Lucky Charms?"

"I'm glad to be home," I tell Emily, "But it was great sharing a room with Brooke."

"Try doing it for weeks and weeks! Then tell me how great it is to share," she says, meaning Nora. "And now Aunt Claire insists on paying her share of the grocery bill with food stamps, but my mom hates the way the checkout people look at her in the market."

"What do the checkout people care?" I ask.

"Who knows if they even *do*?" Emily says. "My mom could just be imagining it. Everyone around here is going completely bonkers. Just a second . . ." I hear Emily close her bedroom door. Then she whispers, "I found out that Nora is so ashamed of all this that instead of telling her friends at school what's going on, she just totally stopped talking to them."

Emily's whisper gets so quiet I can barely hear her. "Now they hate her and think she's a snob for dropping them. So at school she's a total loner."

"Ick! What a mess!" I say. "But remember when Nora told

me about the police with the locks and power drills and her mom swearing and throwing stuff on the front lawn?"

Emily says, "Yeah."

"She seemed OK about it then, even kinda jokey, practically. Remember?"

"Well, I think I'm the only friend she's got now," Emily whispers even quieter.

"And me!" I say.

"And you," she agrees.

"How'd you learn all this?"

"Asked. Caught her crying."

Oh. That's maybe the saddest thing I've ever, ever heard.

Chapter 12

PILLOWS AND CROQUET

Tʜᴀᴛ ɴɪɢʜᴛ, I hobble in from the shower and find Mitch camped out on my couch with his laptop. He has the TV on mute and is bellowing along to his iPod, keeping time with the slap of his flip-flops. I glance at his computer, what I thought was homework is actually SNOOD. He's playing on Armageddon.

There's nothing else to do from my couch so I watch the show Mitch is ignoring on TV. There's a mostly empty white screen with a little, teeny, dot-person crossing the bottom in a sled, like Santa but with dogs for reindeer.

Then more dogs and snow, and people bundled up as lumbering mountains of clothing. The guy talking has what looks like frozen snot in his mustache and beard, and eyebrows. How does a person get snot in his eyebrows? The sunset behind him is gigantic.

I tap Mitch. He pops out one of his earbuds and yells, "YEAH?"

"You don't have to yell," I tell him. Then I ask, "Have you been watching this?"

He shrugs. "It's the Iditarod." Then seeing that I have no idea what he means, he adds, "That dogsled race across Alaska?"

I click on the volume. A woman is baby-talking her sled dogs. Awww! They love her.

Turns out these Iditarod people are amazing! They race spread out miles apart, each one alone with their team of dogs, across frozen rivers, and mountains, and forests, and tundra (which I think is like a desert, but with snow instead of sand). With no hotels or restaurants or bathrooms, carrying every single thing they'll need on their sleds for *weeks*!

I can so totally see myself doing that! Me and my dogs, camping out under the huge, wintry sky. I'd ask Daisy's people in the pink house if I could borrow her to be on my team, although there don't seem to be a lot of cocker spaniels out there pulling sleds. At least not that I see.

My sister is on her phone as she passes through the living room. "Brooke!" I call out, "Look at this! It's totally amazing!"

She adjusts her phone and gigantic fifty-pound backpack and ballet bag and the stack of books in her arms, so I'll know she's too burdened and busy to stop. But she glances at the screen. "The Iditarod?" she asks.

So *Brooke* knew about this before me, too.

"I'm totally going to do that one day!" I tell her.

"You?" she snorts, into the phone and at me. "The one who refuses to even *think* about taking a family ski trip because she's always so delicate and shivery? Have you ever even *seen* real snow?"

"Harrumph!"

Brooke laughs and says to whoever she's still talking to, "My little sister, the one who sleeps with not one, but *two*, blankets all summer."

She climbs the stairs, still talking about me. "And can't eat ice cream unless she nukes it in the microwave first. Orders soda with no ice."

Mitch juts his chin at me and says, "She gotcha!"

I ignore him.

"Hey! What about my pineapple gelato?" I yell. "That was frozen!"

But Brooke doesn't answer.

I turn back to the TV. Now a sled is racing at night. The only light is strapped to the guy's head! Cool!

Mom comes into the room and says, "Time goes so fast! I didn't even realize it was the Iditarod already!"

Well, this is good, I guess; everyone seems back to normal, at least as far as making me feel stupid. "Hey Mom," I say, "Does it snow in Casper, Wyoming?"

Mom nods toward the TV. "Just like that, Sweetie Pie," she says.

I don't know if she's kidding or not, but I know Wyoming is right in the middle of the country, and near the top. So I bet it totally snows there . . .

Wow!

Before going to sleep I text Em. "Did you ever hear of the Iditarod?"

"The idiot Rod?" she writes back. "That would be my Uncle Rodney?"

See why Emily Finkelberg is the absolute best of best friends?

* * *

But I was wrong, life is *not* back to normal. Not that I'm even all that sure what normal is anymore. A woman comes over to look at our house. She's a realtor. Mom introduces me to her.

"Why is a *realtor* looking at our house?"

"To sell it."

"You mean if you get the Wyoming job," I ask Mom. "Right?"

"Either way, Sweetie Pie," Mom says, trying to act all smiley in front of this realtor lady. "There's nothing wrong with downsizing. We don't need all this room," Mom says. "And we certainly don't need a *pool*."

"Yes we do!" I say.

"When's the last time you swam?" Mom asks, still smiling but shooting me don't-be-a-brat warnings with her eyes.

"Yesterday! Every day!" I say. "Well it doesn't count *now* because of my boot!" I say, holding my foot up for sympathy points.

"It's just one possibility," Mom says. "Just checking to see what Noreen thinks we could get in the present market."

Humph. Noreen. I hate her. She's all syrupy sweet, walks through the house complimenting every single thing: "Oh your son's reeking cleats are the perfect touch! And are those last week's crusty dishes in the sink? How homey and delightful!

And the disgustingly filthy powder room truly makes this house a home!"

She and Mom go into Mom's office to talk, while I fume and speed redial Emily although I know, know, know she's in final *Guys and Dolls* rehearsals.

Brooke comes in and sits at the other end of my couch.

"Mom's in her office with a *realtor*," I tell her.

Brooke takes a deep breath and lets it out slowly.

"You should see this realtor *person*," I say. "She's a total phony slime. I can tell. Nasty to the bone. The kind who later, when you rip off her face, a horrible, sticky, insect-larva monster comes oozing out with no blood."

Brooke nods.

"She's got Mom totally fooled. Hypnotized, probably."

Brooke smiles a little fake smile at me.

"She's going to downsize us," I explain. "Shrink us into tiny soulless, plastic Playmobil people, build us a teeny Lego house. Leave us with that sushi doll food from Little Tokyo. Remember? Where the chopsticks are permanently attached to the noodles?"

"Sounds lovely," Brooke says in a calm, airy voice.

"Huh?"

"This is the new mellow, floating me," Brooke explains. "Who takes life as it comes. Who makes lemonade when life gives her lemons. Who accepts the things she cannot change, and trusts in the cosmos."

"Gross!" I say. "Give me back my snarky sister!"

"Do you know why David and I really broke up?" Brooke asks out of nowhere.

"No."

"Do you want to know?"

I nod and say, "Sure."

"Because deep inside, David believes that good things happen to good people, and bad things happen to bad people. He believes that he has had a charmed life, because he deserves it more than someone with leprosy or someone born poor. As if a baby trapped in a burning building is to blame for what is happening to her."

I don't say anything, afraid I'll scare away the moment.

"I didn't really get that about him, until my charmed life got a little less charmed." Brooke stares at her beautiful hands.

"Grrrr! I'd love to uncharm his life right in the nose!" I growl. "With a baseball bat!"

My sister takes another deep, dramatic yoga breath, and lets it out even slower this time. "Now, now, little flower," she says. "We must rise above our evil impulses and embrace the light. Breathe with me, little sister!"

So I grab a couch pillow and whap her with it. Wham!

When she whaps me back I wail, "No fair! My broken foot! My boot! No fair!" So she whaps me twelve times harder. But not half as hard as I whap her!

Mom and the realtor come out of Mom's office and find us shrieking and hooting and sweaty, with pillows everywhere.

The realtor lady's smile doesn't even flicker.

"I'll be thinking of you Friday," she tells Mom.

"What's Friday?" I ask, still panting.

"That's when Casper, Wyoming, is supposed to let me know what they decide."

Oh.

*　*　*

When we pull up after school Thursday, there's a For Sale sign in front of our very own house.

"Deep breaths!" Brooke advises, and goes inside.

I'm standing on the driveway scowling, when a car slows down and stops. I swing my scowl over toward the car as someone gets out of the passenger side, and the car speeds away. Oh! That someone turns into Adam B.!

He smiles and walks toward me.

"Ugly, isn't it?" I say clunking one of my crutches against the wood stake that's stabbed into our lawn.

He nods and says, "Yeah."

"I'd kick it down," I tell him. "But that's how I broke my foot last time."

Adam B. grins.

"Want to come in?" I ask, half because I have to pee and half because my backpack weighs a ton.

Adam B. says, "Sure!"

I crutch up the driveway to the side door hoping no one is around.

"It's bad feng shui to enter where the garbage goes," I blab, "but the front door is only for Jehovah's Witnesses, and those Mormon God-squad boys on bikes, and Mr. Woo, and delivery men and other strangers."

Shut up, Jacki, I tell myself. What if he's a Mormon or a Jehovah's Witness or a delivery boy?

I hear Mitch's music upstairs, and Mom and Brooke are nowhere to be seen. Good.

I ask Adam B. if he's hungry because I am. He shrugs. But first things first, I say, "Well, I have to go to the bathroom, so . . . I'll be right back."

The only bathroom I can get to without stairs is just inches away from where I leave Adam B. I hope Mitch's music is loud enough to drown out my peeing, but just in case, I turn on the water in the sink. I know that's a terrible crime during this drought, with all the water rationing and all, but tough. This is an emergency.

I look in the mirror. Stupid school uniform again, of course, but at least there's no gory lunch stains splattered across my chest, or green clumps of food between my teeth. I'm glad I washed my hair this morning and it's not a particularly bad zit day.

I come out and Adam B. is sitting on my couch! Right where I sleep! It makes me feel all giggly but I do *not* giggle.

And where am I supposed to sit? Right next to him? Way over on the chair? I stall by hobbling into the kitchen saying, "I'll get us something to eat."

But what? Apples? Chips?

He comes into the kitchen and catches me staring blankly into the open refrigerator, doing nothing.

"Where are you moving to?" he asks.

I shrug. "I don't know." That sounds beyond plain ordinary stupid and deep into the world of astoundingly stupid. Who wouldn't know a thing like that?

"See . . . well," I say. "It's complicated." I smile, still standing at the open refrigerator.

He smiles back.

"Maybe Casper, Wyoming, but I hope not," I say, closing the fridge and heading back to my couch. "Maybe . . . um. I don't know." There, cleared that right up.

We sit down, about seventeen and a half inches apart. I notice I didn't actually bring out any snacks. Oh, well. To change the subject I say, "So how come *Ryan* sent the valentine to Emily?"

Adam B. looks a little surprised. "Well, because he wanted to I guess."

"Yeah, but why did *he* do it instead of bangs-boy? V-something. Vazric?"

Adam B. looks totally confused now, and maybe a little afraid. Am I *scaring* him with how loony I am? Or is he looking confused on purpose just to make me feel even loonier than I am?

"You know, the one with the bangs?" I explain.

"Bangs?" he asks.

Is he teasing me, or is he kinda dumb? Or don't boys call bangs *bangs?*

"Wanna watch TV?" I ask, turning it on before he answers.

Ew! Now he'll think I'm a huge vidiot, which he'll probably think is totally repulsive and nauseatingly gross and who could blame him? I wish I'd suggested YouTube instead. I could have showed him the kittens with the Kleenex box.

But it's OK. We click through the channels, making fun of everything. He's funny, which is something I definitely, definitely like in a person.

Oh, no! Here comes Mitch, galumphing down the stairs. Eek! I feel like I've been caught doing something totally illegal. Plus, what if Mitch acts all shocked to death to find an actual boy in our actual house with actual *me?* Terror! I can so picture

166

my brother clutching his chest in a pretend heart attack. Staggering from the shock . . .

But Mitch just says, "Hey man," and Adam B. says, "Hey" back and it's over.

PHEW!

I'm dying for Adam B. to leave so I can text Emily, but I hope he stays forever, too.

Mom comes downstairs and does a sitcom double-take, but then she introduces herself to Adam B. all formal and school principal-esque like she hands out detention slips instead of candy on Halloween.

Adam B. leaps up to shake hands, and it's entirely and completely embarrassing and one hundred percent *awkward*!

Adam B. shifts his weight from foot to foot and tells Mom he recognizes her from Mr. Woo's recital, and Mom totally relaxes because she thinks only really nice boys play piano. And maybe she's right.

Mom finally goes into the kitchen. Maybe to sneak peeks and listen in, and snicker to herself. I hope not. But it turns out that it doesn't matter because Adam B. says he's gotta get home. He takes my cell number, though, and I practically float, crutches, boot, and all, to the front door to let him out.

"Does that mean you think I'm a Jehovah's Witness, piano teaching, God-squad, delivery man?" he asks. "Because I was perfectly happy being garbage."

I fight down the giggles and veer off to lead him to the side door.

He says, "See ya," and I say, "See ya," and he's gone.

Then I scream! And grab my phone to text, "EMILY YOU

WON'T BELIEVE WHO WAS JUST HERE!" But I absolutely can't wait for her to guess, so I add, "ADAM B!!!!!"

* * *

When I finally get Emily live and breathing at the other end of the phone, I say, "Here's how it happened. Ready?"

"Totally."

"Well, I was just standing on the front lawn, looking at the For Sale sign when a car . . ."

"Looking at the *what*?" Emily asks.

"Didn't I tell you about the creepy real estate lady?"

"Um . . . Yeah. But I didn't think . . . ?" I can practically hear Emily making her confused face. But then she takes a big breath and says, "So, an-y-way . . ."

"An-y-way," I repeat, "he got out of a car, and we went inside and Em . . . We sat on MY COUCH!" I pat the very spot.

"That should keep you tossing and turning tonight," Emily giggles.

Mom comes into the living room, clearly wanting my attention.

"Gotta go," I tell Emily. "The Mom wants me."

Em's voice gets sad, "About Montana, right?"

I sigh in answer. Montana, Wyoming, Neptune, what's the difference if it's not *here*?

Mitch plops down next to me on the couch, knocking me over, totally on purpose. I shove him aside. Brooke floats in from I don't know where.

"Later," I say.

And Emily quietly answers, "Gator."

Mom clears her throat with an, "Ahem!" and I put my phone down.

"New Rules," Mom announces.

"No boys on the couch?" I ask.

Mom looks confused. "What?"

"Never mind," I say, glad this isn't about Adam B.

"We already have new rules!" Brooke pipes up from the floor where she's doing dancerly leg stretches. "Sheets, garbage . . ."

"Well, these are *new*, New Rules," Mom says. "Mitchell! Take off those earphones!"

"I can hear every word you say," he says. But his feet keep thumping to the beat.

"Well, new rule number one, Food: We're going to start eating meals at home. And not carry-out or expensive prepared food. Regular meals, cooked on our own stove. And every one of us is responsible for making one dinner a week."

Mom crosses her arms and waits for us to complain but no one does. I remember Grandma saying we should eat at home more to save money. Make our own food.

We're probably all thinking the same thing: none of us knows how to make anything except toast and microwave popcorn.

Finally Mitch says, "I'm the master of grilled cheese!" We all look at him with admiration, hoping it's true.

Mom says, "Excellent."

"Cooking on our table at the Korean barbeque doesn't count, huh?" I ask.

"I'll look for that cookbook Grandma gave me," Brooke

says, eyeing the bookshelves across the room. "And there's always the cooking channel on TV . . ."

Mom nods, satisfied. "New rule part two, number two," she announces, "Reduction of possessions."

We exchange looks.

Then the house phone rings and Mitch nabs it. "Hey, David," he says and is about to hand it to Brooke but she's shaking her head.

"I'm not home!" she whispers and gestures that she's slitting her own throat again and again.

"She's not home, but I'll tell her you called," Mitch says, glaring at Brooke. He hangs up and all disgusted and annoyed he asks, "Why'd you *do* that?"

"They broke up!" I tell him.

"You did?" he asks Brooke.

Mom and Brooke smile at his cluelessness as if it's absolutely adorable. I do *not* see what's so cute about being stupid.

"But what if he needs to tell you something?" Mitch asks.

Brooke just sighs.

"As I was saying," Mom says, "Everyone is to go through all, and I mean ALL of their personal possessions: clothing, toys, books, sports equipment, toiletries, and electronics, in their bedroom, all closets upstairs and down, and garage. Said possessions shall be divided into three categories: 1. Things to keep. 2. Things to throw away. And 3. Things to sell in our garage sale a week from Saturday."

"A garage sale? Us?" I ask, trying to picture that.

"Saturday?" Brooke howls. "But there's a party at Kelsey's!"

"I always have games on Saturday," Mitch says.

Mom holds up her hands to stop us. "Everyone do your best. Ads are already in the paper for our sale. I suspect there will be at least two garage sales before we're done. This one is to get started on simplifying our lives."

"Like Dad always says we should?" I ask.

Mom answers, "Well, *that* was tactful."

"No, I don't mean Dad's right and you're wrong. I just meant . . ."

"That Dad's right and I'm wrong," Mom smiles. "And in this one case that is quite possibly true. I'm a big girl. I can take it."

My brother and sister put on their innocent, not-saying-anything faces, and I try to, too.

"OK," Mom says. "That's our goal: to winnow our possessions down to a level your father would be comfortable with."

"What? No way!" we all complain at once. But Mom just laughs at us.

"If it was Dad's choice," Mitch shudders, clutching his precious iPod, "he'd just have a bungee cord and his bike."

"And a toothbrush!" Brooke says. Even Mom laughs because everyone knows my dad is a fanatic about dental care.

"I'll get some poster board this week," Mom says, changing the subject. "Jacki, you'll make the signs, because you have the best lettering."

I do?

"Brooke and Mitch, you'll hang them up around the neighborhood. The idea is that if we scale down and get rid of the things we don't need, it will make the house show better and the move easier."

"About this move . . ." Mitch begins.

But Mom stops him. "There are still far too many unknowns to even begin discussing the move. But I think we should be prepared."

"I get to look through everyone's giveaways in case I want their stuff," I say, meaning mostly Brooke's.

Brooke's phone rings. I watch her check and ignore it. I wonder when David's going to give up.

Mitch shoots Brooke a look, then asks Mom if there's a new rule part two number three.

Mom smiles, "Not at this time, but stay tuned. Now who wants to make dinner tonight?"

No one answers.

"OK. It's me then," Mom says. "Fine. And who wants to come grocery shopping for future meals?"

No answer to that either.

"When your turn comes you'll just cook whatever I buy?" Mom asks. "Sheep eyes? Turtle skins? Rutabagas?"

Mitch untangles his legs and stands up. "Come on, Ma," he says. "Let's shop."

* * *

"Do you want to start upstairs or in the garage?" Brooke asks me.

First Adam B. on my couch, now Brooke and I doing this together! I hold up my boot and we both say, "Garage."

I never thought about it before but actually, a garage is a strange kind of place. If I were blindfolded and spun around and led into one, I totally bet I could sense its garage-ness and guess where I was instantly.

"Even our *car* has a house," I say.

Brooke is on her way up the ladder to reach the high shelves and she answers, "A dusty one."

I'd meant compared to homeless people, but now that she mentions it, it is pretty sneezy in here. And you wouldn't believe how not-afraid-of-spiders my sister is.

Brooke hands boxes down to me, and I don't even recognize half the junk inside. Old plates and hats and books, badminton racquets and a croquet set. When did we ever play croquet?

But when we hit on baby clothes and baby toys, Brooke climbs down to look through them with me because everything is unbearably cute. Some toys and outfits I half recognize from our oldest photo album, the one with Dad in it.

Brooke pulls out a wooden elf. "I remember this!" she says. "Dad carved it for Mitch. I remember watching the wood curl off the knife." She stuffs it in her pocket.

I drag a box out of the cupboard. "So this is where she went!" I say, lifting out my American Girl Kailey doll, naked but still smiling her happy smile in spite of the awful haircut I gave her. I really didn't get it at the time that her hair would never grow back.

"And look! Here are my Beanie Babies!" Oh, I forgot that I'd decorated so many of them with markers.

"I bet that's all worth some serious money," Brooke says.

"But what if I want to save them for my daughter or something?" I ask.

"I was kidding," Brooke laughs on her way back up the ladder.

A few boxes of boring stuff later, she hands me down a big

heavy one that turns out to be full of old tarnished silver stuff, a tray, a teapot, some ugly bowls.

"Now we're getting somewhere!" Brooke says. "We'll have to polish it up, though. Make it look ritzy."

Everything is piled everywhere when the garage door burps and shudders open.

Mom and Mitch step around our baskets and boxes of assorted junk, carrying bags of groceries. Mitch spots his old action figures and says, "Dude!"

Mom stops to stand in the middle. "My whole life, spread out on the floor of the garage," she says. "Odd."

"Good odd, or bad odd?" I ask.

But she just stares.

My sister looks lost in thought, too, holding what are probably her first ballet slippers. They are teeny, tiny, pink flats, not all that much bigger than my Kailey doll would wear.

Chapter 13

PIE AND MUSICAL CHAIRS

Mom makes onion cheese omelets. They aren't beautiful, but they taste a lot like real omelets! We compliment her like crazy, and she's so proud.

"New Rule part two number three," she says. "Or is it four?"

We all shrug.

"She or he who cooks does *not* have to clean up. Especially on the nights that *I* cook. So, who's going to do the dishes?"

"*All* the dishes?" I cry, looking around at the mess. Eggshells all gloppy on the counter, bowls, onion skins, a cheese grater, a carton of milk standing in a spill . . .

"Well, someone could clear the table," Mom suggests, "and someone else rinse and stack the dishwasher or wash the frying pan."

So we divvy up the tasks and are all busy in the kitchen when my sister says, "Look at us! We are so *Little House on the Prairie*! So wholesome and family-friendly! So Norman Rockwell and apple pie!"

"It could get old fast, though," Mitch says. "Like around now."

I agree. "How many nights a week do we gotta do this?" I ask Mom.

"Well, there are four of us, so *four*," Mom says. "But not necessarily in a *row*."

"Thank goodness! And speaking of American *pie*, did you guys buy any dessert?" I ask.

They say, "No."

"I'd sure like some pie," I say. "Boysenberry."

I can totally see thought bubbles with pictures of pie pop up over all their heads. "The mile high pie at La Belle Epoque?" I suggest.

Within seconds, the dishes and eggshells are abandoned and we're all cramming into Mom's car.

"Well," Mom says. "You can't change the whole world at once. Little steps in the right direction are a start . . ."

We all totally agree, absolutely one hundred percent.

* * *

I'm lying on the couch in the dark, wondering where we're going to move to, and knowing that wherever it is, it would be better with a hamster. I remind myself to remember to ask Madeline if her canned food drive is still on, so I can bring cans in for good luck. But I'm worried about what kind of good luck we'll get. Mom is supposed to hear about Casper, Wyoming, tomorrow.

She says most of the time when people say you'll hear something on a certain day, you don't, but still . . . she might.

So what would happen? Would Mitch really stay with Dad? And what about Brooke? I don't think she means Casper Community College. She probably means Pasadena City College, or Glendale Community College, or Santa Monica College . . . with *Carly*?

Does that mean Brooke would live with Dad, too? And who would live in our house? Total complete strangers?

And where will *I* be? I can't picture *being* in Casper, Wyoming, because I don't know how to picture Casper, Wyoming. I just see the blizzardy whiteness of the Alaskan dogsled race from TV, and I know *that's* not right.

I can't *not* live with Mom wherever she is. But then when would I see Emily and Brooke and Dad and Mitch and Grandma? But if Mom goes and we don't all go with her . . . Well, she's our queen bee! We'll just drone around miserable and buzzy, stinging anyone who gets too close, right?

* * *

Today's All School Assembly is about earthquake preparedness, an all-time favorite. They love to talk about The Big One, which is what we Californians call the earthquake that experts say is absolutely coming, maybe this afternoon, maybe in a hundred and eighty-three years. The Big One will kill most of us and probably leave the rest horribly messed up on a heap of rubble, alone with nothing to eat but each other.

This one's a puppet show.

I imitate the puppet's high squeaky voice, "It's a well-known fact," I tell Em, "that if you talk like this about The Big One, kids won't be as terrified!"

"I know!" Emily squeaks back. "Downtown L.A. ten feet deep in glass from crumbled skyscrapers? Tsunamis washing all the beach communities away! Whee!"

"Mega surfing, dude!"

Ms. Kaufman's head snaps around and she glares at us. What took her so long? She's totally losing her edge.

I turn the other way to look for Brooke and to see if Lauren (or should I say Chubbs?) is nearby. Sitting kitty-corner behind me is Madeline, and the sight of her finally reminds me to ask if her canned food thingie is still going on.

"No," she whispers back, keeping her eyes on Ms. Kaufman. "But you can donate stuff anytime."

"Oh."

"I'm going tomorrow, if you're interested in coming," she adds.

"W-h-h-at?" I stammer. "T-T-Tomorrow?"

"Never mind," Madeline laughs. "Don't worry about it."

But I turn back around and *do* worry about it. The earthquake puppets are having a fabulous time taking out the supplies they'd cleverly remembered to put away in case of emergency. "Look! It's a flashlight!" one squeaks in delirious joy. "And batteries!"

"Oh, boy! And here's our can opener and fresh drinking water!" the other one cheers.

I turn back around and tell Madeline that I could maybe stop by for a little while tomorrow . . . "If there aren't a lot of steps." I say, trying to point to my boot.

"Nope. No steps," Madeline whispers back.

"So, like what time do you go?" I ask her.

"Between eight and nine."

"In the morning?"

Madeline smiles at me and tilts her head sideways.

"Yeah, of course, in the morning," I say. "I totally knew that."

Madeline tilts her head the other way.

"So, I just show up?" I ask. "Like, walk right in the door?" I'm getting nervous already, down to my toes.

"Yep. Just show up. Walk in the door," she says, with a weird smile.

* * *

Now what? All through the rest of the earthquake assembly and French and history I tell myself that I can call Madeline in the morning and tell her I'm sick. Or that my mom won't let me go because we have to get ready for our garage sale because we're moving and we don't even know where, which sounds pretty pathetic, you've got to admit. Or I could say I don't have a ride. Or tell her that my grandfather died, and just not mention that it was almost four years ago.

Mr. Rodriguez calls on me during current events, of course, but I don't let it bother me.

* * *

I'm trudging across the green to math when David falls in step beside me. Uh oh.

"Hey, Jack," he says all friendly, as if he has ever once in his entire life spoken a single word to me at school before. "How're you doing?"

I'm on crutches, sweating in the gritty, hundred and three degree heat, with my enormous fourteen-ton backpack, feeling

179

all tormented and squirmy about going to the shelter tomorrow, so of course I answer, "I'm good."

"How's your sister?" he asks.

Ugh! What I *want* to say is LEAVE ME ALONE! But instead I say, "She's good."

David says, "Great!" And bares his teeth like he's going to bite me! No wait, it's a smile.

* * *

At lunch, I tell Emily and she thinks it's sweet and sad and romantic that David's all heartbroken.

I frown.

"You're not very sympathetic," Emily says.

I frown deeper.

Then, as long as I'm in maximum frown mode, I tell her about Madeline and the Catalina shelter.

And Emily says, "Cool! Can I come?"

"You're just saying that to make me look like an even poopier poop for not wanting to go," I say.

"No, I'm not."

"You are, too."

"I'm not, Jacki. I *want* to come."

"OK, fine. We'll go," I say. "Happy?"

Emily shakes her head, "Am I missing something here?" she asks.

But I don't know what to say. I'm all scrambled about everything.

The bell rings and Emily crunches up her garbage and wrappers and tosses them in the trash from here. "Wow! Good shot!" I say, "That's so *Mitch*!"

Emily bows. "Come early so you get a good seat!" she says on her way inside. It takes me a second to realize that she means to her play tonight, not to Madeline's shelter.

"Are you kidding? I'll be there when the doors open!" I yell after her.

And I am.

Brooke drops me. There's a minute or two in the car when I almost tell her about David stalking me so he can stalk her, but why ruin a nice evening?

I stump into the Theater Arts Building and sneak inside the auditorium to put my jacket across two front seats for Nora and me. But instead of going back out to the lobby till show time, I sit down in the dark, empty theater. I hear voices and things clanging around backstage, but it's quiet out here. The red velvety seats are lumpy and stained from so many years of audiences sneaking snacks in. They were probably beautiful when they were new.

I can almost get why Emily wants to spend forever in places like this. It does feel totally separate from the rest of the planet, even the air is different.

I've seen every single play and skit and talent show Em has ever been in, but I guess that won't necessarily, positively always be true because Casper, Wyoming, called and offered Mom their job right when they said they would, which I guess is a sign that they aren't totally flaky at least.

Mom jumped when the phone rang. She's not usually the jumpy type, but I guess she'd been waiting for the call all day and her nerves were shot.

She put on a whole new Casper, Wyoming, voice which didn't sound like her usual work voice, or her home voice and she laughed a strange nervous laugh, which was totally suspicious. She thanked them all over the place and told them how *flattered* and *honored* she was and . . . well . . . It was enough to make you puke.

What she didn't do though, was say, *Yes, I'll absolutely take the job.*

She said she had to discuss it with her family (yes!) seeing as it would be such a radical zabba zabba life change, she'd think about it seriously over the weekend, and have an answer to give them Monday before noon.

When Mom hung up, with the fake smile still plastered to her face, she looked me in the eye and burst into tears. Poor Mom. She's not the bursting into tears type. In fact the only other time I've ever seen her cry was at Grandpa's funeral, and even that was only for about two minutes at the absolute most.

But today she was all sobs and snot and soon a splitting headache and lying flat on the couch asking for Excedrin and absolute silence. Now I guess I know *why* she's not a crier.

"But are you crying because you're relieved that they want you?" I asked extra quietly, trying not to rattle her headache into a migraine. "Or sad to have to take the job? Or sorry to not take it, or what?"

"All of the above," she moaned. "And then some. Now let me die in peace."

I *wanted* to tiptoe away, but where was I supposed to go? She was on my couch. And she was still lying there when Brooke and I left.

I'd asked Brooke if she wanted to come to the play, but she said, "Can't. Sarah and I are meeting a whole bunch of kids in

Old Town to talk about the prom. Don't worry, I'll be back to get you."

"What *about* the prom?" I asked.

"We've decided to go in a big group thing, no dates."

I said, "That sounds fun," but what I was thinking was, 1. Is David part of that big group? And 2. Whatever happened to the six hundred dollar dress?

There must be something I can do to raise six hundred measly little dollars for her. Look at all the fund-raising stuff going on right here in the lobby. For three bucks you can send some poor, sweaty kid from the drama club scurrying backstage to deliver your note and a red carnation to the actor of your choice. And they're selling crappy ten-cent cookies for a dollar each.

I'd only have to sell . . . um . . . six *hundred* cookies? Oh, that's kind of a lot. Never mind.

Plus for proms isn't there also supposed to be a limousine and corsage and getting your hair done and all that other expensive stuff?

Ick. I'm so entirely sick to death of money!

* * *

Someone in a ton of stage makeup peeks out of the curtain and I wave although I can't tell who he is. The head disappears and the curtains ripple.

I hear him yell, "Emily! Your friend is here."

If I was better at math I'd tell you how many hours there are from now (Friday evening) until Monday before noon, but I *can* tell you it's not all that long. After Emily's play tonight, there will probably be a little ice cream, then sleep.

And tomorrow, me and Emily are supposed to go to Madeline's shelter, unless I get suddenly way too sick.

You might be wondering what I'm dreading so badly, and the answer is: I'm not sure. I know I absolutely don't want one of those experiences that are so horrific and shocking that they make you appreciate what you've been taking for granted your whole life, and make you become a better person, who never complains about anything ever again.

I'd much, much rather just never complain about anything and skip the hairy part.

And I'm also afraid of looking like some kind of spoiled little twerp come to do a good deed a few years early for her college application. Or like I'm there for looky-loos and to feel good about myself, even if that is exactly who I am and what I'm doing there.

Anyway, if I survive the shelter, then tomorrow night I'll be right back here with Mom to watch the second performance of Emily's play.

Sunday, lunch at Dad and Grandma's.

Then back here one last final time, (possibly my last time in this auditorium ever, ever, ever) for the very last performance of *Guys and Dolls*. That's the sad part about theater. You work, work, work, rehearse, rehearse, do the play a few times, and then Poof! It's over and gone! I think that would get to me after a while.

When I asked Emily about that though, she said, "Just like life itself: live, live, live, Poof, dead! Right?"

Wasn't that deep?

Then Emily will go to her cast party, and I'll go home to

sleep, and Plunk! it'll be Monday morning and time for Mom to tell Casper, Wyoming, yes or no, and the future to begin.

* * *

Emily's head pokes out of the curtain. "Comfy?" she asks. "Enough elbow room?"

I look up and down my empty row. "Yeah," I say. "I'm good."

"Good," she says. "Just checking."

I hold up my crutches and say, "Break a leg."

"Will do," she answers. "Later."

And of course I say, "Gator."

As soon as she's gone, the audience starts to pour in. Nora comes running up to the front and gives me a hug. She brought a giant bag of gummy sharks, my favorite!

And the play is GREAT! Especially Emily! I know that if she was a senior, instead of a ninth grader, she absolutely, positively would've been cast as Miss Adelaide, or even Sarah, but the lead roles always go to seniors without fail. And that's OK, because in just a few little bitty years, whether I'm here to see it or not . . .

I applaud till my hands hurt. It was absolutely worth all those hundreds of years of rehearsal! And Emily was right, Shota really can sing like a bird. And I don't mean *tweet*!

* * *

I cannot believe that Emily is allowed to sleep over tonight but she is! First Emily's parents take me and Emily and Nora and

Nora's mom, Aunt Claire (who looks nothing at all like I pictured her), out for major sundaes at Cold Stone. Yumm!

From Emily's stories about poor miserably weepy Aunt Claire, I pictured her hunched and scrawny with stringy pale brown hair and shoulder blades that stick out like a bird whose wings were hacked off, wearing a lacy old-lady blouse buttoned up to her scrawny neck.

But she was all cleavage and red fingernails and lipstick with a giggle in her voice. I'm sure that proves something, but I don't know what.

After ice cream, when they bring me and Em home, Emily sees the For Sale sign for the first time in real life.

"Eewww!" she says, pointing with disgust.

Nora pipes up with, "Grosssssss!"

"I know," I say. "Isn't it awful?"

"Totally," Nora says sympathetically. And for a split second I'm sorry she's not sleeping over, too. We'd invited her, but she absolutely does NOT want to go to the shelter in the morning. Doesn't want to see it, hear about it, think about it . . . The idea makes her woozy and I can see her point, if you know what I mean.

Actually, I think that is an entirely reasonable reason to completely cancel our shelter visit, but no one agrees with me.

Emily's mom gives us a mini-last-minute zabba about getting sleep for the play tomorrow night. Emily and I nod in agreement like bobbleheads until they pull away.

Inside, we get all set up on my couch with snacks and drinks, put in the *Little Shop of Horrors*, and then the worst thing happens. Without meaning to, entirely and completely by accident, we both fall sound asleep and stay that way until morning! Can you believe it? What a tragic and horrible waste!

We wake up shocked and blinking in the light to Brooke saying, "You said you need a ride to the shelter, right? Well, this ship is sailing in ten minutes, with or without you!"

Emily's instantly on her feet. Her stage makeup gone crazy all over her face. "Dibs on the shower!" she calls and tears upstairs.

Good, that gives me a few more minutes with my pillow and . . .

"Up now!" my sister snaps. "I'm totally not kidding!"

So I haul myself up on my crutches and lurch to the bathroom.

We're dressed, and in the car, and at the shelter, in no time. Brooke zooms away and Emily doesn't pause a single second, she just marches right up to the entrance and in. I use my boot and crutches as an excuse to follow slowly behind.

Chicken! I call myself. But even walking slowly, I get there eventually. Near the door is a sign-in kind of table, but the ladies wave me through. There's a cafeteria line with sandwiches and chili. It's pretty quiet and clean and brightly lit. Most people sit alone, eating. It's so totally not the big scary scene I'd feared.

I see Madeline in the far corner so I wave. Emily's heading for her, too, past piles of stacked cots. I wonder if they shake everyone awake one by one, or if there's one loud alarm clock or what? Maybe it's like in the movies where soldiers have to pop out of bed and stand at attention for inspection at the foot of their cots. No, that doesn't make any sense. What would they be inspecting for?

Madeline is thrilled to see us. She's totally in her element, bossing people around, getting everyone organized. They are all like seven years old and younger, so they're used to being bossed and it's not that hard to get them all roped into a game of musical chairs. But why Madeline wants to play a game that makes so many kids *lose*, I do not know.

I'm the one with my back to them, singing "Row, Row, Row Your Boat" and I feel like a creep when I stop and hear them all shuffle and shriek to grab a seat. The truth is I absolutely hate games. If I were in charge of everything, I'd get rid of all games that make winners and losers. I wonder how I'd do that, though. And actually, everyone is laughing and happy and no one's in tears, or running back to tattle to their parents, so maybe it's just me.

After musical chairs, it's Hot Potato, only it's Hot Bert and Ernie, with the two dolls going in opposite directions. At least this one makes two losers at once so no one has to feel bad alone, although like I say, no one seems to feel bad anyway.

This time Emily is the music. She sings "A Bushel and a Peck," of course. That's a Hot Box Girl song from her play.

And one by one, the kids' parents claim them, and the place thins out. I don't know where they all go since they don't have homes, but Madeline says everyone has to be gone by eleven when the shelter closes. Maybe that's when they take up their positions at exit ramps and parking lots, holding up their cardboard "Hungry Iraq War Vet," or "Will Work For Food" signs.

When we get outside, my sister has the windows down and her bare feet up on the dashboard. Her music is blaring and she's on the phone, so I don't feel so bad for making her wait.

As we're walking to the parking lot, Madeline says, "Thanks

for coming. That was fun." Then she adds, "You know the kid with the braids?"

Emily nods, and I say, "Yeah."

"Her mom is in prison so she's homeless with her aunt who is a meth addict and maybe pregnant."

My mouth drops open. "What?!"

"The kid with the braids?" Emily practically yells. "That little girl with the *braids*?"

Madeline nods. Then turning to run for her Dad's car, she says, "See ya!"

* * *

Mom is coming with me to the play tonight. She tells me to pick out what I want her to wear, and of course I pick the green dress the color of brand-new grass that reminds me of springtime and baby sheep going baaaa. I always pick this dress. Mom doesn't really get it but I suspect that she likes that I'm consistent, so I think even if I didn't want to pick the green dress anymore, I still would. But maybe not.

"How did you like the shelter?" Mom asks me when we get in the car.

I start to say, *It wasn't so bad,* but then I remember the braids girl playing musical chairs like any other little girl anywhere. "The bad stuff was invisible," I say.

"It's better that way," Mom says. And maybe she's right, but I'm not sure. The whole *braids* thing has been bugging me all day. I don't know how to think about it, but I don't know how to *stop* thinking about it either.

We stop so Mom can buy flowers for Emily.

"You can get some in the lobby," I remind her.

But Mom scoffs, "Carnations," like carnations are too vile and turdlike to be considered flowers.

I watch her point out the most exotic and expensive ones, stem by stem. When the giant bouquet is ribboned and ready, Mom hands it to me, while she digs in her purse for her credit card. Am I supposed to carry it sideways like Miss America being crowned? Hold it in front of me like a bride? Straight up like the Statue of Liberty? How about on one shoulder like a baseball bat?

"Jacki!" Mom snaps. And I see that the florist is looking at me funny, too.

* * *

Mom likes to sit way back in practically the last row. The play looks totally and completely different from back here. The actors are little wind-up toys, teeny teens, putting on a show in a shoe box.

It never creeped me out before, but this time it feels a little bit spooky to see all these kids, especially Emily, looking so unreal and unfamiliar.

Sometimes I'm with Mom when she runs into someone she hasn't seen for years. She always tells them they haven't changed a bit. Then she later tells me she hardly recognized them. Will that be *me* with people from Palm Canyon Academy one day?

I've been resisting the urge to keep asking Mom what she's thinking every ten seconds, but at intermission I break down. "It's probably about halfway now between Friday and Monday, right?" I ask.

Mom nods, "Just about."

"So, are you thinking yes Casper, Wyoming, or no Casper, Wyoming?"

Mom sighs. "Actually, Sweetie Pie, I was really enjoying not thinking one way or another about Casper, Wyoming."

"Oops," I say. "Sorry."

Chapter 14
WHAC-A-MOLE

I GOOGLE CASPER, Wyoming, and don't get much, but when I try just plain Wyoming, I get Yellowstone National Park! With geysers and bears and buffalo and unbelievably unbelievable scenery. Well, *that* would be cool!

"But Yellowstone is on the whole other end of the state," Brooke tells me. "That's like thinking L.A. is near Big Sur or Yosemite just because we're both in California."

"Oh."

I don't ask Mom about it again until I'm getting into Brooke's car to go to Dad's. If I'd held out just a few more seconds, we would have driven away and I could've felt so proud of my maturity and self-control, especially since I didn't get an answer anyway. All Mom said was, "Family powwow when you kids get home from your father's."

"Want to place bets on her decision?" Brooke asks when we're a half block away.

"I say she takes the job," Mitch says.

I turn and look at him, all sprawled elbows and knees in the backseat. "Really? You think she's going to say *yes*?"

Mitch nods and shrugs.

I look at Brooke. "I don't see what choice she has," Brooke says, agreeing with Mitch. "It's not like a million job offers are pouring in."

"But . . ." There's nothing to say, really. I feel all the energy and hope and happiness seep out of me like a deflating beach ball. Ooof. I'm flat on the car seat, just an empty plastic thing with eyes.

Brooke pokes me with her finger. "Cheer up, Wacky. We'll get through this."

I don't answer, but if I *was* going to answer, it would be to make a horrible, miserable, noise, so hopeless and sad and fed up that anyone who heard it would weep.

I don't have the energy to get out of the car at Dad's house. I just sit there watching a small gray lizard do pushups on a rock, until Grandma comes out to peel me off the car seat and bribe me with chicken curry. I'm not the least teeniest bit hungry, but I go. It's not *her* fault the world is such a mess.

"How come you and my dad aren't all frantic and worried about money like everyone else?" I ask her.

"We're worried," she says. "But I own this house outright, which means I don't have monthly payments anymore. And I get a pension every month from teaching. We live frugally, and fix things when we can, instead of replacing them. We don't buy on credit, I cut coupons and watch for bargains. And your dad brings in some money for incidentals with his baking . . ."

"That doesn't sound too complicated," I say, waiting for the catch.

"Your grandfather and I saved money all our lives, and he left a modest life insurance policy."

I say, "And . . . ?"

"And nothing!" she laughs. "That's the whole story."

I sit at the kitchen table wondering if it's too late. Can I go home and fix a lot of broken things, and cut out coupons and get rid of Mom's credit cards . . . ?

I tell Grandma and Dad that we're going to have to leave a little earlier than usual so I can get to school for Emily's final performance of *Guys and Dolls*.

Grandma says, "Oh! That's a fun one. I love musicals!"

Dad and Mitch groan and gag, so I turn my back on them and ask Grandma if she wants to come with me. "I'm sure they'll still have tickets at the door," I say. "It never, ever sells out completely."

Without missing a beat Grandma says, "Well, I don't think so. How much are the tickets?"

Oh. *That's* what she means by being frugal and modest and not living a snazzy life. Wow! There's no way Mom could think like that. Not even if we fixed every old vacuum cleaner and TV and microwave in the garage, and sewed up every torn towel or sheet or whatever instead of getting new ones from now on, and ate dinner at home every single solitary night. My hopeless deflated feeling returns, and I'm suddenly sooooooo sleepy.

Mitch kicks my good foot. "Get up! It's time to go."

I guess I fell asleep on Grandma's couch. Maybe the sight of any couch will do that to me from now on. I'll walk through the furniture department at Macy's and . . . zzzzzzz. No, wait!

The whole couch thing will be over really, really soon! Next week my boot gets the boot!

But the second I dare to be happy about *that*, I remember that we're going home now, to another family meeting. A big one. And the dreadful dread is back.

* * *

In the car, I get a text and I think it's Emily so I'm confused when it says, "Want to hang out later?" And the name is Brownfeld. Huh?

I scream, "BROOKE!"

She hits the brake and we lurch forward.

"IT MUST BE HIM!" I shriek, shaking the phone at her. "Adam B. for *Brownfeld*!"

Mitch says, "Jeeze! You could've killed us!"

But Brooke just laughs, and drives on.

"What should I say?" I ask, although I'm already texting back, "YES!"

But as soon as I press *send*, I remember Emily's play! Oh no! I furiously send the next text: "Emily's in a play tonight. Want to come?" But we're in a dead zone so my phone says, retry? YES!

Retry? again. YES!

Retry? Grrrr!

I practically throw it out the window.

"Calm down," Brooke says. "Breathe."

The message goes through, and almost instantly he answers. "Sure! Where?"

"Brooke!!" I scream again. "He said *where*? What should I tell him?"

"Tell him to come over and I'll drive you both. I want to get a look at this guy."

See? I told you I have the best sister in the world! Oh my God! I'm going to the play with Adam B. for Brownfeld! I tell him to be at my house by six thirty but it's already four! I have to shower and wash my hair and scream and shave my legs and tell Emily!

We're home and I go crutching at a mad clip in the side door, but there's Mom, waiting. Looking very, very serious.

Oh yeah. The powwow.

*   *   *

Mitch sits on the piano bench, tilting it way back. Brooke is on the floor and I'm on the couch, looking serious but secretly deciding what to wear tonight.

Mom stands. "Well, now that we've all had time to think it over, I want to hear your opinions on the Wyoming . . . situation," she begins. "But first I want to tell you this: no matter what I decide, the house is going to have to go. Let's just hope there's a buyer out there."

I wish Mom would hurry!

"We are not in desperate shape," she continues. "We won't end up on the street, or hungry, but we might never live the kind of life we've been living, at least not for quite a while. But if I take the Casper job, we will be much more financially secure, although in a new place. Now who wants to say what?"

"I think you should do whatever you need to do," Brooke says.

Mom looks the way she used to when we made home-made Mother's Day cards. Sort of sadish-happy and almost weepy-smiling. All she says is one word, kind of whispery, "Brooke."

"Well, I'm not moving to Casper, Wyoming," Mitch says. "I'm sorry but I'm just not. I'll live with Dad or friends, or whatever. But like Brooke says, you gotta do what you gotta do, Ma."

Then everyone looks at me.

I say, "What?"

"Well, what are your feelings?" Mom asks me.

"Mine? I want to live here, and go to school with Emily and keep everything exactly the same, so, what difference does it make what I want? We can't have that, right?"

"That's basically correct," Mom says. "But I can say no to the sweet, generous people in Wyoming, let the lifeboat drift away . . . And take a gamble on being able to cobble together an existence here where our friends and family and roots are. We'd all have to make sacrifices, though, and work together. There's no telling when another job will come along."

It's quiet a second and then Mitch shrugs one shoulder and says, "I'm in." He gets up and sticks his hand in the middle of the room. Brooke puts her hand on his and says, "Me, too."

Oh! It's a football huddle kind of thing. I hop over. Mom and I add our hands to the pile and Mom says, "All right then, we stay. Done deal."

I count to ten so everyone knows that I know how serious this all is, before I zoom away to the shower.

* * *

He is so cute! Look at him! Can you even stand how adorably adorable he is? Wearing a shirt with a collar like at our piano

197

recital. I guess he thinks the play is dress-up, which it's not, of course. But isn't that *so* sweet?

I'm in jeans, though. And a T-shirt.

He shrugs his adorable shoulders and says, "My mom said I had to wear . . ."

Brooke comes down the stairs and I wait for his eyes to bug out of his head, but they don't too badly, which is nice. "This is my sister," I tell him. "She's driving us. Ready?"

I call out, "Bye, Mom," not sure where she is.

Her head pokes out of her office like those animals who tunnel in our yard. She peers at the three of us. "Jacki," she says, "would you please step in here a moment?" Not, *Come here,* but *Would you please* . . . Weird.

I follow her into her burrow. She pulls me inside and closes the door.

"Is this a *date*?" she asks in a hissing little whisper.

I laugh. "No. We're just going to Emily's play!"

"Because, you know you're not allowed to date until you're sixteen," Mom says, squinting up at me.

Up? When did *that* happen?

"Don't worry," I say giving her a kiss on the cheek.

Brooke and Adam B. are waiting by the car. "I got taller than Mom!" I tell them. "Like, *today.*"

Brooke nods. "It happens."

"I was taller than my mom by fourth grade," Adam B. says, "But I freaked when I realized I was taller than my *dad.*"

I'm in the front seat, Adam B. for Brownfeld in the back. It's a tiny bit quiet in the car until Brooke puts in a CD and she and Adam B. talk about music.

When we get to school Brooke flashes me a thumbs-up before she drives off. It almost gives me the giggles.

Oh. I forgot that there'd be so many people I know here. Like half my school. They start buzzing around almost instantly, smelling fresh blood.

Don't embarrass me! Don't embarrass me! I chant under my breath. I try to send psychic messages to the goons I go to school with. *Don't say anything horribly stupid and humiliating. Please don't tell him I threw up on Coach Keefer! Don't tell him I'm the worst student and a klutz and whatever dreadful third grade shameful memories of me you all have on the tip of your tongues.*

And by some miracle, everything goes just fine. Almost suspiciously fine. Madeline has an extra ticket, so we don't have that icky, *who should pay* moment that I'd been dreading a little bit.

I can tell Chloe thinks he's cute by how she's throwing her hair around, and Alison made an *Oh Wow!* at me when he wasn't looking. We all go find seats in a big group, so Adam B. and I don't have to make all the conversation ourselves every second. We sit near Lauren and some other juniors. I ask her if she brought Chubbs.

And she says, "I should have!" Then in an NPR kind of accent she says, "Chubbs simply adores the theater!"

"That's her hamster," I tell Adam B. He frowns and says, "I had a great hamster named Larry, although he was technically a girl."

"What happened to him . . . er . . . her?" I ask.

"She died," Adam B. says, looking so sad for a second.

Is this the perfect boy or what? I'm positive he'll totally love the sneezing panda and the tree-climbing dog, and . . .

The music starts, lights, curtain.

There's Emily! I jab Adam B. with my elbow and point. It's hard not to mouth all the words and sing along, but I don't.

I sneak a peek at Adam B. He doesn't look bored, he just looks nice. Oops! He feels me looking and tips his head my way a little, smiling. I snap back forward and there's my best friend up onstage kicking and singing and being fabulous.

I know it sounds a little crazy, but it's not until halfway through the "Sit Down You're Rocking The Boat" scene that I realize I am absolutely positively really and truly *not* moving to Casper, Wyoming, or any other faraway place! HOORAY!!!

* * *

After the play me and Adam B. have to squish into Brooke's car with Sarah and nine zillion of their friends. They drop us at home and zoom off. I'd meant to ask Sarah how she was doing since her dad's company went bankrupt and all that, but . . . oh well.

We stand in the very quiet driveway a second after they're gone, then I ask Adam B. if he wants to come inside and he says, "Sure."

Either we were robbed and trashed or Mom's been busy while we were gone. *Someone* seems to have pulled every single thing we own out of every drawer and closet. Adam B. and I stand in the living room looking around at the piles and stacks.

I call out, "Hello?"

I hear grunting from Mom's office. I hobble closer, "Mom?"

"Give me a hand with this!" Mom calls out, probably

forgetting that my hands are usually on my crutches. Nonetheless, I crutch over there with Adam B. right behind me.

Mom is trying to pull a big wooden box out of the bottom shelf of her bookcase. I'd never noticed it before. Adam B. hurries over to help her, heroic, noble, sweet boy that he is.

From the way they strain, it looks very heavy and important. The background music should be much more dramatic than the plain drone of these NPR voices. What *is* that box? Maybe the letters from Hogwarts that I secretly spent my entire eleventh birthday waiting for and was sooo heartbroken not to get. Or, maybe it's the priceless jewels that Mom stole when she abandoned her throne as queen of some wildly exotic animal kingdom.

"These are my college textbooks," Mom says, opening the crate onto the grim sight of a bunch of dull dust- and mud-colored books.

She orders Adam B. to help her carry it to her desk. They crab walk across the office with me crutching awkwardly out of the way.

"Where are these from?" Adam asks her.

"I went to UCLA," Mom says.

Oh *yeah*. I totally knew that.

"I hope to sell them on eBay," Mom says.

"Tonight?" I ask.

Mom looks confused, she brushes a hank of hair out of her eyes and says, "What's wrong with tonight?"

I look around at the piles everywhere and say, "N-n-n-othing."

I gesture to Adam B. to follow me and we leave the room while Mom admires her boring old schoolbooks.

"I think she's lost it," I whisper to him.

He nods. "Well, maybe she'll find it again."

I start to say, "No, I mean . . ." but then I see that he understood me all along.

My couch is entirely surrounded with piles. One heap is rain-themed: ponchos, raincoats, rain boots, and umbrellas even though we've been in a drought for years.

Adam B. is examining a mountain of board games. "Scrabble, Mousetrap, Simpson's Monopoly, Chess, Clue, Connect Four." He pulls Whac-A-Mole out of the stack, and says, "Yes!" I didn't even know we still had that.

We clear a spot on the coffee table, he hands me a plastic mallet, and we play. The noises beep and tweet and whirr and we SLAM the moles on the head.

My mom may be going loony, turning the house inside-out in a weird panic, but there's nothing like a good old violent game of Whac-A-Mole to set things straight!

Brooke comes home while we're playing. She stops right inside the door to stare at the crazy mess. After a few seconds of shock, she says, "Wow, Jacki, I *love* what you've done with the place!"

"Not me," I tell her. "Mom."

"Well, it certainly gives it a new and unexpected look," she says.

I offer her a mallet and she drops onto the floor between the pile of raincoats and the stack of old road maps. Adam B. and I let her win that round. SLAM! WHACK!

I didn't even know Mitch was home until he shows up next and says, "Dude! That's my favorite game, like, ever!"

He becomes the fourth player. All mallets taken.

Mom hurries through the room from time to time, carrying armloads of whatever, this way and that, but we just let her be.

I don't know what time Adam B. told his parents he'd be home but when his phone buzzes he jumps. "Uh oh! It's a school night!"

He answers it and says, "Sorry. Leaving right now," and he quickly does.

I peek through the window to watch him hop on his bike and vanish into the dark. I strain further and see him reappear in the glow of the next streetlight but after the next one he disappears completely.

"He's a doll," Brooke says, when he's gone. "A little hottie!"

"Isn't he so sweet?" I ask.

"Oh, please," Mitch mutters in disgust.

"What, Mitchy?" Brooke teases. "Didn't you think he was sweet?"

My brother ducks, as if Brooke's words are stinging, poison arrows. "I'm outta here," he says.

Brooke chases him up the stairs, calling, "And totally cute! Right, Mitchy? Wasn't he a cutie?"

I float to my couch and practically grin myself to sleep.

* * *

Last time I went to school *this* tired, I broke my foot. I am *not* going to break my other foot three teeny tiny days before getting this stupid boot off, although can't you totally picture that happening now, with spring break less than a week away?

I'll crutch extra super carefully all day today. Tiny shuffling steps in slow motion, eyes on the floor. None of the great Olympic armpit swings I've now mastered, the ones that can get me from French to history in five great, flying leaps.

The grand plan for spring break is to sort our junk and have garage sales. It's no trip to Mexico, horseback riding on the beach, eating fabulous tamales and getting our hair braided with beads. But still, no school is NO SCHOOL!

And Emily's family is too broke to go skiing this year! Isn't that fabulous?

Wait. That doesn't sound right.

But it's not like they're terrifyingly broke. They just can't afford to take Nora and Aunt Claire along, and Emily says it wouldn't feel right to go off on a ski trip and leave them behind.

She says the snow is skimpy this year anyway, because there wasn't enough rain, or because of global warming or who-knows-what. I guess serious skiers like fat snow. Hey, I wonder if that Iditarod man is still racing. Or did he freeze into an Alaskan mansicle ice statue with dogsicles and snotsicles?

Anyway, most years while Emily's family is skiing and mine is in Mexico, I spend half my time missing her, and the other half looking for souvenirs to bring back for her. But this year we'll spend spring break together, having sleepovers and just hanging out! Doesn't that sound perfect? Nora will be tagging along, but still.

Add in the wondrously wonderful fact that Adam B. . . . well . . . that there *is* an Adam B., who isn't too cool to play Whac-A-Mole and who loved his girl/boy hamster, and who has a sweet soft smile, and is funny and . . . Oops! I'm supposed to be paying attention to how I walk today.

Little careful baby steps.

*　*　*

Where's Em? I didn't see her before school and I have so much to tell her that it practically hurts! I hope she's not ditching although I bet she was up late, late, late at the cast party last night, because a lot of the actors are seniors and if they're anything like Brooke, they never come home unless they're grounded.

There's all the Adam B. details to tell her, of course, but she doesn't even know that I'm not moving to Wyoming! I almost told her backstage after her play last night, but I didn't want to be like David. Remember how he made Brooke's ballet recital all about his own stupid wink? Ew.

*　*　*

Finally, finally, Emily shows up at lunch and says, "Guess what?"

"No, *you* guess what!" I say. I've been waiting all night and morning for this!

"No, Jacki *you* have to!" Emily insists.

So I say, "OK, what?"

"Brad Pitt kissed me!"

"Huh?" I ask, a little confused.

"Shota! And I kissed him. A lot. And it was really great!"

I want to take a half second to think about this, but instead I say, "Wow, I didn't even know you still liked him."

"Well, I always kinda . . . I dunno." she says. "But it was

the cast party and we drove over together with Mark, you know the senior who played Harry the Horse? And we just kind of stayed together most of the . . . Hey! Where did you find Adam B. last night?"

"I didn't *find* him," I say. "Me and Adam B. came to the play together! On a date-ish thing!" I wait for shock and amazement and cheers, but I don't get much of anything.

"EMILY!" I practically yell. Other kids turn to look, but who cares?

"What?" she snaps. She's not one bit happy either.

Oh. I want her to care about my *date*, but of course she wants to talk about *kissing* Shota. And she's right. Kissing is huge! We've probably spent nine hundred thousand hours wondering what our first kisses would be like, and now it has actually happened in real life to one of us and that's an enormous big deal and I should be excited.

But, *Shota?* What can I say? That he sure can sing? That he ate rabbit poop when he was six? I feel giggles start bubbling like Pepsi burps but I stomp them down because I am absolutely positive that this is *not* the time to laugh about Shota in any way. But all that un-giggling takes time and I guess I've waited too long because now when I ask, "How was kissing?" Emily looks annoyed or something. Hurt? Mad?

"Let's rewind," she finally says. "Start over."

I'm so glad she said that. "Yes, let's!"

And we smile at each other, but it's *still* not entirely, completely one hundred percent all right, and I have a stomachache growing and want to cry a tiny bit.

"Are you mad at me?" she asks.

"No!" I answer. "I'm not even the tiniest speck mad!"

"Well, you sounded grossed out that I kissed Shota. Like you think I'm a—"

"No, I don't think *anything*. I was just surprised is all."

"OK then," Emily says.

But it doesn't feel OK. I wish there was an undo button in real life.

Bip. I'd delete the whole morning, except for the part where Brooke woke me. "Shhhh! Mom passed out in her office!" she said. "Let's sneak out and let her sleep!"

Brooke and Mitch and I had drive-through McBreakfast, which would've made Mom furious. That might be why it was so entirely and absolutely scrumptiously delicious.

But now, I feel sick. I don't know if it was my greasy morning McPigout or that Emily and I are . . . Well, not *fighting* exactly . . . but . . .

"I'm not moving to Wyoming," I blurt out.

Emily's head whips around, her hair lashes me in the face.

"WHAT?!" she screams.

"You heard me."

"For sure?"

I nod. "Yep."

Em drops her lunch and flings her arms around me in a shrieking squeezing hug. We have a nice long scream in each other's ears and . . . all's well with the world.

Chapter 15
GRILLED CHEESE AND KANGAROOS

M<small>R.</small> RODRIGUEZ IS ZABBAING ON about how this is the worst depression since the Great Depression, but there's no way I'm going to be the one to ask what was so great about it, because it sure sounds pretty seriously un-great to me. Why don't they call it the Not-So-Great, or the Really-Not-One-Tiny-Bit-Great-Depression?

Now he says he wants to talk about the resilience of the human spirit through adversity, which is fine, but first I think he better tell us what *resilience* means. I don't ask, though, in case I'm the only one in the dark on this.

Madeline's hand is up. What a shock.

"I volunteer at the Catalina shelter," she begins. "And I see it all the time."

That sentence, you'll notice, does *not* define resilience. It could mean athletes' feet or bristly facial hair. No. The *bristly facial hair of the human spirit* doesn't work.

"People who are happy even though . . . well . . . it doesn't look like they have anything to be happy about," Madeline continues. "I mean, nothing good has happened to them, as far as anyone can tell, in a long, long time, if ever." She takes a deep, Madeline breath. "And sometimes, they'll come in with some awful piece of news, like that they were turned away from the hospital, or got mugged, and just a few minutes later, they're cheerful again!"

"Maybe they're just stupid," Ben says. "And don't know enough to be depressed."

"No. I think some people are just naturally happier than others," Madeline says. "What will make one guy totally miserable won't even bother someone else. I really believe that."

"Well, that's different from resilience," Mr. Rodriguez says. "Resilience infers recovery. Bouncing back after a setback."

Ah ha!

Lacey raises her hand. "Maybe everyone has their own personal private happiness set point. You know Ben's would be," she holds her hand down just an inch off the floor, "like one and a half."

We all laugh.

Lacey puts her hand on her own chest, Pledge of Allegiance style, and says, "I'd be in the middle, of course, because I am, as we all know, perfectly well balanced and normal."

We laugh again.

"And Jacki," she continues, holding her hand as high over her head as she can reach, "Will be a hundred."

I say, "Who, me?" And the whole class cracks up even harder.

"Everyone else will be somewhere along the grid," Lacey explains. "And maybe that's where they bob back to, like a pool float."

Mr. Rodriguez nods. "That may be," he says. "In which case, no matter how good or bad the economy is, people will basically adjust and survive."

"Except for the people who won't," Ben adds.

"But they probably wouldn't have anyway," Lacey says. "Probably would have found something to be gloom and doom about."

And then everyone starts talking and arguing, but I'm stuck back there on Lacey saying I'm a hundred on the optimistic scale. Miss Silly Pants Smiley Face, or whatever it was my sister called me.

Olivia speaks up, "I've heard that people who win the lottery think their lives are going to be so fantastic, and then a lot of them are totally depressed afterward when they find out they are still themselves."

YES! The lottery! Why didn't I think of that? We should be buying lottery tickets every single day! I mean, *someone* has to win, right?

* * *

The most wonderful part of Emily's play being over is that now she has tons of free time after school and can come home with me! I tried to prepare her for what Mom has been up to, but it turns out *I* wasn't even prepared myself. Remember how torn up the house looked last night when Adam B. was over? Well magnify and multiply and quadruple that a few dozen times.

Brooke and Emily and I weave our way through the living room following a *cha-plink cha-plink* noise to the den. Turns out it's some kind of sticker-putter-oner machine. Mom has cha-plinked little price stickers on everything in sight and is going mad cha-plinking a metal sales rack full of clothes.

"Hi, Mom!"

"Oh, hi!" She blinks, entirely surprised to see us.

I'm tempted to explain that we live here. Are her kids. But instead I ask, "Where'd these racks come from? I didn't know we had these."

"We didn't," she explains, going back to her cha-plinking. "I bought them."

"Oh. And that price tag gun?" Brooke asks.

Mom nods.

Brooke pushes me and Emily toward the kitchen, hiding her snickers behind her hair. When we're far enough away she bursts out laughing, a little teeny bit insanely, with just the least little bit of hysterical crazy-osity.

"What's so funny?" I ask. "Mom's totally flipped!"

Brooke nods, tears are starting to stream. It's *that* kind of laughing.

"I bet she spent more on . . ." Brooke tries. ". . . the clothes racks . . ." She slides to the floor laughing and sputter-ing. But, since she's Brooke, she does it in a perfectly graceful ballet-looking way.

Emily opens the pantry and pulls out the cereal. Good idea. I get bowls and spoons. Oops, no milk. Just an empty carton staying nice and cold in the fridge. I wonder if Mom ate today.

Brooke's still laughing, but it's simmering down.

I find a package of burritos in the freezer. "Does it matter how long this has been here?" I ask Emily.

She steps over Brooke's legs to come look at the box. "I

don't think so," she says. "I mean don't they find ancient animals frozen in ice caps for millions of years and then eat them?"

I shake the burrito box. "Mmmmm! Woolly Mammoth Burritos! Little brown tufts of fur, tomatoes . . ."

We nuke it and go out by the pool.

The lounge chairs, table, and umbrella have all been price-tagged. I feel my first sad ping of, O*h! I'll miss this table!* Although I don't know for sure if you *can* actually miss a table. Nonetheless, I wonder how many pings I'm going to feel before this is over.

"It's just that your mom is used to working," Emily says. "All that excess energy."

"It'll be the designer boutique garage sale of the century," Brooke says with a snort, and I'm afraid she's going to melt down again.

I send her inside to find Mom and see if she'd like a piece of Wooly Mammoth Burrito. It's not bad, actually.

Mom comes out by the pool and does take a tiny piece, but she doesn't sit down to eat it. Munch, munch, munch on the run.

"Mom. It's only Monday," I say. "Your garage sale isn't till Saturday, right?"

"Got to be ready!" she says. "You girls better start on your rooms!"

I point to my boot, but then I say, "Oh, wow! I practically forgot this was ever coming off! But it's happening Wednesday! I'll be going up and down stairs just like anyone else! Sleeping up there even!"

"Yep," Mom says, "you're losing *that* excuse."

"Do you think Coach Keefer's going to make me go back to track?" I ask in a sudden panic.

Brooke laughs, "Something tells me she won't be in any huge hurry."

"But you'll have to break something else and barf on her again to get out of sports next year," Emily says.

Next year.

I cringe, waiting for my mom or my sister to say that I won't be there to deal with Coach Keefer next year, but they don't. I suppose this would be the perfect time to tell Emily about it, but I don't want to do it in front of everybody like this.

"I'm so used to you on crutches," Emily says.

"Me too, actually," I say, glad to change the subject. "Isn't it funny how fast things go from being new and weird to normal and ho-hum?" Hey, getting used to things, resilience, that's kind of what Mr. Rodriguez was talking about today.

Which reminds me that I completely forgot my Win the California Lottery Economic Recovery Plan! I tell Mom and Brooke and Emily about it and Mom says, "Save your dollar, Sweetie Pie. You've got about an equal chance of winning whether you buy a ticket or not."

"But there's *no* chance at all if you don't buy a ticket!" I say.

And Mom says, "Exactly."

* * *

"Now about that kiss," I ask, after Mom has returned to her mega-stupendous garage sale preparations, and Brooke has gone back to school to get Mitch.

213

Emily falls back in her lounge chair, marked $5.00, and says, "Kiss*es*!"

I repeat, "Kiss*es*."

"I've been thinking about how to describe this all day," she says. "And the best I can do is say it's like falling asleep."

"Boring?"

"No, not *boring*, you goofball. Like that second when you start to fall . . . as in *fall* asleep. When you're sort of between two worlds . . ."

I think about that. "I wonder if that's why they call it *falling in love*?"

Emily shrugs. "Well, it does make a person sort of dizzy. Because you kind of stay in that fall the whole kiss."

"I'm afraid of heights," I remind her.

She knows that my very worst most horrible nightmares are always about falling. She's been with me when I've woken up all gaspy and sweaty and wild eyed mid-fall, at the split second that I realize I cannot land safely no matter how I wiggle around or position myself. It makes me shudder to think about it.

"I know, but it's not scary," Em says. "More like tumbly. You don't think about landing and shattering on impact. You just . . . float. At least I did. It was fun!"

"Well it must be," I say. "But some people think scary rides are fun . . ."

"You'll like it," Emily says. "I promise. Think Adam B."

"I have been," I say. "But I can't imagine not totally cracking up if he came at me all serious and smoochy with his eyes closed and his lips all puckered up." I giggle and make kissy fish lips at Em.

"I'll bet you a million dollars you won't laugh," Em says.

And we do a very fancy handshake that goes on for so long I practically forget what we're shaking about.

* * *

Mitch makes grilled cheese sandwiches for dinner. Remember when he said he was the *master* of the grilled cheese? Well, that may have been a tiny exaggeration, not that I could've done any better or burnt them any less, necessarily. But after dinner, while we're all talking about where to go OUT for dinner tomorrow night, my phone rings and it says *Brownfeld*!

I've talked on the phone a few million times before, and a bunch of those calls were boys, but something about Adam B.'s voice, right there, in my ear, right up next to my face, well . . . It did not feel like something I could do in front of my whole entire family.

"Hey! The dishes!" Mom calls as I crutch out of there to my couch. But I hear Brooke whisper to let me go.

"I'm grounded," Adam B. says.

"Because you were here so late?" I ask.

"Yep."

"Oops, sorry," I say. "For how long?"

"Depends on my dad's mood," he says. "But you know, I meant to tell you that my brother Josh is in show business, too. Like your friend Emily."

"Yeah?"

"Yep. He's one of those guys dressed like Spiderman outside the Chinese, in Hollywood."

"Really? Posing for pictures with the tourists?"

"That's him."

"Wow! I bet that gets awfully hot."

"Not as bad as the Darth Vader costume." Adam B.'s voice drops to a whisper. "I'm not supposed to use the phone while under house arrest. I'll call you when I can," and he's gone.

I'm just standing here, holding my phone and possibly grinning, when Mitch walks into the room, takes one look at me and says, "I'm going to throw up."

* * *

Boot is OFF! I'm free!

It's so weird. Just my pale skinny foot all naked in my sandal. When I get home I'm going to polish each toenail a different color to celebrate!

The still amazingly pregnant doctor asks if I've been walking without the boot and I say, "No. Could I have been?"

And she says, "Sure, a little at a time wouldn't have hurt this last week or so."

No one told me that. But so what? I'm free now!!!

The doctor tells Mom to make sure I drink enough milk and eat enough calcium-rich foods. Mom nods in a terribly serious, medical way that's a little tiny bit funny.

And here I am, *walking* up the stairs to my room! Right foot, left foot, no problem-o!

My room looks pretty much the same but quieter or something. Like it fell asleep waiting for me. Wake up! I'm back!

I open the top drawer of my dresser. Mom wants me to go through all my stuff and decide what to sell. My underwear and socks?

Ew. What kind of perv would buy used panties?

Next drawer. My shorts and T-shirts?

No.

This is silly.

Brooke appears in my bedroom doorway and says, "Time to go to Dad's. Race you downstairs?"

I practically knock her over, barreling out of the room. We thunder down the stairs shrieking. Mitch stumbles into our path and we nearly flatten him.

"Don't forget to drink milk!" Mom calls after us.

* * *

My brother brags to Grandma about his brilliant grilled cheese success, and she's completely and entirely thrilled.

"Aren't you afraid I'll turn into a better cook than you?" Mitch asks.

And she laughs, "Are you kidding? I'd love that! Someone to pass the magic measuring spoon down to! The spoon that was carved by one of our ancient ancestors and has been in our family for countless generations."

I bet she's kidding about that. Right?

We tell them we're having a garage sale Saturday and Dad says, "I know. I'm going to come sort out my old camping gear and archery sets and whatnot that are rotting away in the attic."

"We have an *attic*?" I ask. No one else looks shocked or even interested in this news. Don't they know there's always amazing stuff in attics? Ask anyone!

"Half the mysteries in the world involve attics!" I remind them.

"Trust me," Dad says. "There's nothing even remotely mysterious about this one. But it's time to haul all that stuff out and see if anyone wants to buy it at the garage sale." He says this, too, as if there's nothing totally and bizarrely wacky about his obviously having spoken *directly to Mom*, or about his coming over to our house on purpose, when it's not even an emergency.

Brooke kicks me under the table and I kick Grandma. Oops! I'd meant to kick Mitch, but I don't have great aim, plus I'm new at having regular feet.

We eat our spinach lasagna, chew, swallow, chew, swallow, in total and complete silence.

"What?" Dad finally asks.

Brooke is the oldest, so we turn to her. "Nothing," she says. "We're just a wee bit surprised. That's all."

"By what?"

"Well, it's not like you and Mom are great chums," she says.

Dad shrugs as if it's no big deal and says, "In hard times, people pull together."

Grandma stands up and says, "Who wants carrot cake?"

"Me!"

* * *

On the way home Brooke says, "Mom's going to have to take you guys to school tomorrow."

Mitch says, "You're skipping?"

And then I realize, tomorrow is March twenty-fourth! The day the schools start to post their acceptances on-line! I used to have the date totally engraved in my brain but I guess I didn't know it still mattered.

"She's going to be busy!" I explain to my brother, pretending

218

I'd remembered all along. "The colleges start posting tomorrow. And tomorrow can start at twelve-oh-one, midnight tonight, right?" I ask.

Brooke nods.

I look at my beautiful, courageously brave sister, and wish, wish, wish there was something wonderful I could do for her. Tomorrow is the day she's been waiting and working toward forever and ever, and now it's going to be the end, instead of the beginning. Poor Brooke!

I say, "You seem so calm."

"I know," she says. "I'm surprised, too."

"Well," Mitch says, "what'll you do if someplace accepts you?"

"*If*?" I shriek, swinging into the backseat to slug him, but he dodges my fist.

"*If* anyone accepts me," Brooke says, "I plan to call and write them and beg them to hold a spot for me for next year, and I'll spend the year knocking myself out getting financial aid and scholarships and a job or two and loans and whatever else there is out there."

"And you'll take classes at the community college, right?" I ask.

"Probably. Unless I'm working full time. A lot of people take a year off to work between high school and college," Brooke explains. "I won't be the first." The car completely fills with silence for a second, and then she says, "It'll be fine."

"I'm going to buy lottery tickets," I reassure her.

"Someone should tell Jacki that you've got to be twenty-one to buy lottery tickets," Mitch stage-whispers from the backseat.

Brooke looks at him in her rearview mirror and stage-whispers back, "It's OK. She'll be twenty-one by the time she actually remembers to buy one."

And they both laugh, ha ha, at me.

There's a car in the driveway. Adam B.'s?

No, that's just stupid because 1. Adam B. is my age, and there doesn't even need to be a 2. Because number one is entirely and completely enough, unless someone drove him.

"How do you like it?" Mom asks when she sees us.

"Like what?" Mitch asks, going straight for the fridge even though we ate seventeen seconds ago at Grandma's.

"My new car! Isn't it cute?"

"The one in the driveway?" I ask.

"Yep! It's a Toyota Corolla," Mom beams. "Payments are less than half what I was paying before!"

Brooke smiles, "Nice," and runs upstairs.

Mitch grunts.

I'm not a car person, but I figure *someone* has to pretend to be interested, so I say, "Let's name it!"

Mom laughs, "I haven't named a car in at least twenty years."

She and I look out the window at it. It looks like a car.

"First we have to get to know its personality," Mom says, "before we can pick an appropriate name."

"You didn't get to know *me* before you named me," I remind her.

Mom says, "True. So, it's little, and it's black, and it's . . . um . . . basic."

"Poppy seed?" I suggest.

But Mom says, "How about The Dot? Like a pencil dot? Or the dot on the letter i?"

"Perfect!" I say. "Want to take me and The Dot to Emily's?"

But Mom just laughs and says, "I've got too much to do for the garage sale."

* * *

It feels strange to be back in my bed, but strange in a good way. The living room windows faced the street, so car headlights used to swoop through the drapes and race across the walls all night. From back here, though, it's all velvety darkness. I watch the glow-in-the-dark stars on my ceiling fade to black.

Brooke's bedroom door is closed but I fall asleep to the sound of her voice murmuring away and her super fast tap-tap-typing at her computer.

I'm sound asleep when I hear Brooke scream! Bam! BAM! My heart slams around in my chest and my throat clamps closed. Fire? The Big One? No, the room isn't pitching. COLLEGE! I reach for my crutches . . . practically knock over my light turning it on. Where am I? My room! No crutches!

I dash for Brooke's room. Mom is already there. They are jumping with their arms around each other. That's a good thing! No one jumps for sad!

"What? Where?" I scream, jumping too, but all alone.

"N! Y! U!" Brooke screams. Her phone is ringing and the house phone is ringing. "NYU!" Brooke shrieks again. "YES!!!"

Mitch is leaning in the doorway, smiling sleepily.

221

Mom is grinning ear to ear and hugging herself.

"SARAH!" Brooke yells into the phone. "I got NYU!"

I look at the clock and it's two fifteen. Wow!

Things calm down after a while. Brooke is on the phone with friends and back at her computer. I'm just crawling back into my bed when she screams again. "SWARTHMORE!"

* * *

Since no one wakes up in time for school, Mom says we should go apartment hunting. Actually, first she suggests we bash and clang around the house doing garage sale stuff, but Mitch and I say she should probably get out of the house since she's been home, home, home for days.

And we should let my sister sleep because last night was just the beginning. The whole last week of March can be just as loony. All the colleges have to let everyone know if they're in or not by April Fool's Day.

Some schools don't post on-line, so there's also the craziness of waiting for the mail. I can so totally picture all the high school seniors in the country trailing their mail carriers like cats after the tuna wagon! No, I don't know what a tuna wagon would be, but you know what I mean.

Of course, Mitch suggests we go to Amoeba Records in Hollywood. That's always where he wants to go because it's the biggest music store in town, or in the universe, I forget which. Amoeba is my brother's Holy Land Happy Place. He once told me he wants his ashes spread there when he dies.

I want to go to the zoo and see the kangaroos because I just saw a hilariously hilarious video of a kangaroo who goes boinging up to an unsuspecting golfer and gives him a huge kaboom kick with his big back feet! POW! The golf guy goes flying, SPLASH!, into a water hole.

I love kangaroos.

But Mom thinks the only worthy excuse for skipping a day of school is to find our next home. Mitch looks miserable about it, but I tell him that at least we get to help pick our new place and not just come home one day to a new hive.

I say, "And maybe we'll find an apartment building where everyone's really nice, and we'll all get to be such great friends that we'll pop in and out of each other's apartments without even knocking, like on a TV sitcom!"

Mitch rolls his eyes.

"And we'll get to know The Dot!" I tell him.

"Oh boy," he says, but he's kidding.

Mom says, "If there's time, maybe we'll stop at Amoeba later."

"Promise?" Mitch asks.

And Mom says, "No."

I watch him weigh the non-promise in his mind and decide that *any* chance of going to Amoeba is way, way better than none.

*   *   *

Mom has circled ads in *The Recycler*, which is a newspaper full of stuff no one wants anymore. Some of the ads refer to apartments as *units*.

"Ah! What a lovely *unit*!" I say in robot speak. "We'll have a *unit* warming party, and get one of those embroidered pillows that say *Unit Sweet Unit*, or *There's No Place Like Unit*." I crack myself up.

But it turns out I absolutely love the first *unit* in Los Feliz! It has one of those bumpy red tile roofs and archways everywhere and the walls curve into the ceilings with no angles anywhere and look like white frosting.

See how totally important the windowsills and doors are, all dark wood and serious? This is absolutely not a place for fart jokes or a pink couch, not that we have a pink couch, but I'm just saying.

I'd be artistic here, in a classy way with excellent posture. Maybe I'd study mythology and ancient languages and wear my hair in one long braid.

But Mom says it's too expensive. Breathtakingly expensive. Way more than our house payment each month, so never mind.

Next is a gigantic walled city in Glendale with rows of identical cement balconies where people keep their barbeque grills and dead plants. Before we even see the apartment, the woman tells us that the *complex* has an arcade room, an exercise room, an enormous TV in the screening room, a hair and nail salon called LuLu's, two swimming pools, and a mini-mart.

She takes us up in a mirrored elevator to a unit with sliding glass doors on one side but no other windows anywhere. Not one. I feel the people living and breathing upstairs and downstairs and on both sides. It's like being a book on a shelf.

On our way out, the woman asks if she mentioned the concierge service, and dry-cleaner, and 24-hour patrolled security parking. "It's like life on a cruise ship!" she says.

Mom shudders.

From there, The Dot takes us to a dark, maybe not actually *damp*, but it looks like it *wants* to be damp, duplex that's totally one hundred percent gloomy and depressing. We back away while the landlady is still talking. Sorry!

None of these are in our neighborhood, so I guess I wouldn't be going to school with Adam B. if we move here, but I love the next unit so much that I don't even care! It has a twinkly ceiling and cottage cheese walls. There's a sparkly bar-counter thing in the living room that you're supposed to put tall stools by, and a tiny, kidney shaped pool in the courtyard with a sea horse throwing up in it. Well, a fountain of a sea horse, with water gushing from its mouth.

I can totally picture myself out there in a bright polka-dot bikini and big earrings, white sunglasses, and a wide hat. I'll be sipping a cold drink with an extremely long straw, flipping through the pages of *Teen Vogue*.

But Mom thinks it's cheesy and more like a cheap hotel than an apartment, and she doesn't think the green, long-haired carpet is one tiny bit funny. "It's for old-time, wanna-be starlets," Mom says. "Can't you feel the desperation and despair?"

"Um . . . no."

Mitch is getting sulky and even kicking him doesn't seem to help, so we stop at the Golden Dragon for dim sum. "This is going to be harder than I thought," Mom says.

In spite of my brother's grumblings, we decide to check out one more place. I figure it's going to be like Goldilocks with the Bears' porridge. Some were too zabba, others were too zooba, but this one will be just right! Right?

Wrong.

The description in the paper made it sound like such a charming, cozy guest house. Actually, those are exactly the words it used: *charming, cozy, guest house*. Ha! Whoever wrote that must be on crack and actually, from the look of this place, that's completely, one hundred percent possible.

It kind of *tilts* in an entirely cement yard, surrounded by razor wire. No grass. No tree, not even weeds want to live here.

We peer at it through the car windows, past a mailbox that's completely tagged to death and covered with graffiti.

"This we can afford," Mom says. "But I can pretty much promise that whoever rents this *charming, cozy, guest house* has only one other housing option, and that's the tent city of cardboard boxes on skid row."

"We just need to look closer to Amoeba Records," my brother says, as if that will solve everything.

Chapter 16

EAGLES AND PINGS

WE GET HOME AND FIND MY SISTER sitting like a Brooke statue in the center of the couch.

"Princeton has been added to my *yes* list," she says, with a blank face and an empty voice. I guess she's done jumping and shrieking.

Brooke has been so brave lately, it kind of had me partway fooled into thinking all this was OK with her. There are no sniffs or tears, and no trace of there having been any, but still, even *Brooke* doesn't sit *that* straight.

Mom shoos me and Mitch upstairs and goes to Brooke herself.

* * *

"Man, it's emotional around here," Mitch says, sinking into my beanbag.

"You don't think Mom meant it that the *cozy, charming, guest house* is the only one we can afford, do you?" I ask him. "She was kidding, right?"

227

"Totally," Mitch says. But I can tell he's not so sure, either.

"What are you going to miss most about Palm Canyon?" I ask him. "The team?"

"What kind of question is that?" Mitch asks all cranky and irritated like I'm poking him with sticks. "How am I supposed to know what I'm going to miss? I'm still there every day."

"I know, but . . ."

"Well," he says, wrestling right back up out of my bean-bag. "It's sure been fun talking to you." In a second, his music is BLASTING!

* * *

I close my door and check my phone. There are thirty-two messages from Emily. That makes me feel sooo much better! I check the time. Yep! She should be out of school by now, so I call her.

But she answers and says, "Can't talk. I'm at Zushi with Shota!"

"Shota?" I ask. "Just the two of you?"

Emily giggles, so I guess that's a *yes*. "Later," she chirps.

And all I can say to *that* is, "Gator."

* * *

The garage sale is crazy! People show up at seven in the morning while we're still setting up, and there's no getting rid of them. They remind me of the seagulls at The Clam & Crab who wait for you to throw scraps, but keep a close, suspicious eye on each other. They can't stand it if another gull gets a single solitary crumb.

Emily and Nora slept over last night, but Emily either just

plain didn't want to talk about eating sushi with Shota, or she didn't want to talk about it in front of Nora, or I forgot to ask, or all of the above. Maybe it's because Mom has been working all of us to the bone since the girls got here yesterday and none of us has had a chance to breathe let alone talk about anything.

We tell my mom that most garage sales just heap everything in piles on blankets, and have boxes of stuff to rummage through, but she says that's reprehensible and shows that the sellers have contempt for their merchandise.

Dad was here for a while last night and back again early this morning with fresh bagels and cream cheese. He's making endless trips up through the hole in the ceiling to the attic. I tried *four* different times to climb that stupid ladder, but froze three rungs from the top all four times!

Good thing I don't have my heart set on being a firefighter or an eagle-cam camera placer, or a roofer, or tightrope walker, or house painter, or a window-washer for skyscrapers, trapeze artist, or bridge painter.

The only even slightly interesting thing Dad brings down is a tiny camp stove like the frozen-snot guy had on the Iditarod. That race has to be over by *now*, right? It's weird to think that while I'm living my life, going to school, hunting apartments, and eating woolly mammoths, people are still being dragged across Alaska by their dogs, and other people with braids are sleeping on cots in the Catalina shelter. It makes a girl's chest hurt, thinking about how many ways there are to be alive.

* * *

And it's impossible to believe that the boring, normal junk that Dad keeps dragging down from the attic is all that's up there. I send Emily up as a spy after making her swear on her life not to withhold any information no matter how terrifyingly gruesome: decaying skeletal remains, ghostly warnings written in blood on the walls, I can take it.

But she comes down with the worst report of all: "It's a snore," she says. "I'm sorry."

"Are you sure?"

"Positive."

"You looked everywhere?"

"There is no *everywhere*. No hidden corners, just one not very interesting rectangle of nothing."

I have to believe her—she's my best friend—but it's hard, and the disappointment is terrible. I'm tempted to secretly ask Nora to go up and double-check, but if Emily found out she'd probably kill me for doubting her. And if I was actually willing to *die* for this, I'd just go up the last three rungs, right?

"Your job," Mom says pointing at Mitch, "is to help people carry their loot to their cars. Mine is to answer difficult questions, such as, *Will you take two dollars instead of five?* And your job," Mom points to Dad, "is to stay out of my way and try to be helpful."

Dad stands at attention, military style, and salutes her.

Wow, that was like a friendly teasing joke sort of thing! Awesome!

Mom has the sales staff: me, Emily, Nora, and Brooke, wearing bright red fanny packs that look stupid on everyone except Brooke, of course. The packs jingle because they're stocked for making change.

Brooke's phone rings often and she still ignores a whole lot of the calls, but maybe they aren't all David. I absolutely can't blame the guy for missing Brooke horribly and wanting her back, but I'm afraid he's just going to show up here being handsome, with flowers and puppies and who knows what? I mean, she liked him *once*, what's to keep her from liking him again?

After that first rush of serious seagull-esque customers there's usually more of us sellers than there are shoppers. But people come and go and it's fun. Brooke's friend Sarah stops by for a while, and I remember that I keep forgetting to ask Brooke about Sarah's (and Madeline's) dad losing his job and all that. I must absolutely remind myself later.

Sarah *looks* fine, but maybe her unhappiness is invisible, like the braids girl and the others at the shelter.

Whole huge families pile out of cars and swarm the yard for a few minutes, then squeeze back in their cars and vanish. Other people stay forever, examining every little thing and asking tons of questions.

Familiar furniture and clothes leave in the arms of strangers, but I don't feel much *ping* about any of it. I saw Mitch snatch his old Pokemon cards away from a kid who looked interested, but that's the only time I saw any of us change our mind. I do have to look the other way when strangers paw through the box of Brooke's leotards and old dance costumes, but that's a different *ping*.

Look at that little girl, so hard at work, arranging my Beanie Babies into piles on the grass. She's not sorting by color, or kind of animal. Maybe it's just which ones she likes best, second best, and like that. When I can't stand the suspense for another second, I go over and ask her.

She looks up at me like I'm as dumb as dirt, which stings from someone who's three, and patiently explains, "I'm looking for the magic ones."

Of course!

Now it's absolutely clear to me that everyone here is doing exactly that! Even the older lady sniffing the place mats is searching for the magic ones, right?

* * *

And talk about magic: how long have Dad and Brooke been sitting together on the front porch? They're talking and smiling!

A father and daughter hanging out, chatting on the steps might not seem like such a big deal, but trust me, it totally is. I'm not sure why my sister has been so crabby with Dad lately, but she seems constantly, perpetually annoyed with him. And when she acts all cold and unfriendly, he backs off and leaves her alone.

Sometimes I want to shake him and yell, FIX THIS! Instead I usually just get a stomachache.

But now . . . Hooray!

I nudge Mitch and point to the porch.

He nods a few times, but it could be in time to his music. "I told you she's a Mom-Clone," he says a little too loudly. "If Mom's not hating Dad, then Brooke's not hating him."

No, that's stupid, right?

As much as I'd absolutely love, love, love to hide behind a shrub and eavesdrop on them, I don't do it. And I control the urge to scoop them into a big squishy-squeezey family hug, to show how happy I am that two of the people I love most in the whole entire world are friends again.

Instead, I pry my eyeballs off them and force myself to dig through the bag of bagels. I find the last sesame seed one and have my own small, private, but totally yummy celebration.

* * *

My dad and brother just left for Mitch's game in La Cresenta, and—drum roll, bugle call, megaphone announcement—the neighborhood boys, starring Adam B. for Brownfeld, show up!

I'm so glad to see him . . . er . . . them.

And I'm so curious what Emily will think of seeing blond Ryan of the valentine and bangs-boy Vazken again.

Adam B. isn't ungrounded; he says he's just not all that grounded during the day on the weekend.

I say, "I'm glad."

And he says, "Me, too."

Have I mentioned that he is sweet and adorable and adorably sweet and incredibly nice, and that I like him a little?

* * *

By one thirty, the garage sailors have all sailed away and it's down to us and our version of silence: birds, neighborhood air conditioners, pool filters, leaf blowers, and cars.

There's still tons of unsold stuff, but a whole lot is gone, too. We're all sprawled on the grass, sweating, drinking lemonade, swatting flies.

I tell everyone about the Beanie Baby girl.

"So which one did she pick?" Emily asks.

"A brown dog," I explain, realizing that it was a cocker spaniel like Daisy. Then I say, "She picked out about five other ones, too, but her mother said she could only get one."

233

Emily says, "You were asking, like a quarter each? Weren't you?"

"Yep."

Ryan says, "What a mean mom."

"And what if that's not how the magic works?" Vazken asks. "What if meanie babies have to be *together* to have power? And now, thanks to that cheap mom, they're so far separated that the chances are one in a billion that they'll ever be correctly combined again. Maybe that moment was the last hope for life on Earth, and now we're doomed!"

Nora (who has been really, really quiet until now) speaks up and says, "First of all, they are *Beanie* Babies, not *meanie* babies, and second of all, I chased that kid to the car and gave her the other ones she wanted."

Emily laughs, surprised. "You did?"

Nora blushes a little and says, "Yes." Then she turns to me and says, "I know they weren't mine to give away, but I didn't think you'd mind. And I could pay you back . . ."

"No, no! Of course that's great," I say. "I just feel bad that I didn't think of that myself!"

"So," Nora says, looking at Vazken, "we're not a bit doomed. It's all going to be fine."

Adam B. holds up his Dixie cup of lemonade as if he's toasting Nora, and says, "Good work, saving the world and humankind and stuff!" And Nora blushes even more.

I told you he was sweet.

Uh oh! Mom's heading straight for us and I bet she's going to make everyone get up and lug all this left-over junk back into the house. We're way, way too hot and tired. I'm about to whine and protest when she says, "I called Goodwill and they'll pick up the rest of this Monday morning."

"Really? I thought you said we were going to have a bunch of garage sales," I say.

"Nope. Changed my mind," she says. "You all look like you could use a swim."

And she's sooo entirely and completely right! I've been in my boot so long I got completely out of the habit of even *thinking* of swimming.

"Might as well use the pool while we've got it," Mom adds. Then she says, "And maybe we'll order pizza in a little bit?"

The boys stand and whirl away on their boards and bikes to get swim trunks or shorts or whatever, and it's suddenly me and Emily and Nora alone on the lawn. "Life is really interesting," I say.

And they totally agree.

* * *

We have a complete blast, and swim till we're soggy. My sister joins us for a while, and I think the boys are going to have heart attacks and drown when they see her in a bathing suit, but they manage to survive. We play Aqua ball and water basketball and have chicken fights and play Marco Polo and the boys dunk each other and push each other off the board.

I can't tell for sure if Emily *like* likes, or just likes Ryan but if she does, it will be so totally one hundred percent fun to give her Ryan's old valentine. I can't wait for the whole Shota thing to just blow away like dandelion fluff, not because he's a bad sport in baseball but because if I'm really and truly not going to return to Palm Canyon next year, I want Emily to have someone way better than Shota as her closest friend there.

In fact, I think I better start scoping everyone out and seriously considering who to leave her to. My first thought is Lauren, but that's just because of Chubbs.

We're all shivery and wrapped in towels like six colorful eggrolls when my brother and Dad appear. I introduce my dad to the boys and I know they just assume that he lives here with us, and who can blame them? I know it doesn't matter the teeniest bit who they think lives where, but still, it makes me almost feel a little like I'm lying, if that makes any sense.

Mom comes out with pizza, and everyone eats.

"OK, let's tally up!" she says, dumping her cash box and our fanny packs on the table.

"Minus your overhead," Brooke reminds her. "Fanny packs, clothes racks, price tags, and that price sticker gun thing." Brooke giggles.

"The ad in the paper," I add. "The poster boards. And is that cash box new?"

"Whatever," Mom says, as she counts. "The important thing is that three different people asked about the *house*. And I saw several take flyers."

Oh. The house. *Ping*! There will be no more swimming with my best friends and the neighborhood boys, or having the incredibly adorable and sweet Adam B. just magically appear in front of the house.

"And," Mom says, pushing the entire pile of money across the table to my sister, "Here's $509.75 toward your prom dress."

Brooke looks entirely and completely flabbergasted. She says, "What?"

Mom shrugs and takes a slice of pizza. *Mom* eating pizza? Do you know how many calories are in a slice of pizza? Well, neither do I, but I know it's a whole lot! Meanwhile, Brooke's face is going through all kinds of contortions, and she's not going anywhere near the money.

I look around. Emily is trying to pretend she's not watching this scene, but of course she is because she gets it completely. The boys are clueless and just acting like boys, and Nora is totally absorbed in her pizza. She is the slowest eater I have ever seen in my entire life. Dad and Mitch are standing by the flowerbed, discussing Mitch's game in intense zabba zabba detail.

Finally Brooke says, "Aw, Mom, you're the best. But I'm not her anymore."

"Not who?"

"That girl who felt entitled to a new gown, when people were going broke around me."

Mom reaches out and touches Brooke's cheek.

I nudge Emily that we should leave them alone.

* * *

Some stuff we decide to keep and carry back inside. But we shove most of the unsold garage sale junk closer to the curb and Mom sticks a sign on it that says *free*.

In the morning it looks like raccoons or coyotes got into our garbage because everything is thrown around. It's creepy to think that while we were sleeping, people were coming by, picking through our pile, and carrying things away.

I picture hordes of them, stooped and faceless in long, brown hooded robes, grunting and sniffing around in the dark—giving myself a serious case of the willies.

I scurry downstairs.

Mom is drinking tea, looking out the kitchen window when I come down.

"Do you think they look up garage sale addresses in the newspaper, then go later to see what's left?" I ask her. "Or are there always people just roaming around looking every-where for stuff every night?"

Mom shrugs, "Both, maybe. I was just thinking it's like roadkill, when the crows and ants and tiny organisms come and clean up the mess."

"What? Ew!"

"Well, Jacki, if there weren't scavengers we'd be up to our necks in dead bodies."

"EEWWW!"

Mom laughs. "We'd sure rather someone use our vacuum cleaners and old shoes than have them just end up in a landfill somewhere, right?"

"Maybe we should take the rest up to the Catalina shel-ter," I say, remembering that I forgot *again* to ask Brooke about Sarah and Madeline's dad.

Mom shrugs, "The shelter, Goodwill, scavengers . . . One way or another, it'll get to the poor."

Mitch stumbles in, half asleep. He shuffles to the fridge, pulls out a slice of pizza, and chews with his eyes closed.

"So," Mom says, all cheery voiced, "who wants to go apartment hunting this morning?"

"I pass," Mitch says with his mouth full.

Then my brain suddenly comes up with the greatest idea that it has ever hatched out! Now I'm all awake and jumpy with yes-ness and excitement and how perfectly perfect my idea is!

"Mom! Let's look in Emily's neighborhood!"

"Woodland Hills?" Mom asks, wrinkling her nose. "*The valley?*"

"Yes! Absolutely! Pretty please? Can we?"

Mom squints at me.

I bat my eyelashes.

Mom looks at Mitch.

He shrugs.

"*Woodland Hills?*" Mom asks again. Then she mutters, "I've heard they've got a good public school system . . ."

And I've got her! Hooray!

I tear up to my room where I left my phone. "Emily! I scream at her tired hello. "You have to promise that your family is never, ever going to move!"

"Huh?"

"That would just so figure, right? We move to your neighborhood and you move away?"

"You're moving here?" Emily squeals. "That's GREAT! Beyond great!" she's entirely awake now. "Where?"

"We haven't actually *looked* at apartments yet, but we're going to today!"

"Oh."

"No, don't worry! I plan to *love* all of them and talk Mom into one for absolutely sure! Isn't that brilliant? You may praise and worship me!"

Emily laughs. "Excellent! And you know what? When we're sixteen we can share a car!"

"A purple one!"

"Totally purple!" Emily says. "But a cheap old one with character, so we can plaster stickers all over it and no one will mind. How fabulous would that be? Go to Melrose, the beach, Disneyland, whenever we want, drive together to school . . ."

"I'm probably not going to Palm Canyon next year." There. I said it.

It's suddenly quiet.

"Emily?"

More quiet.

I say, "My mom says she doesn't think we can afford it. Me and Mitch will probably most likely go to a public high school."

No answer.

"Em? Are you there?"

Boom, crash. All that noise is my heart slamming around against my ribs. My sweat stings on my sunburn. "Emily? Say something!"

Emily says, "Well, I'm thinking."

"Think out loud!" I say. "It's not like I can see your face, you know."

"I'm wearing a thinking face," she explains.

I'm so glad she isn't asking how long I've known about

this. But *how long* I've known isn't really the point anyway. And the relief of finally, finally telling her makes me feel light and floaty.

"Still thinking?" I ask.

"Yes," she says. "And here's what I'm thinking, ready?"

"Ready."

"How about if I transfer to public with you?"

"Yes! YES! That would be fantastic! Completely and entirely beyond fantastic! Wow! We'd be the new girls together!"

I can so totally picture us marching in, side by side, cute with a capital Q, and amazing as can be. Everyone will stop and stare, then part like the Red Sea making a path of awe and admiration for us to pass through! There will be applause! And hey! We won't be wearing uniforms!

"Your parents will never let you," I say hope, hope, hoping I'm entirely dead wrong.

"They were talking about switching Nora to our neighborhood school so Aunt Claire doesn't have to keep driving her to her old one, especially since Nora is like completely miserable there. And if *she's* going to the local . . ."

I change my vision to the THREE of us marching in, shoulder to shoulder, ready to take over, even though Nora will still be in middle school because she's younger.

Emily and I scream and talk over each other and scream some more until Brooke's in my bedroom door, yelling, "SHUT UP! JACKI! SOME PEOPLE ARE SLEEPING!"

So then we scream quietly.

Emily says, "My dad was just saying how crazy and scary and expensive everything is. I'd save him boatloads of money!"

"Yes! YES!"

"OK," Emily says. "You go find an apartment. I'll talk to my parents. We'll meet back here!"

I say, "Excellent! Later!"

And Emily answers, "It's a plan! Gator!"

Chapter 17
ALPACAS AND
ORANGE BLOSSOMS

I'M FABULOUS COMPANY AND PERFECTLY CHEERFUL. I don't complain about being hot-cold-tired-hungry-bored-thirsty, and don't say a word about Mom's boring radio in The Dot. I point out charming Woodland Hills-esque details like pigeons on the telephone wires and trees in bloom. Mostly I've got my eyeballs totally and completely focused on Mom and the split second she seems interested in anything, I'm all over it. Like in the very first place when she stops to look at the fireplace, I get all excited. Never mind that it's ninety-seven degrees out today.

"Wow! Cool!" I say. "Abe Lincoln studied by firelight, right? I think we learned that in school. It would be fun to do my homework by firelight, and I bet I'd get way better grades."

"We have a fireplace now, Jacki," Mom says. "You know that brick thing in the den?"

And in another gigantic ninety zillion unit building called The Birch Wood, Mom likes the little white office off the kitchen with a built-in desk and bookshelves.

"Oh this is sooo cute!" I coo. "It's just perfect for you! Your computer could go here . . ."

Mom squints at me, "OK, Jacki, cut it out," she says. "You're not fooling anyone."

I zip my lips shut and Mom nods her approval.

The next one is listed as a four-plex. Trees are practically holding hands over the street forming a tunnel of branches as we pull up in front of The Citrus Gardens.

It looks like a fairy-tale castle mixed with a library. There are turrets!

I turn to Mom. "Un-zippppp?" I ask.

She raises her hand, "Don't bother. I can see it all over your face. This place looks just like you."

I nod frantically.

Mom doesn't look like she *hates* it. We get out of The Dot and ring the manager-on-premises' doorbell. A woman comes to the door carrying what I think at first is a dog. She opens the screen door and I see that she's giving a bottle to a . . . ?

"It's an alpaca," she says. My son has a ranch up in Santa Ynez but this one's mamma didn't make it so she needs mothering round the clock." The woman blows her bangs off her sweaty forehead and says, "But how can I help you?"

"Can I pet her?" I ask in total, pure, one hundred percent awe. And my hand cannot believe how soft that alpaca baby is. I've never, ever touched anything so soft and so unbearably and perfectly and adorably sweet.

I hear Mom sigh behind me. "You've done it now," she tells the lady. "I'll never get my daughter out of here." Then she tells the woman, whose name turns out to be Harriet, that we're here about the apartment.

244

"Great," Harriet says. "Let me just put the baby in her crate."

"I'll stay with her!" I say.

"Don't you want to see the apartment, too?" Harriet asks.

"Yes," I say, "but . . ."

"I'm sure Harriet doesn't want to leave a total stranger alone in her . . ."

Harriet cuts Mom off by telling me I can give the baby the rest of her bottle if I like!

If I like?

I clamber into the pen. Harriet tells me to sit cross-legged and she lays the baby on my lap. Nothing has ever, ever in the history of the world felt as amazingly wonderful.

"Does she have a name?" I ask in a whisper.

Harriet says, "I've been calling her Rose."

"Rose."

Mom *does* like the apartment. She says the turrets are stairwells and each apartment is a tiny townhouse which means it has an upstairs and a downstairs. She says there's a stained-glass window in the hallway and the way she says that I can tell she's a big fan of stained-glass windows in hallways although I never knew that about her before. But maybe she didn't know it either.

As we're leaving (which I really don't want to do), Mom and Harriet see that Rose peed on my shorts a little bit and Harriet runs to get a wet towel and soap and all that to clean it up. But I don't mind a tiny, little, dribble of alpaca pee.

I tell them about how hysterical Coach Keefer got when I puked on her, and Harriet says I remind her of herself when she was younger. I don't know if she means she used to throw up

245

on her coaches, or because I like alpacas or what, but if it means I'm going to be like her when I'm old, that's OK. As old ladies go, I wouldn't mind being like her when I'm one. She has a cool apartment and a baby alpaca and seems really happy.

"But the apartment is for rent right *now*," Mom explains back in The Dot. "And we can't actually move anywhere until we sell our house."

Clunk! That's my poor tragically broken and disappointed heart dropping to the saddest, deepest pit of my gut.

"So why are we even looking?" I ask.

"To see what's out there," Mom says. "Explore our options. And anyway, places like The Birch Wood have units available all the time because they're so huge."

I sigh. The Birch Wood is no longer acceptable, little white built-in office off the kitchen or not.

Mom sighs, too.

"Did you feel how soft Rose was?" I ask her.

"Rose isn't going to live there forever, you know," Mom says. "I assume she'll go back to the ranch when she's bigger."

"Still."

"Talk about a fresh start, though," Mom says after a few seconds. "The Citrus Gardens is certainly a departure from anywhere I've ever lived in my life."

"Me too," I say.

"And as landlords go, it's hard to imagine Harriet being a sleaze."

"Impossible," I agree.

"Well," Mom says, "we'll just have to see what happens."

* * *

Now I'm all in a knot. Anyone in their right mind who takes one look at The Citrus Gardens, even just from the curb, is going to totally love, love, love it and want to rent it. How can they *not*? And once they meet Harriet and Rose . . . well, forget it.

I wish we could just freeze it in time till we're ready, or camouflage it from the street like with a gigantically huge movie screen playing a loop of some boring, shabby rental . . . maybe the cozy, charming guest house! Or we could cover the whole building with a lot of branches so it'll look like . . . um, like a pile of branches. And we should for sure take Harriet's ad out of the recycler and off craigslist!

* * *

"An *alpaca*?" Emily says. "What's that?"

"Like a little llama."

Emily goes, "Hmmm," probably trying to imagine a llama, but Rose's sweet cute softness is unimaginable. The look in her huge eyes and long eyelashes while I was feeding her . . . well . . . What can I say? It was just the absolute high point of my entire existence, that's all.

"OK," Emily says, "I just googled alpaca and am looking at a picture of one on Wikipedia. It's cute. Big, though. Like a pony?"

"I don't know. Rose is just a baby," I say. "So, what did your parents say?"

"Blah blah, quality of public education . . ." Emily answers, perfectly imitating her dad's New Jersey accent. "California public school system . . . funding cuts to education. Teacher layoffs . . . budget slash . . . pass the salad. We'll think about it later."

"Do you think they *will* think about it?" I ask.

"Well, I plan to bring it up every hour on the hour, but," I feel Emily sigh. "Who knows? It reeks being a kid. I hate not having a drop of control over my own life."

I'm about to agree, but then I remember my mom in The Dot. She doesn't seem to have all that much power over her life either, and she's entirely and completely grown up.

* * *

"The rooms are tiny. Charming, but tiny. It's three bedrooms, two baths," I hear Mom telling Brooke. "So you and Jacki would have to share a room."

I freeze in the hall and try not to breathe so I can hear what my sister thinks of that.

"That's fine," Brooke says, without missing a beat.

Yaaay! I wait a couple seconds so they won't know that I was eavesdropping, then I sail into the kitchen. It smells faintly of Hortensia Day.

"I hear you fell in love," Brooke says. I think she's going to tease me about Adam B. but she says, "So I'm guessing you're going into the alpaca biz. Do a little breeding, shearing, spin alpaca wool for blankets? Am I right? You and Emily getting a little farm up in Los Robles?"

"Where's that?" I ask, and Brooke points to the ceiling.

"Upstairs?" I ask.

"North."

"Anyway," Mom says, wiping the counters and back-splash, "Noreen is going to have the realtor open house here Wednesday morning, which means two things: 1. The house has to look perfect, and 2. None of us can be here. Noreen says we're supposed to have flowers around in vases, and boil cinnamon on the stove so it smells like apple pie baking."

"Sneaky," Brooke says.

"And another trick is keeping things sparse, only a few books on the shelves, no piles of magazines, newspapers. Surfaces empty, so everything looks roomy. As if there's plenty of space for all the buyers' own clutter."

"And everyone falls for this?" I ask.

Mom shrugs, "I guess so. Wednesday's open house is just for other real estate people. Then next Saturday it'll open to Joe and Josephine Public. So basically, from now on, the whole house has to always be neat enough for realtors to bring prospective buyers through at a moment's notice."

So that's what the scrubbing is about.

At that exact second the front doorbell rings and I say, "Wow! That was fast." But it's not a realtor, it's David.

Brooke grabs her purse and runs out the door with him.

I scowl at Mom. "What's *that* about?"

"They were together a long time, Jacki," Mom says. "It's hard to just get over that instantaneously."

"Well, she should try harder," I say.

"Emotions are never quite as tidy as one might wish," Mom answers, reaching up to wash the cabinet doors. The phone rings and Mom juts her chin at it, "Can you grab that?" she asks.

It's a lady asking for my mom.

Mom reaches her sudsy, yellow rubber glove for the phone, and I go stare into the pantry waiting for something yummy to pop out. But wait, Mom's voice sounds really, really weird.

I poke my head out to see if she looks good weird or bad

weird but she just looks totally weird in every possible direction.

"I can be there in an hour," she says. "Thanks."

Then she hangs up and stands perfectly still with her mouth open, looking me right in the eye but for sure not noticing I'm even there.

Oh no! It's the Return of the Casper Wyoming Zombie Un-Dead! Isn't this exactly how she looked and acted then?

She says, "I . . . I . . ."

"Mom?"

Suddenly she springs to life and starts dashing around, pulling off her rubber gloves and flinging them sort of in the direction of the sink, she yanks off her ponytail thingie, shakes out her hair, kicks off her flip-flops and looks at her hands. "My nails are a wreck!" she cries, as if that's the end of life as we know it.

She charges upstairs and I follow her, saying, "Who was that?"

Mom turns, grabs me by the shoulders in an almost scary way, brings her face close to mine and says three letters, "NPR."

I don't get it.

"National Public Radio!" she says. Then lets go of my shoulders and I stagger backward, practically falling onto her bed.

"I *know* what NPR is, Mom," I say. "But what about it?"

She's in her bathroom now, starting the shower and ripping her clothes off.

"A job," she says, and slams the shower door behind her. The steam takes over in no time. It's scented like orange blossom.

Chapter 18

COCONUT MACAROONS
AND JELLY DONUTS

Mom DASHES OUT THE DOOR, returns immediately for something she forgot and leaves again. The house is entirely quiet. It's two thirty on Monday, which means if it wasn't spring break, I'd be in English. I'd never have thought about alpacas, let alone held one and fed it a bottle. I wouldn't know that Mom is on her way to an interview, or that Brooke is out with Dartmouth Dave.

I sit on the couch, and realize that it has already changed back to being *the* couch instead of *my* couch and that's OK, too.

I call Emily but her parents are at work and she doesn't have a ride. She sounds bored. Crabby.

"What about Aunt Claire?" I ask.

"She's busy being entirely crazy out of her mind hysterical," Emily explains.

"Can't she do that while she drives you here?"

"I wish," Emily says. "Anyway, Nora and I are watching *Chicago* . . . So, later?"

"OK, Gator."

I call my dad. "Hi."

He says, "Jack-o'-lantern! Good to hear your voice. What's up?'

"Nothing."

"Everything all right?"

"Yeah."

"Did the phone dial itself?"

"Huh?"

"Is there a reason you called?"

"No."

"Do you . . . um . . . want to go out for gelato, by any chance?" he asks.

And I realize there's nothing I want more in the whole entire world, except maybe an alpaca like Rose, and a hamster like Chubbs, and to move to Harriet's apartment with turrets, and to go to school with Emily, and for Mom to get this job with NPR since she loves them so much, and for Brooke to go to the college she wants, far away from David.

I say, "Sure!"

"Give me twenty minutes," Dad says.

And in eighteen minutes and nine seconds he rides up on his bike.

On the bus to The Gelato Joint we pretend we're new to the planet. We're whispering very, very quietly about the bizarrely exotic earth-sights out the window, but our fellow passengers still look at us funny.

My dad gets half strawberry and half dark chocolate. I get pineapple because even though the others look great, and everyone always tells me how delicious they are, the pineapple is so perfectly one hundred percent wonderful that I can't *not* order it.

Dad says I could try half and half like he does, but then I'd only have half as much pineapple.

We walk, and eat, and discuss the problem. "How about if you had gelato three times a day," Dad says. "*Then* do you think you could substitute one serving every few days with another flavor?"

"Maybe," I say. "But what if it backfired and made me sick of pineapple? That would be terrible!"

Dad nods his head seriously. "That happened to me with coconut macaroons," he says. "I went through a phase where I couldn't get enough of them, and then suddenly, just the thought of them made me queasy. In fact, let's not talk about it."

We walk a few steps. Then I turn to him and say, "Coconut macaroon!" And he pretends to barf.

"So, you like one of those boys in particular?" Dad asks.

"Boys?"

"The ones that were at the house yesterday," he says.

"Kinda."

"Which one?"

I say, "Guess."

Dad says, ". . . Um . . . the really cute one?"

I yell, "Wow! That's amazing!" Then I feel myself blushing. "Was I that obvious?"

My dad laughs. "Jacki, I was kidding! I have no idea which of those boys you think is *cutest*! They all look like puppies to me!"

I peer over at him doing my best Mom-squint. I know he's laughing at me, but I'm used to it.

"How did you and Mom ever get together?" I ask. "You're so entirely and completely different."

"We are that," he says. "Sometimes opposites attract, at least for a little while, although I don't recommend it."

I wonder if me and Adam B. are opposites. I have no idea what the opposite of me would be.

"And she sure was a great kisser," Dad says.

"Who, *Mom*? Ew! Ew! Ew! Now I have to have my ears cut off! My head replaced! My memory scrubbed!" I swat my dad and yell, "DON'T tell me stuff like that!"

"Sorry."

And then I tell him about the braids girl at the shelter, and Emily's Cousin Nora and Aunt Claire, and the eviction police, and Brooke going to community college, and Rose the alpaca. I spill for so many miles that we're almost back at the bus stop when Dad says, "What an interesting time this is in your life. One tap could tip your future in so many possible directions!"

"Yep, I do feel a little like I'm at the edge of a cliff," I agree.

"But in a great way!" Dad says. And I realize that he too would be a hundred on Lacey's optimism scale.

* * *

Mom's flat on the couch with another headache when I get home.

Mitch is thrilled to see me, not because he missed me so terribly but because he's been Mom-sitting. The second I'm home he disappears.

254

Mom's arm is flung across her eyes. She doesn't even peek out when I move her feet and sit on the couch.

"How was the interview?" I ask in a whisper.

"I don't know."

"Did you like the people?"

"Very much."

"Did they like you?"

"I don't know."

"Do you want the job?"

"Yes. No. More than anything. But I don't think we can afford it."

"Can't afford a job? I thought we couldn't afford for you *not* to have a job."

Mom sighs.

I'm not sure what else to ask, but then Mom says, "It's your turn to make dinner. Wake me when it's ready."

"*Huh?*"

*　*　*

So here I am, peering into the refrigerator at one curling, dried out slice of pizza with a bite missing. Next to it is a soggy clump of old woolly mammoth burrito on a greasy paper plate. There's a package of ground turkey, which is sort of pinkish and makes me gag a little. Some ketchup. A carton of eggs that reminds me that I forgot to ask Dad about our vegetable garden. And a slightly shriveled apple.

I call Grandma and list the items for her.

"I see," she says, and I know she's thinking that my mom is a terrible, awful mother and it's a miracle that my brother and sister and I have lived as long as we have.

"What's in the pantry?" she asks.

I go over and peer in. The lightbulb burned out weeks ago, so it's hard to see.

"Um . . . Cap'n Crunch . . . and . . ."

"Any noodles or rice?" Grandma asks.

"Yes! Look, a whole box of mac and cheese!"

"You mean the kind with the packet of bright orange cheese powder?"

"Yes."

"What else? Any tomato sauce, maybe?"

"No. Just tomato paste. Ew. What would you paste with tomatoes?"

Grandma laughs, then says, "That was a joke, right?"

I don't answer.

She asks, "How about an onion?"

"I doubt it."

Grandma says, "All right. Is that everything?"

I figure she doesn't want to know about the Pop-Tarts or instant cocoa or Diet Cokes so I say, "Yep, that's it."

"Great! We're making a beautiful pasta dish we'll call Turkey-Noodle-Cassa-Roodle. Are you ready?"

I giggle, "Ready!"

"Open the macaroni and cheese box and throw out the cheese. Now, get a skillet to brown the turkey . . ."

"*Skillet*?"

"Frying pan?" Grandma tries. "Do you know what this reminds me of?" she asks while I clang around in the pots and pans.

"What?"

"Sometimes, when there are technical difficulties on the

space shuttle, the engineers back on Earth have to talk the astronauts step by step through a tricky, antigravity repair job in space."

"Cool!" I say. "*I'm* the astronaut, right?"

* * *

Mom and Mitch are totally and completely awed by my dinner. I know Brooke would be impressed, too, but she's *still* not home.

"Considering cooking school?" Mom asks, but I think she's probably kidding.

* * *

It's not that I'm waiting up for Brooke, exactly, it's just that I'm . . . well, waiting up for Brooke. I wonder if this is the kind of mother I'll be one day, looking out the window and at the clock every three and a half seconds, checking for text messages and constantly seeing if the land line has a dial tone, in case she's trying to call.

Brooke's not even late yet. She's got forty-five more minutes before her eleven o'clock curfew.

But I've been on high alert since about nine. That's when I told Emily that Brooke left eight zillion hours ago with David, and Emily said, "Maybe they eloped!"

"That's not funny," I said.

"Aw, come on," Emily said. "Not even a little funny?"

"No."

"How about a little romantic?"

"Eew! No!"

"Little bit . . . interesting at least?"

"NO!" I barked. "It's a little nothing but horrible!"

"But if they got married and Brooke moved with him to Boston or New York or wherever David's going with his wink, we could visit them!" Em said. "Woot! Woot! Road trip! Cross-country train!"

One tiny cell in my brain almost perks up for a micro-second, but then Em adds, "And you've got to admit they'd have gorgeous babies!"

"No babies!" I walk outside and straight into a spider web! "EEEK!" I leap and wiggle and swat myself all over, feeling creepy-crawly-cob-webby spiders in my hair, down my neck. I hate, hate, hate that feeling!

Emily said, "Gee, I had no idea you were so anti-baby!"

I didn't explain that it was spiders not babies I was shriek-ing about.

Then Emily said, "But seriously, he probably dropped Brooke at the library, or at the dance studio, or Sarah's or something hours ago. Don't worry."

But here I am. And even YouTube isn't helping.

I go on a Mom hunt and find her at her desk. Really, I just want to see if she's worried about Brooke or if I'm the looniest one in this bin. Turns out Mom's just as worried, but about entirely different stuff. You guessed it: money.

"If I get the NPR job," she says as soon as I walk in. "And that's a big *if*, but hypothetically speaking, I'd make basically half of what I used to."

She looks up at me, and repeats, "Half."

I know I'm supposed to have some reaction here, but what? Tell her I'll only buy shirts, no pants? Or eat half a sandwich at lunch instead of a whole?

Truth is, I'm tired of this whole recession depression, thing. I'm over it. So what if we're half as rich? The *important* question is: Is Brooke going to come home, 1. Soon? 2. Married? And 3. . . . I never can remember my threes by the time I get there.

"I don't think we can make it on half, do you?" Mom asks me, as if I have even the teeniest speck of an idea what we're even talking about half of. A quazillion-billion dollars a year? An hour?

"Yes," I say. "We'll be fine. Absolutely."

And Mom nods seriously, which would be funny if it wasn't so weird.

Then Brooke is at Mom's office door, and I give a little gasp, maybe a little jump, because I so totally didn't hear her coming. It's that silent, dancerly float-walk she does. She'll be an excellent cat burglar, if it comes to that.

"Hi, guys," she says.

I want to march over and demand answers. Are you married? Where were you? Were you with *him* all this time? Don't you remember you said he was a snob? All that stuff about good people and leprosy?

Instead I say, "Hi," and look at her hand. No wedding ring at least. And he's not standing next to her, ready to make their wedding announcement. HOORAY!

"I have something important to tell you," Brooke says, and—oh no! Is she blushing?? I want to put my fingers in my ears and SCREAM to drown out whatever she's going to say. But I don't.

"Sit down," Brooke says.

Plunk! I'm sitting.

"I've made some decisions over the last few days," she says, looking from me to Mom. "And I've been making plans. I wanted to be sure it was all more or less a sure thing before I told you."

Tell my heart to shut up, or I won't even hear what she says!

"Ms. Valentina and Sarah and I have been talking," Brooke says.

Huh? Ms. Valentina, her dance teacher? Sarah?

"It began," Brooke says, "when I told Ms. Valentina that I'd be staying in town for another year, and she offered me a job as her assistant."

"That's great!" Mom says, "Valentina's studio is one of the finest in . . ."

"Hold on," Brooke says, "I'm not done. It was really, really sweet of her and I was touched. But teaching little rich girls to dance . . . well, it didn't feel like enough. So I was talking to Sarah about it . . . about what to do with this unexpected year that has been handed to us . . . and she and I thought maybe Ms. Valentina would be willing . . ."

Mom and I are both leaning closer to Brooke.

"I'm not explaining this very well, am I?" she asks with a giggle.

"Go on," Mom says.

"Well, Ms. Valentina is going to back Sarah and me in a program to teach kids who would never otherwise get dance lessons . . . like I was before, but on a much larger scale, and for pay. Ms. Valentina will sponsor us. Sarah will be the foundation's business manager, arrange fund-raising events, getting donations. That's what she wants to study anyway, community nonprofit arts events."

"Wait. What?" I ask.

"I'll get paid to teach," Brooke explains. "But the kids will get the dance classes for free."

"That sounds wonderful!" Mom says. "And it will look even more impressive on next year's applications. The scholarship money will pour in."

"More importantly," Brooke says, "it will be a year worth living."

I laugh. "All years are worth living."

Brooke shrugs and says, "Some are spent waiting to live."

I'm not super positive what she means, but I can tell she really means it.

"And," Brooke says, "when Sarah and I do eventually leave, our dance program should be able to keep running without us."

Brooke looks so happy! But I *have* to ask, "What's it got to do with David?"

Brooke looks confused. "David?"

"Never mind," I giggle. The conversation goes on, but now that I'm absolutely sure that it's one hundred percent about dance, I can listen less and enjoy it more. I can't wait to tell Emily!

Then Mom tells my sister about her NPR interview. "I think I have to turn it down if they offer it, though," Mom says. "The pay is . . ."

I say, "What? But you *love* NPR!"

My sister agrees. "Look Mom, you and I have always done

everything *right*. My perfect grades and test scores. Your perfect job and investments . . . but it all fell apart anyway."

Mom sighs.

"So as long as even the safe things are risky," my sister says, "we might as well take our risks on the things that really matter to us." Brooke reaches out and touches Mom's arm. "Maybe we're supposed to take the risks that count."

I can tell Mom's listening.

I'm pretty sure Brooke means that Mom should grab the NPR job if she wants it, and I totally agree—as long as she doesn't make *me* listen to it all the time!

If the choices in life are to be happy, or not—well, that's an easy one, don't you think?

* * *

And I bet you can guess the rest, right?

Mom got the NPR job and says that it was me and Brooke who gave her the courage to take it. I'm not sure what *I* had to do with it, but I'm happy to take the credit. Now Mom's exhausted all the time and frazzled with meetings and deadlines and spreadsheets and budgets and pressure and stress and all the other stuff she loves. Buzzzz! The return of the happy worker bee!

Brooke and Sarah work their butts off, too, and seem to be having a total blast with their dance project. And Mitch is Mitch: the same, but maybe a little taller.

We sold our house to a family who seem really nice: a pregnant woman and her husband and their incredibly cute toddler. They're new to Los Angeles and say they're from the Midwest where the economy is even worse!

Maybe they look like my parents did when we bought our house—back when Brooke was three and I was in Mom's belly, and Mitch was still in the future. The new owners say they first saw the house during our garage sale, and Emily swears on her life that it's the exact same little girl who was looking for the magic Beanie Babies. Remember the one who Nora chased after and gave the freebies to? But Nora and I are both pretty positive that little girl was blond and this one is Korean, but who knows?

I just hope they'll be happy.

Mom says they asked her if she knew anyone who cleans houses and Mom was so excited to give them Hortensia's phone number. At the mention of her name my nose instantly remembers the clean minty smell of Hortensia Day. I think it's cool that these kids will grow up in our house smelling what we smelled, at least on Wednesdays.

Do you think that will make them turn out like us? Will that little girl be a good student and amazing dancer . . . and the baby that's not born yet will be like me, whatever that is. And when the me-kid is nine, will the parents get divorced? And then a few years later, will the mom lose her job? And the daughter break her foot and . . .

No, that's just stooopid.

Anyway, as soon as the new family made a bid on our house, Mom called Harriet to see if the apartment was still available. I stood with my fingers crossed, hope, hope, hoping and it worked! Harriet said YES! She says she couldn't possibly rent it to anyone else after I let Rose urinate on me like that.

Saved by a pee!

"In these awful economic times," Mom says, "I doubt

Harriet had to drive many cash-wielding potential tenants away with a club to save it for us."

But still.

Rose is so much bigger that it's impossible to believe she ever fit on my lap. Now she works as a living lawnmower, and everyone loves her to bits, but especially me.

And since we're eating most meals at home, I've discovered that I like to cook and that I'm pretty good at it! Dad's sure I have natural bread-baking talent, so one day next week I'm going to bring my bike and sleep at his and Grandma's house. Dad says we'll get up way, way before dawn and bike to the bakery in the dark. He says it's a beautiful, peaceful time, clear and quiet with stars in the sky and smooth, empty streets.

"The delivery people already know all about you," Dad told me.

It's weird to picture him talking about me to strangers. Does he whip out a wallet full of pictures? Does he *have* a wallet full of pictures? Does he even have a *wallet*?

He says that after the cleanup crews and before the customers, there's an entirely separate world alive and awake. "You'll meet the produce and egg guys, the meat guys, the flower market lady, the other bakers, the police . . . The early hours of the bakery are home to a whole secret society that few people even know exist."

Doesn't that sound incredibly cool in so many, many ways? I can't wait!

And remember the plants we once knew as itty-bitty baby seeds cuddled in egg cartons? Well, we watched them grow, uncurling leaf by leaf, making flowers, then tiny miniature green vegetables that grew bigger, and changed color, until they were huge and ripe and perfect.

It felt a teeny, tiny bit . . . well . . . *violent*, I admit, to yank them out of the ground and chop them up. But Grandma showed me how to make them into stew and everyone agreed it was terrific!

Now our garden is full of tomatoes and raspberries. And we're growing our own pumpkin for Halloween. Dad makes a lot of lame jokes about Jack-o'-lantern's jack-o'-lantern, but I'm sooo looking forward to the pumpkin pie that I don't mind a bit.

Plus Dad says maybe there will be enough for Emily and Nora to have a home-grown pumpkin for their house too, and Emily loves, loves, loves the idea. Halloween is her absolute favorite holiday of course, not just for the candy but for the makeup and drama and costumes.

And, speaking of costumes, we spend endless hours planning what we'll wear to school that first un-uniformed day— if Emily's parents let her transfer to public with me. As of now, we're thinking black jeans and purple T-shirts, because Emily's favorite color is that real deep, almost blue, purple that I like a lot, too.

If I told you that leaving the house I'd lived in my whole life was entirely and completely one hundred percent easy, I'd be lying. It was sad and spooky to walk through the emptying rooms on moving day, knowing that one big huge part of my life was totally over. Almost like that part of me was dead, except for the memories and some photos.

The new family will have their own furniture and hang

different art on the walls. And except for Hortensia Day, it'll smell like their food, and soap, their hair products, and B.O. instead of ours.

I didn't cry, but just as my eyeballs were thinking of giving it a try, Dad rode up with a pink bakery box of jelly donuts. I'm pretty sure it's impossible to be a hundred percent sad around jelly donuts.

And tonight, Brooke and Sarah's little ballet students are performing outdoors at Barnsdale Art Park. I invited Adam B. to come with me. We'll bring a picnic and it will be wonderful: a full moon, a soft breeze, night-blooming jasmine scenting the air. Brooke promised to French braid my hair if I'll take her turn cooking.

This might be the perfect night to settle that million-dollar bet with Emily. Remember? The one about whether I'll be able to keep a straight face if Adam B. tries to kiss me?

And if I burst out laughing with a snorting, spit-spraying heee-haw, then I'll use my million dollar winnings to buy . . . Well, Brooke doesn't need that six hundred-dollar prom dress anymore, and I know she's going to get all kinds of scholarships for school, and Mom loves her new job, and we all love the apartment. So hmm . . . maybe I'll just donate it to the Catalina Shelter.

But more importantly, Adam B. will probably wear a shirt with a collar tonight because I think he knows how incredibly adorable he looks when he's dressed up. And even if he doesn't know, his Mom will probably make him. And he'll smile his soft smile and there I'll be, the luckiest girl in the world.

AMY GOLDMAN KOSS

Amy Goldman Koss is the author of several highly praised teen novels, including *The Girls*, an ALA Best Book for Young Adults, an ALA Quick Picks Top Ten selection, and an IRA Young Adult Choice; *The Cheat*, winner of the IRA-CBC Children's Choice Award; and *Side Effects*, an ALA Best Book for Young Adults, a *Kirkus* Best Book for Young Adults, and a New York Public Library Best Book for the Teen Age. She is also the author of *Poison Ivy*, praised by *Horn Book* for its "honesty and unforgettable voice" and by *Publishers Weekly* as "fascinating and intriguing." She lives in Glendale, California, with her family. Visit her online at: www.amygoldmankoss.net.